D1365243

ALONE
IN A CROWDED ROOM

An Adoption Story

Constance Bierkan

This is a work of fiction. All of the characters, names, incidents, organizations, and dialogue in this novel are either the products of the author's imagination or are used fictitiously.

LifeRich Publishing is a registered trademark of The Reader's Digest Association, Inc.

LifeRich Publishing books may be ordered through booksellers or by contacting:

LifeRich Publishing
1663 Liberty Drive
Bloomington, IN 47403
www.liferichpublishing.com
1 (888) 238-8637

Because of the dynamic nature of the Internet, any web addresses or links contained in this book may have changed since publication and may no longer be valid. The views expressed in this work are solely those of the author and do not necessarily reflect the views of the publisher, and the publisher hereby disclaims any responsibility for them.

Any people depicted in stock imagery provided by Thinkstock are models, and such images are being used for illustrative purposes only.
Certain stock imagery © Thinkstock.

ISBN: 978-1-4897-1291-2 (sc)
ISBN: 978-1-4897-1292-9 (hc)
ISBN: 978-1-4897-1290-5 (e)

Library of Congress Control Number: 2017908020

Print information available on the last page.

LifeRich Publishing rev. date: 09/18/2017

Sometimes, only one person is missing
and the whole world seems depopulated...

Alphonse de Lamartine
(1790 - 1869)

I dedicate my story to
Carolyn Evans Campbell,
teacher, poet, writer, painter and musician,
without whose devoted encouragement my journey
would not have found its written expression.

…and to Kurt, my husband and best friend, without
whose love and support I would be utterly lost.

CONTENTS

FOREWORD

On the very day when a child, destined for adoption is born, a heartbreaking trauma occurs. Until recently, this is an upheaval professionals in the field of adoption have never deigned to recognize as the single most influential trait of any adoptee's psyche. Whether one wants to admit it or not, the shock of instantly separating from one's mother is so great, that the injury stays with her for the rest of her life, worn like an invisible skin. That the adoptee is obviously there when the event occurs is often discounted. Of course, she knows what it feels like to be abandoned by her mother and then handed over to strangers. Suddenly and inexplicably severed from the one with whom she has bonded in utero for forty weeks? Taken from the sole individual to whom she is genetically, historically, emotionally, psychologically, even spiritually connected? No one should ever deny a newborn adoptee her feelings of that devastating loss. She's been orphaned for heaven's sake!

Yet doctors ignore this fact back in 1952. After all, what does an innocent baby, even a newborn with eyes swollen shut and a squirming wrinkled body covered in cheesy vernix, know? In the '50's doctors would have said, *nothing*. Today, however, experts assert adopted babies can tell you plenty because they have all sorts of questions, doubts, fears and anxiety within hours of birth and relinquishment. They just cannot tell you with their words.

> *"… the comparison between [the death of an infant's mother]*
> *and relinquishment at the time of adoption is valid, because*

for the child abandonment is a kind of death, not only of the mother, but of part of the Self, that core-being or essence of oneself which makes one feel whole."
(*Primal Wound; Mac Newton Verrier*)

Adoption has been considered the best solution for the biological mother who doesn't keep the baby, or the unborn child, herself, as well as the infertile couple who want a child to love and raise. Nevertheless, misconceptions abound. The fantasy that all will be well by joining a relinquished infant to a new family, no matter how well intentioned the players may be, ignores the potential for much confusion, distrust, fear of impermanence and more abandonment on the part of that child as she matures. There can be no denying that the connection between a child and her birth mother is sacrosanct. To believe there is no hole as big as a crater left in the child's subconscious when separation occurs is nothing short of equivocation. And to presume it totally viable to replace one's natural mother is glossing over a harsher reality. No one can fully replace the biological mother. Better to embrace the fact that there absolutely is a mystical, mysterious and unique bond between an infant and her mother. Better to accept the fact a baby is entirely capable of finding her mother's face in a crowd, identifying her in a photograph, singling out her voice, or smelling her essence sight unseen. Better to acknowledge this magnificent bond between mother and child as instinctual and intuitive; unconscious perhaps, but undeniable. Better to understand there absolutely is no replacement for one's mother and that this is not to be construed as an insult to the adopting parent. There is an increasing number of biological mothers and adoptees searching for each other across the globe. Why do you suppose that is? Because in some unreadable manner they crave each other!

There has to be an understanding that should this bond between mother and child be cut, expect a wound to open up almost immediately. Today, that wound is recognized as real, and it is understood by the medical community that preventing this injury from festering as the child develops will become an ongoing task for both the adoptive parents and clinicians alike. In the past adoption was scarcely discussed, and as a result, the child often felt his abandonment more acutely. She was either labeled or it was all very hush-hush with secrets and sometimes even shame thrown in. So, it is up to the adoptive parents to treat adoption as more than just a concept. It requires candor, courage, and selflessness in helping a child to understand her heritage and how she came to be with them and not her biological parents. That she might some day want to search for her birth parents reflects not at all on the adoptive family. Rather it is her birthright, which is entirely separate from her replacement family. She should never be discouraged from doing so, though that is a lot to ask of the adoptive parents. Indeed, it is an emotionally charged hurdle many cannot overcome.

"Although the idea of searching to reconnect with the biological mother is filled with conflict and anxiety, it should not be regarded as pathological.It should, in fact, be regarded as healthy. We all need and [most of us have] the biological, historical, emotional and existential connection which is denied so many adoptees. For them, searching might be seen as an attempt to heal the primal wound about which there are no conscious thoughts, only feelings, and somatic memories and an aching sense of loss."

(Primal Wound; Mac Newton Verrier)

BOXING DAY

It was December 26th, 1951, six weeks before Mama's due date. An orange sun was just cresting the horizon where farms not yet awakened by the sound of crowing roosters or lowing dairy cows lay blanketed under five inches of freshly fallen snow. Mama, her ex-boyfriend, who shall remain nameless, and Gramma were sneaking out of town. It was pitiful, three grown-ups tiptoe-ing around the car in dawn's lengthening shadows. I ought to know. I was there. Though I wasn't born yet.

Mama must have flung the rear passenger door open too hard and plunked herself heavily into the back seat of his car. It jostled me inside her womb and knowing me, I probably kicked in protest. Besides, I heard the man bark, "Hey, watch it! You almost took the door off its hinges."

"Well, I didn't, so quit your complaining."

"Would've helped you..."

"I'd have asked."

The car was a brand new '52 four-door Chevy Deluxe Bel Air, a gift the man's father had given him as a graduation present from college. A top-of-the-line hardtop coupe, screaming LOOK AT ME, I bet Mama neither cared for the two tone paint job nor any of the other flashy accessories it boasted.

"It's a bit over the top if you ask me, but then nobody's askin', so I guess I'll keep my mouth shut." Mama snorted as she slid across the leather seat. Apparently, a standard cloth was too ordinary for her college-graduate-ex-honey. She had to concede, though, the leather did smell pretty good - even in her delicate condition. I kinda liked it, too.

"Good idea, Missy, about keepin' your trap shut," warned Gramma. "I'll hear no nonsense today." Mama probably sat and stared out the split glass windshield, deliberately ignoring how her once-upon-a-time-beau, now ex, fussed over her mother. His ceremoniously getting her settled in the front seat, tucking her heavy woolen skirt and coat in and around her, gently shutting the heavy door with a soft thud and then loading the suitcases into the trunk were all simply a means to avoid eye contact with Mama. I'm guessing she made darn sure she was in his direct line of sight in the rearview mirror She could smirk and scowl and make him as uncomfortable as possible throughout the journey.

Gramma probably stared straight ahead, too. Knees pressed tightly together under wintertime layers, lips pursed, she probably clutched on her lap a small pocket book with both gloved hands. Mother and daughter, one in the front and one in the back, both clenching their teeth, neither uttering a word. I kept quiet, too.

A drowsy sort of snowfall began to dapple the windows while rays of sunshine reached into the interior to glint off the metal dash board. Dust motes swirled in the bright beam of light creating an evangelical tableau of righteousness inside the car where Mama, pregnant and unmarried, was spotlighted as an unrepentant sinner. Looming over the two eyes of the split windshield an awning, looking every bit like a giant uni-eyebrow gave the car's countenance the same scowling expression as Mama's. *Typical*, she thought, *this after-market awning option is all about making a statement; a dumb, snobbish and ugly one. What did I ever see in this self-important show-off?*

"He's got dollars, but not much sense," she whispered to me as he climbed behind the steering wheel. When he reversed too aggressively out the snow-packed driveway, Mama grabbed the handrail and glowered at him in the mirror. I could feel her bracing her feet wide apart in order to better balance me in her womb, which no doubt weighed heavily in her lap. I could tell neither of us was comfortable. I stayed quiet and didn't complain, following her example.

In those days it would have taken six hours to make the journey to Chicago as Eisenhower's federal highway system had yet to be built. On two lane roads through farming hamlets and small towns of no more than a few hundred in population, the trip was made all the more painfully slow by the absurd silence within that Chevy. It echoed miserably to the snowy stillness outside. Fields of pigs and sheep, cattle too, were becoming fewer and fewer as they neared the Windy City, Chicago's apt nickname. Farms, most of them in tidy shape, though some dilapidated, boasted tractors sitting out front now idled by the winter season. And studded sheet metal silos bursting with stored grain were a testament to the success and/or wealth of a farmer by how many he had out back. They glinted in the white glare of the sun on snow. Red barns and loafing sheds dotted the landscape, too. These were Mama's favorites because the earthiness spoke to her as it would me when I grew up. What was most curious, though, was how man-made boundaries of hedgerows and fencing disappeared under the deep snow. Fences, which usually made for dependable distinctions between what's yours and what's mine, simply disappeared. It was a reminder that not too much faith could be put in such artificial delineations. I think Mama must have always believed that with fences you actually had more freedom, that you knew your place or where you belonged. In a vacuum where everything is erased with white, you don't know where you are, and are trapped by the endless expanse of being neither here nor there. I grew up thinking that very same thing. Where else would I have come up with such a concept if not Mama?

Occasionally, though, a small Currier & Ives town surprised Mama along the way. I could feel her longing because she leaned her forehead against the frosted window and sighed wistfully as she looked into those charming houses. Picket fences festooned with boughs of fir, front porches decked with garlands of holly, mistletoe swaying above so many front doors were all testaments of hope and joy. There were families inside gathered around Christmas trees enjoying the aftermath of her most favorite holiday, one her family could ill afford. Folks enjoying leftovers of turkey sandwiches jammed with white meat, cranberry sauce, lettuce and mayo, a fistful of Lay's potato chips on the side and a cold glass of fresh milk to wash it down. She probably caught sight of children playing on brightly colored braided rugs with toys delivered by Santa Claus; moms and dads reading the Saturday Evening Post while a fire crackled in the grate; and puppies or kittens diving into discarded wrapping paper and ribbons. All along the way, she watched idyllic Norman Rockwell moments unfold and wondered, *that's s'posed to be me in there.*

I knew big tears were sliding down her cheeks, hanging first from her nose and then her chin. And as each mile of road propelled us unwillingly closer to the city where our lives were about to be forever altered, I felt her posture sag, turning me into a pretzel. With unblinking eyes forward as if in a trance, and with only the slightest movement of her hand back and forth across my bottom, she caressed her rounded midriff. I was grateful for the affection. I know I would have wanted to transmit it back to her if I could. Weeks earlier, she said goodbye to her beau, her college sweetheart, the man who had promised to marry and keep her always, after he refused to marry her. Said his parents could never abide a shotgun wedding and besides, wives were supposed to be virgins. So she willingly withdrew from this moron. But parting with the baby she was keeping safe and who kept her warm these past seven months? Me, in other words? That was a test she couldn't fathom enduring. Me neither.

As we entered the outskirts of Chicago from the south side, Mama couldn't bear the silence anymore. "Would it be too much to ask for the radio to be turned on?"

Gramma probably looked over her shoulder at Mama in the back seat with a frown of rebuke and Mama probably shrugged her shoulders. Rolling by junk yards with endless spans of chain link fencing was just too boring for words. Railroad tracks, side by side and crowded with sooty boxcars full of coal, mooing livestock or modern wares were depressing. Factory smoke stacks spewing thick chemical fumes and endless stockyards filled with cargo containers lent a foreign cast to the panorama surrounding the car. She became frightened. Even frozen Lake Michigan, sparkling under a canopy of snowflakes like a vision in a snow globe, couldn't engage her. There was no hope in that landscape, just an ominous chill spreading as far as the eye could see. Skyscrapers looming ahead made her feel very small as the city streets morphed into towering cement canyons. Up ahead was a gray landscape of steel, concrete, stone and mortar confronting them. With a hoar frost spreading its sheet of icy gray across their path, even the men and women walking briskly to and fro were gray in countenance and dress. So, too, drifts of slush. Grey. This urban jungle was home for the next six weeks, and Mama felt decidedly queasy. Adding to her misery, she thought if she coughed or sneezed, she might wet her underpants.

"Are we there yet?" she asked petulantly. "It may surprise one of you to know that a girl in my condition needs to visit the john more than once on a six-hour road trip."

"Almost there," he said glancing in the rearview mirror. "Sit tight." And with that he turned the radio on.

Mike Wallace's familiar voice invaded our space with the top-of-the-hour news. The impending expiration to the Marshall Plan being the headline, all three of the grown-ups listened. Unable to fathom what $13.3 billion dollars even looked like, Mama, I could tell, yawned with the tedium of it all. She seemed annoyed, nonetheless, by so much money going toward rebuilding Europe and not America after the war. *Who's gonna rebuild Pearl Harbor?* she wondered. *Didn't our boys die saving them from annihilation? Those Japs should be paying us!* Next was a story about Libya becoming independent from Italy. *So what?* Finally, this: a sailor in Sweden is fined for kissing in public and the court calls his actions "obnoxious behavior repulsive to the public moral." At that Mama rolled her eyes and caught her ex's eye in the mirror. His expression probably revealed, *wow, good thing I don't live in Sweden. My sorry ass would be in jail!* His response was to quickly change the station. Soft strains of Perry Como's hit, *If*, filled the car with its sentimental lyrics:

> If they made me a king
> I'd be but a slave to you
> If I had everything
> I'd still be a slave to you
> If I ruled the night...

So much for promises in the heat of the moment. Gramma must have thought so, too because she snapped the radio off. "What claptrap! That gobbledygook is what got you two idiots into trouble in the first place! It's why we're all sitting here now."

Even I, inside Mama's womb, could feel Gramma's anger as it radiated all the way into the back seat where we were stretched out across the bench. When I think about the grandmother I'd never know today, I don't blame her, really. How she must have been mortified by Mama's condition. In those days it was so taboo. And since the Spermatozoa was refusing to marry Mama, claiming he had a fiancée waiting back home, I imagine it was all she could do to get my mama away from home before my granddaddy found out. But escorting her daughter to a home for unwed mothers would have been the last thing she ever would have imagined doing. Worse, the very man who got Mama pregnant was doing the driving. He insisted the three of them go together.

You know, there's something wrong with that. Here he abandons my mama, and me for that matter, but wants to escort her to Illinois. Why? To make sure she goes through with the whole adoption business? Because he doesn't trust her? Because she might run away and hit him up later for child support? Because he feels guilty and wants to do the right thing? Is this the right thing? Phooey! It stinks and it will always stink! Was money involved? Maybe Daddy-O is footing the bill for Junior Sperm Donor's indiscretion. Here they are, all three of them, a very strange trio, sneaking out of town on a false pretext. As for me, I'm just tagging along for the ride making it a cosy unwanted little foursome. The sham concocted to explain Mama's phony move to Chicago was that she was going to a new job with better pay and greater opportunity. Not until later would the non-engagement be called off due to the difficulties of a long-distance courtship. So, that's how things like an out-of-wedlock pregnancy were handled in those days. Shame, lies, secrecy culminating in banishment. Cover it up and make it all go away. Especially in a quiet midwestern town where a Catholic university's influence ran far and wide.

"If either of you ever speak of this to anyone, and I do mean anyone," Gramma warned raising her voice, "there will be hell to pay! It will ruin each of our family's names. Do you hear me?" She wagged a finger in Sperm Donor's face and then turned to inflict the same upon Mama. "Once that baby is born and given away, life can continue as if nothing has ever happened." There was silence as she hesitated to consider her next words. "You, young man, can say one thousand *Hail-Mary's* or whatever you do to be absolved, I don't give a damn. Just don't go forth once cleansed and do it all over again!"

Giving a baby away wasn't going to make the slate clean, but Gramma seemed convinced giving me up for adoption was the right thing, the only thing to do. Of course it's what the sperm donor, the devout Catholic, wanted as well. It got him off the hook. I can't really blame him too much. He was a product of those ignorant times also. Nevertheless, Mama and I were stranded, soon to be separated, left to cope with a decision ostensibly made by others affecting the rest of our lives. Absolution, adoption? Neither would make the anguish of what was about to happen go away. Who's fooling who?

The snow squeaked and creaked beneath the white walled tires as it came to a slow stop outside The Cradle, Home for Unwed Mothers. Two fresh-faced thirty-something-year-old women trotted down the snow-dusted stairs to greet us curbside. They were twin visions in white with brown fur-lined snow boots pulled over their white stockings. Each wore identical starched white pinafores with white long-sleeved collared blouses and white cardigans which zipped, instead of buttoned, up the front. Toothy smiles of lipsticked lips discharging phony cheer made them ghoulish in the fog. I could feel Mama recoil, so I did too. When Spermatozoid leapt out of the Chevy to shake their hands with much too much enthusiasm, he slipped and fell to his hands and knees. As he did so with all arms and legs spiraling every which way, a fat envelope fell out of his coat pocket and skated across the sidewalk. We all froze.

"Excuse me," Mama murmured. "Is there a ladies room I can use?"

"Come, dear. Let's get you inside. The others can follow," the one nurse said.

Sperm Bupkis, having regained his footing, retrieved the fat envelope, and pressed it into the other nurse's hands saying loud enough for even me to hear, "That ought to take care of everything. Lemme know if you need more." He then turned toward the car and motioned my mama's mama to follow. "Come. We need to get going. I don't want to get home too long after dark."

Mama must have stopped on the stairs and turned around when she heard the car doors open and clunk closed. Marooned on the slick pavement below were her three mismatched suitcases and canvas knitting bag, the needles poking out like antennae. She watched with a hate-laced stare as the Bel Air pulled away into heavy traffic. A sea of red tail lights glistened on the slushy streets as traffic backed up. All too quickly the car carrying the father of her child and her own mother disappeared from view while gusts of steam billowing through manholes in the street seemed to swallow them up. Into those gray streets, gray slush and gray crowds of gray strangers they disappeared while Mama remained rooted under her gray cloud of dread. She turned back towards the front entrance and curled her arm under her belly to lift me off her bladder. But it was too late.

"Oh, my!" whispered the nurse standing next to Mama and me. A small yellow puddle melted the snow between Mama's feet. "Come along, Dearie. Let's get you settled." With neither a word nor a tear, Mama entered the building still cradling her belly. Her panties were soaked, her spirits were crushed and me? I lay very still.

I can only imagine the isolation Mama must have felt when not just Sperm Donor, but also her mother of seemingly little compassion, abandoned her on the doorstep. Mama's new home was a cold and austere Victorian building of stone and dark recesses. And it was located in a noisy and utterly unfriendly city where the terrain was made up of cold, angular surfaces with scarcely any character or charm. She was so far from the farmhouse where she grew up amidst geese in the front yard and flowering shrubs in colorful disarray crowding around the front steps. How suddenly very homesick she must have felt, but she'd never go back home now. Not after this. How could she return to a place where all her life she believed she was safe but discovered she really wasn't? That would be counter-intuitive for anyone's emotional well-being. I'm pretty sure she must have shut down that day, never to speak of this betrayal again. Never to allow herself to feel this anguish or any other for as long as she lived. That would be her mantra going forward if there even were a *forward*. I wouldn't be at all surprised if a part of her heart slammed closed that day. Mine would have, given the same circumstances.

I think Mama might have been pleasantly surprised, though, when she got inside the building. The room to which she was assigned for her lying-in at The Cradle was actually cozy. She hesitated in the doorway caressing her belly where I snoozed. "This room's kinda pretty," she whispered to me."Like a hotel."

I guess if one were to be hidden away from the world and eventually robbed of one's baby, then the prison cell should be comfy. It was definitely a far cry from what she was accustomed. El-shaped, the shorter section was lined on two walls with painted white bookshelves and cabinetry underneath. This was fashioned into a cozy alcove filled with novels, a Gideon's Bible and a wide assortment of magazines such as *Family Circle, The Ladies Home Journal* and *The American Girl*. Within this nook was a large, overstuffed armchair of forest green twill with a chenille throw of variegated greens, violets and blues tossed across the back. Even the footstool in front matched the chair as did a kidney-shaped pillow for a pregnant girl's aching back.

"Oh sweetheart, if only you could see this place!" she murmured. Against the long wall in the adjacent space was a double-sized bed! Not a cot which could be folded up and tucked in a corner like the one at home. This had hand-painted head and foot boards with rounded newel posts at all four corners. A pretty laurel-shaped garland of roses adorned the center of each pearl-gray panel. The spread was white; a soft chenille with pom-pom trim coaxing a small smile from her lips. I know because she let loose a contented sigh as she stroked the fabric with her long tapered fingers. On either side of the bed were matching night stands and ceramic bedside table lamps with pleated dusty rose shades yielding a warm, homey glow. Across from the bed a window, flanked by draperies of pink roses on leafy green vines twisting their way from floor to ceiling added another layer of extravagance she'd never enjoyed before. When she took a peek outside, Mama was grateful her view was of the garden below and not a noisy chaotic city street of endless gray.

Mama set about putting her few things away in the closet and dresser. When she was almost finished, she found a letter in the bottom of her suitcase. The envelope was not addressed, but she knew it was from him.

> Dear girl,
>   If you are reading this it means you are unpacked and settling in. This is good, very good.

I am convinced you are doing the right thing by relinquishing the baby. Ours was a licentious passion. It was wrong. Lust, to characterize it honestly, is what our relationship was all about and what we did was a cardinal sin. I've made things right by confessing to Father Navin and he has graciously bestowed his absolution upon me. Though this has not come without a great deal of prayer and church service on my part. You are making things right, too. What better way is there for you to start over with a clean slate than by giving the infant to someone who can love and raise it, someone unable to conceive perhaps. This is such an act of charity you will be proud of. Maybe not now, but someday, I'm sure.

You always knew I was never going to be able to marry you. My parents never thought we'd make a good match. Going against them would have meant a disinheritance for certain. Where would we have been then?

Besides, my high school sweetheart, you know, the one I promised to marry after I graduated college has been waiting patiently all these years. Mom and Dad approve of her pedigree. Did I ever tell you she was named Debutante of the Year last Christmas and just discovered her great, great, great grandfather fought in the Revolutionary War? Not only that, she is a devout Catholic and familiar with our customs. Remember when I asked if you'd consider becoming a Catholic and you said, 'No!'? Anyway, that's water over the dam. It's high time I put a ring on that gal's finger and enter the family business. I'm all grown up now. No more romps for me, although it sure was fun. You were the very bestest, my dear, gotta admit that.

Thanks for the memories, kiddo,
Your Honey-Bear.

Mama was very still for a long time. Poor Mama, she was never given a say. The guy who refused to recognize me and the gramma who colluded in this farce of my going *poof!* never asked Mama what she wanted, because they were too afraid of what she'd say. Naturally, Gramma and Sperm Donor insisted that carrying the baby to term and giving it - *wow, I'm an it* - up for adoption was for the best. It suited them. But why didn't

Mama stick up for herself? Or me? She must have been so hotly ashamed by the fall from upon whatever pedestal she once stood, to object. Oh, but there was rancor all right. I could feel it in her tensed body, muscles so tight it felt like a vise squeezing the air out of my raisin-sized lungs. There were restless nights too, when she tossed and turned, flipping me like a pancake on a hot griddle. And the silence whenever anyone else was in the room with us was deafening. Thank goodness she sang to me whenever we were alone. She even read fairy tales to me from her frayed copy of Hans Christian Andersen late at night. I breathed the lavender she dabbed behind each of her ears after a bath while she stroked my bottom nestled just behind her belly button. Everyone else in the house was asleep, so it was just the two of us. That was the best. It made me think she really wanted to keep me, or maybe that's just wishful thinking on my part. But honestly, where would she go if she were to keep me? Since Sperm Donor wouldn't marry Mama, and her parents would have thrown her out of the house if she kept me, could she live in a flophouse with a newborn? Hardly. How could she support herself and me if there were no one to care for me while she worked? Mama didn't have a college degree in her pocket, nor any personal savings either as she lived at home with her elderly parents, supporting them with every penny she earned.

An abortion might have been possible by way of a back-alley quack, but not only was it illegal and dangerous in those days, but it was also unthinkably immoral by many; certainly more controversial then compared to today. Besides, it would have been a terrible threat to her health and future pregnancies. So, Mama was cornered.

Though some might have blamed her for her indiscretion, and as a result think me an unfortunate victim, I have never felt as sorry for myself as I have for her. Throughout my life, I've always felt truly sad for the mother I'd never know growing up. The predicament in which she found herself must have been terrible. And I've always considered Sperm Donor nothing but a jerk. If he'd not known about me, I might have cut him some slack, but he did know. Not only were they dating for over a couple of years, which must have misled her into believing marriage was in the cards, but he also deserted her. There was nothing gallant about the Sperm Donor escorting her to The Cradle in Chicago. Maybe my gramma thought it kind, but as far as I am concerned that charade of chivalry was purely a self-righteous penitence foisted upon a girl left vulnerable. He, I'm certain, just wanted to make sure she didn't skip out and have me in secret leaving him exposed to financial responsibility.

It's been said the fifties was the plastic generation. A time when conformity to social norms made for a rather unimaginative and pedestrian ho-hum daily existence. A decade when most external influences such as television, radio, comics and the movies were sanitized to reflect the rise in evangelical Christianity or a return to social decorum after the war. In truth, this was a time when teenagers were setting themselves apart from their parents and demanding new images, symbols and role models; ones with more edge and rebelliousness. Teenagers, a term rarely used until the fifties, were no longer interested in the happy-go-lucky examples of cheerful conformity or boring respect for familial authority. Youth was beginning to see themselves as a distinct group. Their attempts to forge an identity separate from adults was rapidly taking hold. This change in attitude was brought about in large part by America's increased affluence of post World War II. Before the war many young people worked full-time straight out of high school in order to support their families, but in the fifties more and more wanted to go away to college and get out into the world. Young women, if they were not college-bound sought marriage as a means to escape the parental scene. Adults or parents struggled to understand this collective shift of youth, but only if and when they even saw it as such. Perhaps, this phenomenon was inspired by returning G.I.'s who had a lot of wild oats to sow, and the kids of the fifties wanted to emulate that defiant, devil-may-care, freer pattern of behavior. Whatever the causes, by 1955 *Time* magazine published a special issue entitled "Teenagers on the Rampage" while thirteen states banned comic books for supposedly causing not only delinquency but dyslexia, too. Psychologist Robert Linder claimed, "The youth today is touched with madness, literally sick with an aberrant condition of the mind." It's important to make the distinction, however, that youthful rebellion in those days, as opposed to later in the mid-sixties, was aimed at parents and the confines of daily life, not at society or government as a whole.

Even though the fifties are remembered for the advent of poodle skirts, Rock 'n Roll, the *Howdy Doody* and *I Love Lucy* shows, slinkies, hula hoops, drive-in movies and frozen dinners, this was a time of strife. No one personally noticed or understood the social upheaval in which they individually found themselves. Not until much later when looking back through the 20/20 lens of the social sciences and demography did the view become clearer. A pity, because many were hurt by this lack of insight. Mama and her mama. Me, too.

They said I was too young
to be anyone's mother
They never asked me
what I wanted to do
They said my baby should have
a mother and a father
They never gave me a choice
or helped me see it through
They never mentioned
the wound in my heart
They just said go on with life
and pretend it didn't happen
They never warned me I might grieve
all the years we'd be apart
They never said flesh and blood
would be amputated from me
They said I'd get married and
other children would call me mom
They never said one person
cannot replace another
They said don't worry
she'll have a good life
They never listened to how
the pain of not knowing
would cut just like a knife
(Anonymous)

GROUNDHOG DAY

At 2:16 on February 2nd, I was expelled from Mama's warm, protective womb and ripped from my maternal soulmate before I could even take a first breath. Spanked, poked, prodded, then tightly swaddled in a rough and standard-issue blanket, I was unceremoniously dropped into the arms of the first of many faceless strangers to come along; all of them well-intended, I've no doubt, but none of them my Mama. Imprisoned by a wooly facsimile of a straightjacket, I could neither protest, nor question what was happening to me. All I could sense was my mother's lavender fragrance, so familiar after nine months of my living inside her, grow more and more faint. A total stranger transported me out of the birthing room and through a long, narrow ward filled with winter light. Mama, lying on rumpled blood-stained sheets with her arms outstretched in supplication was my first and last memory I ever had of her. There were no tender hugs of greeting or farewell. No comforting words whispered in my ear. No feathery kisses caressing my wrinkled brow. Tenderness or familiarity was verboten. Only Mama's once melodic and smoky voice morphing into primal anguish echoed pitifully in my ears as they carted me down that long linoleum-tiled corridor. A defenseless infant, I was torn from the only physical and emotional connection I'd ever known. Mama, who had nourished and protected me in her womb for over forty weeks was gone in literally a heartbeat. Just like that, a visceral, integral part of me vanished. Her essence was snuffed out. Extinguished.

Incapable of expressing my feelings of loss with words, my sense of exile quickly lodged itself in my chest and beneath the folds of my soft, pillowy arms and babyish legs. All I knew at the time was that I lost my mother, an act so abrupt and final it instantly became a wound. No one could see it embedded in my hammering little heart. Even I never really recognized it until much, much later in life; when I was willing to glimpse the pain, actually own it or do something about it. Only my incessant crying, fitful sleep and objections to bottled pablum demonstrated my protest. Those first few days were filled with nothing but a rebellion. I was madder than a hornet.

Let's face it. That was the day, my very first day outside the womb when I lost my identity. Forever. From then on I'd be borrowing whatever identity someone foreign or alien to me might bestow. February 2nd was the day I forever became the newbie, the outsider, the stranger in town. I'd be the guest or the visitor who wouldn't, or in some cases, shouldn't overstay her welcome. It marked the beginning of a lifetime of feeling like I never belonged. Or the day a hole in my soul was peeled wide open, leaving me exposed to sorrows and losses I couldn't name. I'd have to learn how to swim in a pool of strangers, some of them kind for sure, and some not so generous of spirit. Would I be resilient enough to withstand the pressures of my unique circumstances or would I fail? Would I be labeled, experience name-calling? Worse yet, would I be called "bastard" and condemned to a bias for which I had no responsibility? Would people think me different or even weird? Who would I be or become without my foundation? Who would keep me safe like Mama while I lay so contentedly under her beating heart?

More importantly, would Mama ever rescue me? Would she reclaim me, say she was sorry, that it was all a big mistake, scoop me up in her arms to never let me go again? Would my father recant his holier-than-thou position and rescue me by marrying Mama? I'd have learned to forgive him if he had. Or would the grandmother I never formally met find a way to tell Mama's father and siblings about me and together find a way to bring me back to the farm? Oh, to be with the family whose voices were the music I knew by heart because I memorized them all on day one from inside Mama's womb. There were footsteps I could easily differentiate sight unseen. Some were heavy, scuff-sounding steps as though someone were walking around with his work boots on and the laces untied. Others were either slippered indoor footfalls like those of young women in socks or the sharp uneven clicks always in a hurry but with a slight limp. It'd be so wonderful to be back home where the screen door always slapped in the summertime; where the bees buzzed and hovered over the purple clematis under a kitchen window spotted with soapy sink water. I'd be able to smell again the sweet aroma of cut hay from the back forty in August. Even a pungent whiff of manure from the barn throughout the year would be so welcome.

I'd be such a good little girl. Really and truly, I would. Cross my heart and hope to die…

NO MAN'S LAND

I was moved to The Cradle's nursery on February 8th and remained there until April. Why it was six days before I was moved there, though, is a mystery. There were no reports of my having had any neonatal difficulties requiring hospitalization, so why such a delay from Maternity Ward to Nursery? I could speculate Mama had such an upsetting melt-down after I was born, pitching a fit to beat all breakdowns, that The Cradle's Trustees granted her a week to reconsider her decision to relinquish me. Highly unusual for them to be so lenient, letting a new mom wobble like that, but they could have been afraid of a lawsuit.

I remember that nursery clearly. I know it sounds impossible, but I do. It was yellow. Four walls of a pale, acidic hue no doubt meant to soothe, though its cheer seemed to be always out of reach. I can still feel that bland, antiseptic nothingness during those months. I didn't know it then but it was abandonment, and for many years afterward, I've hated being alone. Nothing adorned the walls save for an afternoon shadow stretching at a distorted angle across the room. The metallic bars of my crib loomed very large and ominously against the wall across from where I lay, mimicking the actual ones which surrounded my swaddled body holding me prisoner. The setting sun's rays pouring into my room made everything eerie as those rails lunged grotesquely on that blank canvas of my nursery. Darkness always came soon after that. And in February, March, and April during a Chicago winter, this was a good thing because night lasted for hours. It filled the stark vacuum I hated so much.

I remember the nursery noises, too. A fierce hissing followed by an insistent clanging of radiator pipes as they came to life made me jerk awake every morning. Squeaking rubber soles on linoleum floors always seemed to be on the move. A cacophony of urban noises braying outside my window was loud, angry, and argumentative. Honking cars battled for the last word; police car and ambulance sirens screamed in the distance; fire engines trumpeted their passage as they hurtled down the street, a diminishing racket echoing between the high-rises in their wake. I don't think I liked those noises very much, but they were better than the nothingness of my vacuum. I missed Mama's nursery rhymes and fairy tales. There was no cooing after I was born, no lavender either. And no one stroked my bottom every day and all day the way Mama had when I was still with her.

They say I refused the bottle. With great gusto, apparently, for I could bellow like a soldier, turn beet-red and pass out. Any fool would have seen I wanted Mama's breast. But that was not to be, so I let 'em know how I felt about it. Those poor nurses had a very hungry baby on their hands; with a temper to match any redhead's. They probably felt pretty helpless as I staged one hunger strike after another. For what it's worth I've since learned food fills the void, that dreaded vacuum.

It's funny. While I can readily remember the sights and sounds of my first three months, I have no recall of anyone singing me a lullaby or just holding me in their arms. No eyes to gaze into with my own blurred, newborn vision. I only remember nurses in white garb from head to toe wearing white masks across their noses and mouths. They didn't all just look alike but they all sounded the same, too. Speaking in irritating sing-songy, high-pitched chirps they just made me instantly annoyed. My nonstop crying, fitful sleep and objections to bottled milk were my only means then of broadcasting displeasure. These clues seemed to go unnoticed, at least it felt like it to me. How do I know they didn't notice? Because Mama didn't come back for me.

Eventually, I saw there were no good outcomes from my arduous campaign against motherlessness, so I stopped my caterwauling. Not only did I adapt to that infernal bottle (because I was so damn hungry), but I actually grew plump enough to be presentable. This meant I was ready for prime time. It happened to be April 1st when the staff at The

Cradle introduced me to Mr. and Mrs. Saunders. Apparently, The Cradle volunteers were unaware that this was the day meant for sending folks on a fool's errand, looking for things that didn't exist. A day set aside for playing pranks on one another, trying to get people to believe ridiculous or really dumb ideas.

Caroline, the volunteer holding me in her arms, hesitates in the corridor where lithographs of Chicago's famous architecture hang on the walls. Black and white drawings of the historic Water Tower, Chicago Library, Michigan Avenue Bridge, Wrigley Building, Merchandise Mart, or Tribune Tower to name but a few line the walls on both sides. Outside the "Belonging Room," she quickly smoothes my hand-crocheted jacket one last time, straightens the woolen booties on my squirming, kicking feet and rearranges the knitted beanie which has slipped down over my eyes. *Brother! Best not look too goofy!* According to photographs, the Saunders are seated ramrod erect, she with a stylishly tailored dark gray designer suit of worsted wool, a silk blouse of soft pink, buttoned at the nape of her neck with cultured pearls, and flannel accented pumps. He is sporting a three-piece, navy blue pinstriped suit with a starched shirt positively gleaming behind his narrow red tie. Brand new wing tips peek from his creased cuffs. Both are impeccably groomed with movie-star good looks. Luke Saunders, a dead-ringer for Gary Cooper, stands up as a matter of politeness when Caroline enters. This provokes a bizarre kind of fluttering and twittering on her part, which for a moment makes all of us think she is about to drop me on the floor. The supervisor, Mrs. Rogers, a much more stern matron, maintains her composure and clears her throat as a warning. As I am brought further into the room to be held out for display, my heart suddenly skips a beat when I see the pretty lady up close. There is something strangely familiar. Is it the hair, tumbling to her shoulders in soft auburn waves, parted on the side? Or is it a look in her dark brown, almost black eyes which are so mesmerizing? Maybe it is the lavender she's dabbed behind each earlobe. Whatever it is, I feel a psychic pull. So much so, I lean out toward her with outstretched roly-poly arms.

"May I hold her?" asks the pretty lady. Tears are welling up in her eyes and her arms are reaching out to me with gimme-gimme wiggling fingers.

"Of course," the volunteer says. "Here you go."

As soon as she plunks me onto her slender knees, Jacqueline Saunders turns me toward her lovely face, bends low so our foreheads are touching and murmurs a whole lot of words I don't understand, but whose sounds nonetheless are utterly melodic. I sink Buddha-style even deeper into her lap. She caresses my back with gentle, circular strokes never leaving my gaze. How does she know I love that? Wow, this is as close to how I felt when Mama was still around.

"My turn," the handsome man interrupts. I am moved to his lap and soon I'm gawping into his blue eyes. When he begins wiggling his ears back and forth, my toothless grin quickly turns to laughter. Gales of baby giggles soon fill the room, which flow all the way down the hall. Even the supervisor, intent on remaining impassive, can't resist the smallest of smiles.

"Can you tell us about her parents?" Luke asks the supervisor who's there to observe.

"This is a closed adoption, Mr. Saunders. We cannot provide you with the names of her birth mother or father in order to preserve the natural parents' privacy." This was said with exaggerated patience. "It's policy to match a child with his or her adoptive parents as best we know how using all the tools we showed you in our earlier interviews."

"No, no. We completely understand, don't we, dear?" interjects the pretty lady, shaking her head at the handsome man in an obvious scold.

"Yes, my mistake."

"Good," says the supervisor. "It's important this little one comes to you if, in fact, she does come to you, with a clean slate. No need to start out life together with a nugget of information that might prejudice you. Do you have any other concerns?"

"No, not really," the pretty lady says. "It's just she strikes me as a bit of a big girl. How old did you say she is?"

The supervisor lifts me from Gary Cooper's arms and moves to leave. "Come back tomorrow at eleven o'clock. We'll have our final decision for you then. You both must be very tired. After all, this has been a long and strenuous interview process, especially as it's been long-distance and out-of-state. I'm sure Virginia beckons."

The process of adopting a child in those days was grueling; maybe, not as much as today, but it still involved mountains of paperwork. This typically consisted of autobiographies of prospective adopting parents, references (personal and work related), medical histories, fingerprinting, credit checks, proof of education and employment, criminal and child abuse background checks, recorded interviews, plus the dreaded home visit reports, all of which easily filled a legal accordion file to the gills.

"Yes," Luke admits. "We are indeed looking forward to getting home, but I assure you it won't be a happy return if we aren't bringing this delightful little ray of sunshine with us!" and he points at me with a wink of his eye.

HOME SWEET HOME

My first home was Old Town Alexandria. I was brought to a charming little carriage house located one block north of King Street and across the street from a police station replete with bars across the first story windows. It was a trendy place to live even in the fifties, primarily attracting the younger set - newlyweds, up-and-comers, those who were making a bid for the big-time in our nation's capitol. With its cobblestone streets, red brick sidewalks, the Potomac River waterfront to the east, and the District of Columbia just a short commute away, this was a *neat-o* place to live. Even though ours was a modest home, the address was just right.

America's history positively seeped from every corner of town. Centuries-old architecture, galleries, restaurants and museums such as the Stabler-Leadbeater Apothecary appealed to the intellectually élite such as lawyers, which is what Daddy recently became when he joined Covington & Burling LLP, and career politicians, in which Mother's family was involved. Old-Town Alexandria was the city George Washington had always called home. So, too, my parents, diamonds-in-the rough, Daddy from Conifer, Colorado and Mother Red Hook, New York respectively. They loved following in Washington's illustrious footsteps, frequenting his favorite watering hole, Gadsby's Tavern, and choosing Christ Church as their place of worship. They enjoyed discussing politics, she a Democrat and he a freshly minted Republican, when visiting supposed haunted hotspots. They argued politics while pushing a perambulator, I usually benumbed by the heat or too many pulls at a bottle of creamy whole milk.

"Whatever possessed you to join the Republican Party?" Jackie asks as they sit down on a bench facing the river where sailboats scud every which way across the Potomac. While she waits for Luke to consider his reply she fusses over me, finally pulling the light blanket off my body.

"Once you have to meet a payroll and/or pay taxes, one's viewpoint is usually altered."

"That flies in the face of inclusion and fairness!"

"I'm not interested in my hard-earned income going towards those who sit around on their asses all day."

"But they can't help their poverty. They didn't ask to be born in a ghetto. What's happened to you, Luke?"

"Nothing's happened to me, Jackie." He runs his fingers through his hair. "I've just wised up, that's all. You know what they say. 'If you're not a liberal at twenty you have no heart and if you're not a conservative at forty you have no brain.'"

"First of all, you're not forty and secondly, not everyone is as lucky as you."

"Lucky? Are you kidding me? I busted my butt to get where I am today!"

"Well, you don't have to raise your voice…" she whines, reaching for a Kleenex as if to wipe away an emerging tear.

"Jackie, you are the lucky one! You married and inherited wealth before I even came along. Easy for you to keep pushing altruism. You receive income without ever leaving the house."

"And you get to enjoy that very income thanks to me!" she retorts. I guess I must have started to cry. "Now look what you've done. You've upset Alex." I am lifted from the confines of my steamy pram and propped in her lap facing outward.

"I don't think you even understand what I mean by 'altruism', do you?" He glances at his watch and abruptly stands. "I need to get back to the office. Let's go."

"But it's Sunday. Why do you always need to go into the office on a Sunday? It's not as if you don't already work a sixty-five-hour workweek. Lexie and I never see you anymore." As Mother puts me back into the sauna of my baby buggy she is working on an impressive pout. I consider doing the same but decide against it. That's what designated family peace-makers do. We learn early how not to be the one making waves.

"Aw c'mon, Jackie. Making partner is an odyssey of pain and sacrifice, you know that. The only way for me to get ahead is to either bill a whole bunch of hours or get a high-powered case." He brushes her chin lightly with his thumb. "And right now, it's billable hours."

Mother says nothing all the way back to the house, where Daddy leaves her on the doorstep to catch a cab to the office.

"Don't wait up," he shouts over his shoulder. "And read Atlas Shrugged. That'll explain the evils of altruism."

Once the sun's rays reach into my buggy and knock me out all over again, I sleep in the afternoon glow of our tiny back yard.

"Altruism. What the heck is so terrible about being altruistic?" she mutters under her breath as she opens and begins leafing through the Webster's dictionary. A massive tome, this, it rests on its own mahogany pedestal, a wedding gift from the William Wrigley family for her first marriage to Oliver Hart. Running her finger under the word, she reads: *feelings and behavior that show a desire to help other people and a lack of selfishness...* Aloud, she says, "I don't get it. How can being selfless or giving to others be a bad thing?" She tosses her head as if to dislodge the confusion and comes outside to rescue me from the sizzling sinking sun.

Well into my adult years I have learned that according to Ayn Rand altruism is evil. It implies man must exist solely for the sake of others and not for his or her own sake. If selflessness, self-sacrifice or service to others is the highest virtue to which man can aspire, what then of the self? It is a fool's errand to presume others will look out for one's Self. To Ayn Rand's way of thinking, and Daddy's for that matter, man must be responsible for his own Self; he honors his Self by nurturing his self-esteem and expecting others to do the same with their Selves. This is not to be confused with charity, which comes from the Self willingly, not by coercion. I don't believe Mother has been able to wrap her arms around this concept.

GETTING ACQUAINTED

Mother settles me in her lap with my head resting in the crook of her arm at a forty-five-degree angle. Tucking a cloth diaper under my chin and over my onesie, she tilts the glass bottle just right so the nipple and neck are completely filled with formula. No more sucking air, for me, thank goodness. She used to lay me on a pillow and prop the bottle with a rolled up towel so her hands were free to hold a book while reading it and smoke a cigarette with the other. But that practice has stopped, thanks to the pediatrician's recommendation she ditch the book and cigs during my feedings. Looking back, my bottle feedings may be why or how she finally quit smoking altogether. Two packs a day was her habit for a long, long time. Not even her former father-in-law's promise of money, a cruise or a new wardrobe from Bergdorf Goodman on 5th Avenue convinced her to stop.

That's the way with addiction. One can only kick a habit if and when one is ready and committed to success. Bribes and coercion simply do not work, as I have sadly learned much later. Mother claims it is her love for me which got her to quit, and I'm happy about that. I grab the bottle hovering above my head with pudgy little fists, bring it down to my waiting lips and gaze adoringly into Mother's face. How happy I am to have her focused on me and wanting to talk.

"Maybe, tonight is as good a night as any to tell you my story. Would you like to hear about Mother before she met you?"

No doubt my response comes in the form of little sighs, coos and contented gasps as I chug-a-lug the warm, cream-laden milk. I probably even blink a worshipful assent with long, feathery eyelashes, continuing to stare in the face of my new mother, a woman with whom I am still getting acquainted and in whom I desperately seek kinship.

I was born in Brooklyn in 1918, just a few months shy of Germany's surrender to the allies of World War I. This was the war to end all wars, and it not only marked the collapse of the German empire but also the Russian, Ottoman, and Austro-Hungarian empires as well. That was a big deal, Honey, because the autocrat, plutocrat, and aristocrat were to be no more. Down with the monarchy and up with the people. I digress. Over three hundred and forty thousand Americans died or were wounded in that God-awful war. While twenty-five years later the second World War dwarfed these numbers, those stats from 1918 were record-breaking. My family lost so many cousins… from both sides.

In the aftermath of the Great War, my birth coincided with an economic recession hitting much of Europe. Here at home, it was no different. While this turned out to be a brief and modest economic downturn, a more severe decline occurred when I was three. You see, the war had drawn so many men and women into the labor force to work in factories, that these factory workers who had migrated from the countryside into urban centers were now out of work what with manufacturing slowing and the demand for wartime goods way down. In other words, I was born into instant deprivation. You will never know how awful it was. Homemade pea soup was the staple five nights a week. Two-day-old bread could be had if the baker didn't run out before it was my mother's turn at the counter. She'd have to wait in a long line snaking around the corner and down the block for several hours. Our coats were threadbare. My baby clothes were fashioned from my mother's maternity dresses. My father, Martin, was never home. Always in search of a daily wage, he was. Their crudely furnished walk up, though, was neat and tidy and spotless. My parents were totally at the mercy of a postwar economy trying to sort itself out. The only good outcome of WW I in America was women, who having been drawn into the workforce, earned great respect for their competency as demonstrated when the men were away. So much so that by 1920 Woodrow Wilson urged Congress to give women the right to vote, declaring, "We have made partners of the women in this war. Shall we admit them only to a partnership of suffering, sacrifice and toil and not to a partnership of privilege and right?" I'll never forget those words for as long as I live. They are engraved across my brow.

To complicate this hardship, the flu pandemic of 1918 was in full swing by the time I was born. It lasted a good eighteen to twenty-four months, claiming six hundred and seventy-five thousand American lives - twice that of the war. Can you believe it? Families barricaded themselves in their homes against the threat of infection for fear of exposing their infants to the greatest of dangers. You have no idea, little one, how terrible it was! I'm actually pretty lucky I even made it to term as pregnant women were particularly vulnerable. Do you know I never even knew what my parents looked like until I was a year old because their faces were hidden behind masks?

Mother knew her facts, all right. She never tired of repeating the hardships surrounding her childhood, and I've often wondered why she dwelled on them so. She has recounted variations of this story at least once or twice every year since I was born. She must have wanted me to know how lucky I was, or how grateful I ought to be, but did she ever stop to consider her words *What if **you** never saw your mother's face?* Ah well, those were very difficult times for Mother.

GETTING BETTER ACQUAINTED

I remember autumn nights when daylight was nearly finished and a grandfather's clock chimed the hour. It caused me to jerk awake, stretch my chubby arms and legs with the widest of yawns and open my eyes to stare at my new mother. She shifted me to her other shoulder and I buried my nose into the soft folds of her neck because her skin was like softened butter. And what vestiges of lavender still lingered behind her ears I inhaled deeply because this was a scent reminding me of my first mommy, even though I didn't exactly know that then.

Up and down my spine my new mother stroked my back with the palm of her hand. Then lightly running her fingertips in pitter-patter circles across my diapered bottom, she crooned a poem. To coax me back to sleep, she walked around the house, swaying from one leg to the other as first, she took a step forward, then sideways or backward and onward again. She repeated this sequence with floaty pirouettes over and over again, a dance without end. Total nirvana. Mother sashayed across a sea of bare floorboards from one rug to the next as though we were island-hopping. She snapped on the front porch light, then pulled the draperies closed in the front room. Remembering to leave a lamp on in the front hall for Daddy, she returned to the now darkened sitting room where a narrow beam of light unfurled across the threshold like a stripe. Over our faded hooked rug, coffee table and sofa it stretched and climbed up the wall to the ceiling where it disappeared into the shadows. Surreal, yes, but I felt cocooned in the semi-darkness. Coddled by a velvet darkness so silky and soothing to my skin I was reminded of my first mommy's womb.

Mother liked to wrap my strawberry blond curls around her forefinger. She giggled to see the coil spring back when she let go. I often grabbed a hank of her auburn hair, too, waving it in clumsy straight-armed tugs. It was a game to amuse us both. Mother threw her long slender legs onto the sofa to stretch out on her side. Resting her head on the arm of the couch, she gathered me to her chest. She picked up on one of her stories and I listened as these were my lullaby.

When I was twelve, I was just a slip of a girl. They said I was gamine because of my colt-like arms and legs, but really I was quite delicate preferring to think of myself as a ballerina. My mother, Maisie, was very sick for a long time. She just lay in her bed, pale and concave. When she died it felt sudden because I'd always only known her to be sick, not lying on her deathbed. She died the same day my father gave me a doll, a rare luxury during those Depression years. It came from the Lost and Found box at the Waldorf-Astoria where your grandfather worked. After six weeks of waiting, he was told he could bring it home to me since no one claimed it. I didn't cry the night my mother died, nor for weeks later. I'm not sure I ever shed a tear, to tell you the truth. And I never played with that doll either. I left it in the gutter outside our walk-up.

Mother was always vague when recounting this episode. At times she attributed the cause of death to another flu pandemic, that of 1930, and at others it was cancer. What she did emphasize repeatedly, and still does to this day, is how terrible it was to lose a mother. Ironic.

My father shipped me off to Red Hook to live with an aunt I barely knew, maybe only met once or twice. She already had a brood of her own and was constantly irritated by all of them. Why she took in one more mouth to feed I only could figure later when I was older. That's when I was obliged to pay her room and board. Hers was a cluttered household of seven slovenly, ill-mannered Protestants, who ridiculed my Catholicism, hid my rosary beads every Sunday morning and colored in my mother's bible, the only thing I had of hers. Grandpa claims he had no choice in putting me in this situation, so strapped for money he was. The only wages he earned came from a janitorial job with the Waldorf Hotel. That wasn't much, I can assure you. He told me later, though, that he was so bewildered by the prospect of raising an adolescent girl on his own that he needed to place me with a woman who would know what

*to do. That made me feel even worse. Like chattel, I can assure you. By the time
I was fourteen, I was actually obliged to pay my aunt rent! The others didn't,
of course, and so mine was a true Cinderella story, though Prince Charming
was yet to show. Odd jobs at Woolworth's, the soda fountain down the street,
or Five and Dime around the corner did the trick. I kept to myself, made school
my focus and went to work. By midnight when homework was done and I was
burrowed under the covers, I'd pray fervently for a ticket out of there.*

She stopped at this point and shifted our positions so we could spoon.
Mother changed her tack and instead whispered a poem into my ear. It
was a verse I would come to know by heart:

> I didn't give you the gift of life,
> But in my heart I know.
> The love I feel is deep and real,
> As if it had been so.
> For us to have each other
> Is like a dream come true!
> No, I didn't give you
> The gift of life,
> Life gave me the gift of you.
> (Anonymous)

Poor Mother. When I recall this poem from the recesses of my mind I
am struck by how much she has needed me. As an adopted child deprived
of her birthright, I'd have thought the need was all mine. Unlike the dolly
she discarded in the gutter, I must have filled a chasm left deep and raw
by all her tragic losses.It was more about how I could fill her cup and
less about filling mine. She couldn't help it, and I learned very early that
protecting her was the right thing to do, even if it cost me dearly. There
were many nights when I stared into Mother's eyes, ever seeking me in
her gaze. Eventually, my legs always went limp and I sagged transfixed
by the effort. Night after night, I fell asleep to the melancholy of her
youth, dozing to the tick-tock of that clock ticking precious seconds. It's
as though I were marking each one until the day I'd connect with the
mother who held me in her arms.

MOTHER'S FIRST TRUE LOVE

Sitting in a sunbeam with her head buried in F. Scott Fitzgerald's latest novel, Tender is the Night, Jackie does not notice the young man approaching. She is too engrossed in a steamy romance, transported to sun-drenched beaches along the French Riviera. Idly stroking the bumble bee brooch on the right lapel of her summer dress, then tucking her hair behind one ear, her lips curl upward in a private smile as she turns the page.

"I don't mean to bother you, Miss, but would you be so kind as to tell me where the European History section is?" He stands backlit by the pool of sun which previously highlighted Jackie's bent auburn head. His hands are stuffed into seersucker slacks, a trouser originally worn by the underclass, but now the latest rage of preppy undergraduates with a penchant for reverse snobbery. A boyish grin of amusement awaits Jackie's answer.

"You're new," she says, probably placing a thumb in her book to hold the place where she's been interrupted. "Who would like to know, if I may ask?" It seems to her he is not a Brooklyn College student, but with the sun behind him, it is difficult to really tell. It isn't uncommon for locals to wander on to campus in search of coeds, so she feels justified in asking.

"I'm here for summer school," he says all in a rush. "And I'm not a townie even though I live in Park Slope."

"Well, I am a 'townie' but don't have the pleasure of living in Park Slope!" She arches one eyebrow.

"Sorry, I guess I deserved that. I just meant..."

"I know what you meant." I imagine she flashed him one heck of a smile before saying, "Second floor, turn left at the top of the stairs and go all the way to the back." She flips her book open, signaling dismissal.

"Thanks." But before he turns toward the stairs he says, "Great book, by the by. You're gonna cry crocodile tears."

Jackie doesn't lift her head from her book until she is sure he is far enough up the stairwell. When she does, he is on the third step crouched below the polished handrail of the banister pointing a finger at her.

"Ah hah, gotcha!" An impish grin lights up his face, and his eyes, so profoundly blue, sparkle from across the wide lobby. He strides back to where she is sitting, braces both arms against her desk and leans into her space. "Look, I know this is forward of me, but I just have to ask. Are you seeing anyone?"

"You may ask, but I don't need to tell."

"Wow, coy. Lemme rephrase the question. Wanna go out sometime?"

Undoubtedly, Jackie must have looked him over very carefully, noting the most sincere-looking, gentle soul of a man she'd ever encountered. Kind, definitely cheeky, but above all safe was her assessment.

"Depends on when."

"Are you free tonight?"

She hesitates before saying softly, "As a matter of fact, I am."

"Swell! Eight o'clock. Wear dancing shoes."

"Sure, but with whom will I be dancing?"

"Oh, for the love of Pete!" He smacks the side of his head in expert *duh* fashion. The name's Oliver Hart. And you are…?"

"Jackie.

"Jackie what?"

"I'll tell you at the end of the evening." She waits a beat. "Maybe."

There are photos of the Harts' home in Park Slope. Aurora Crescent, as it was once known before being donated to the Park Slope Academy, is featured in a Lifestyle section of the New York Times. Three floors of the Italianate style, with an emphasis on all things Renaissance soar impressively against an ocean of a sky. There are exaggerated eaves supported by hand-carved wooden corbels; flat red-tiled roofs with wide projections; and a stucco facade of burnt umber. In one picture a vacant wrap-around porch, extending to three sides of the first floor, screams for white wicker furniture. But the granite stairs, blended with white quartz climbing from the street to the house, are the mansion's show stopper.

Seventy-five years ago, Jackie was ushered up those very front steps to meet the Harts, her future in-laws. She was not only impressed by the house but also by the renown of its occupants. As a result, she was as nervous as a kitten. Never before had she been invited to so stately a residence. I imagine Oliver cradled her elbow with a light hand as she carried a bouquet of white peonies in one hand and a box of Whitman's chocolates wrapped in pink tissue in the other. At the first landing, where the granite stairs took a sharp left turn, she probably stopped to catch her breath and gape at Oliver's childhood home. Soaring upward toward an azure sky dotted with soft pillowy clouds, the mansion looked, as it does to this day, more like it was painted on a vast canvas, a stage backdrop for a Broadway play. *This is your home?* she must have thought wide-eyed.

In one night shot, the mansion's squared cupola, reminiscent of a Tuscan campanile, or watch tower, boasts panoramic views of a twinkling lower Manhattan and East River. The Statue of Liberty's beacon of welcome illuminates a path across New York Harbor. Whenever I look at this photo it makes my heart always skip a beat. As I study these old photos I don't know why, but I envision an Indian summer when the windows of this great house are thrown wide open and laughter spills to the gardens below. Strains of Duke Ellington's Mood Indigo are carried on a gentle breeze. The fragrant allure of honeysuckle and jasmine mingle with rose and orange day lilies.

That day, Jackie stood on the precipice of a lifestyle she'd only read about. After years of soup for supper and out-of-fashion hand-me-downs for a wardrobe, her hands trembled with anticipation. Nevertheless, she straightened her back, composed her breathing and smiled shyly. Mr. and Mrs. Hart, who were waiting at the front door, both beamed their greetings. Mrs. Hart, or Alexandra as she would soon be called, first shook Jackie's hand, but then gently pulled her in for a warm embrace, shucking all convention. Jackie, at first taken aback, wasted little time in returning the hug so starved was she for maternal affection. Meanwhile, the formidable Jackson Hart shook Oliver's hand in that peculiar way of men. Maintaining a masculine distance he grasped his son's elbow with the other hand and led him through the door. In the vestibule, Jackie immediately noticed the plush Oriental rugs laid at intervals on top of the waxed parquet stretching down the length of the house into the walnut-paneled dining room and across the hallway into a double parlor with library beyond. Undoubtedly, these swallowed all noise from any footsteps, be they Mr. Hart's deliberate ones, a child's scamper, or the cook's, or housekeeper's or chauffeur's inconspicuous errands through the house.

When Mr. Hart approaches Jackie with an outstretched hand, he pauses studying her face. With arms akimbo and scratching his bald spot he remarks, "I know you, but how is the question?" Before Jackie can respond he exclaims, "I know! You're the girl who won all those academic prizes! Well, I never..." He slaps Oliver on the back as if to congratulate him.

"A pleasure to make your acquaintance, sir," she whispers barely looking up.

"Come, come. No need to be bashful. You must stand tall and be proud of your accomplishments. I hope you took that scholarship to, let me see, where was it, the New York School of Design?"

"No, sir. That wasn't meant to be," she says, eyes still fixed upon their four shoes; one a dull and scuffed pair facing his polished to a gleam.

"Now that's a shame, indeed. But here you are, and I am so happy Ollie has had the good sense to introduce us to such an intelligent young lady."

Jackie finally makes eye contact and smiles gratefully. Shame on Ollie for not telling her ahead of time that his father was the former Superintendent of Schools for New York's five boroughs. Not noticing the maid lifting the flowers and chocolate from her hands, she allows herself to be propelled into the parlor by the one man who would eventually play the most pivotal role in the rest of her life. As she looks over her shoulder, Oliver and his mother are deep in animated conversation.

It was not but a few weeks later, Oliver is scooting across the front seat of his Packard to rest his arm lightly across Jackie's narrow shoulders. In silence, they stare across Upper New York Bay at the twinkling lights of Manhattan. The Statue of Liberty holds her beacon high, its shining light pointing toward Ellis Island, never at rest from the daily chaos of immigration. The Brooklyn ferry is gliding across the water, yellow lights festively buoyant in the distance. Oliver has already lowered the fawn-colored convertible top and grabbed a lap rug from the boot, but Jackie is comfy without it. The car's sheen of inky midnight blue melds into the darkness where they sit under a vault of stars hanging low. Oliver has parked atop a hill behind a stand of willows, out of sight from the street. All is quiet save for the caroling crickets' love songs punctuating the night. A single blue stripe of moonlight reaches across the waterway in front of them, the man in the moon seemingly smiling directly at them. Occasionally, though, a scrim of cloud drifts across that happy face rendering him no longer so decipherable.

"I'm in love with you, Jackie Beecham. You know that, right?" He hugs her tightly to him. Then turning to face her and looking earnestly into her eyes he covers her demurely folded hands with his own. "Ever since that day at the library six weeks ago I knew I'd be asking you to marry me."

"Why Oliver Carlton Hart, is this a proposal?"

"Um, I think it just might be…" He begins utterly deadpan, but because she turns away so sharply in her seat, he gushes, "Of course, it's a proposal, you silly goose. Say 'yes'!"

Looking up and down at him as if he might have forgotten something, Jackie goes back to gazing at the moonlit view.

Oliver, cursing to himself, leaps out the car, frantically pats first one then the other pocket, finds what he is looking for and drops down on bended knee in the open driver's side doorway of the Packard. "Jackie, this is not a question. It's an order. Marry me!"

He must have looked pretty darn silly kneeling on the grass on the driver's side what with Jackie all the way over on the passenger side, but she leans across the seat until she is virtually lying down and cups his face with both hands.

"You wonderful man, what took you so long?" she asks with a feathery voice, soft as down. She kisses him with her generous mouth, he gazing into her eyes, those dark pools of liquid brown he'd come to love so much. Her long dark lashes flutter against the pillows of her cheeks. Letting go of all inhibitions, Jackie allows herself to be pulled out of the car and into Oliver's arms.

No doubt, they kiss for hours, huddled on the ground under a night sky slowly evaporating into morning. Like a stage curtain being pulled up to the rafters to reveal the next scene, a glorious turning point is dawning.

"Is that a 'yes'?"

"Mmm hmm."

"Love you."

"Love you more.

"So is that a 'yes'?"

"It is a 'yes'. Yes."

Oliver was the love of Mother's life. When making her frequent return visits to the past, a place she consistently preferred to linger throughout her lifetime, she conjured Oliver as if it were still 1940 and America had not yet entered the war. While I was growing up, she often chronicled her whirlwind romance and first two years of married bliss with nothing less than an ardent longing for him. He was so attentive and adoring of her. As Mother told it, she doubted he would ever have pulled a single all-nighter at the office, the implication being he never aroused Mother's suspicions of infidelity the way Daddy had. I came to think of Oliver as someone who could have just as easily adopted me. As a result, I often fantasized about what he might have been like as my father, he always being described as so available and affectionate. The daddy I knew was aloof and undemonstrative. Perhaps this comparison was a habit learned from Mother. After all, Oliver's ghost lived in my present day after day, year after year long after tragedy struck.

HEARTBREAK

**CONGRESSMAN JACKSON H. HART'S SON
DIES IN ALASKAN MOUNTAINS 18 SEPTEMBER 1944**

A C-47A airplane has crashed 17 miles east-northeast of Mt. McKinley into an unnamed shoulder, killing all 19 aboard. The C-47 was approximately 35 miles off course en route from Anchorage to Fairbanks with 16 aboard heading on furlough from service in the Aleutians. The crew, flying at 12,000 feet when they encountered a severe downdraft, was forced to go on instruments into the clouds. The C-47 hit belly first with the fuselage splitting open, then caromed down a precipitous slope coming to rest a third of a mile down from the point of impact. The government could neither find nor recover the casualties because of avalanche dangers and the rugged surrounding area. 1/Lt. Oliver C. Hart is survived by his new bride, Jacqueline Beecham Hart.

Since that dreadful day, I don't believe Mother has ever recovered. She wears grief like a shawl, it permanently draped over her slender shoulders and across her heart. Invisible though it may be, I can see its glistening gossamer threads are woven with a lifetime of tears. Much like a web spun to capture prey, this diaphanous net has claimed a third victim: first her mother in 1930; then her own fertility six years later; and ultimately Oliver, the love of her life. With his death being the final heartbreak in a string of tragedies taking possession of most of her twenty-six years, she has been unable to transcend misery. Over the course of a lifetime, I've watched how she rarely ever feels genuine joy thrumming in her chest. Nor is her smile ever that of a truly elated woman. There's simply an imperceptible layer of unrelenting sorrow barring her from stepping out into her present reality where goodness is tangible. It seems as though she is perpetually encumbered by these three devastating losses. It's as though she subsists within a silent scream. And having adapted to a state of melancholy from which she can't or won't ever escape, it appears she has grown accustomed to this emotional stasis.

As a result, Mother has always been a stranger to me, living in a cocoon of papery layers designed to shield her from ever being emotionally available to others. Perhaps, it is her way of never being touched by any more trauma. It's as if she were still curled up on those cold, bare floorboards of her Anchorage apartment where she collapsed upon hearing the heartbreaking news. *Your husband's army transport plane is missing, ma'am. They're saying the C-47 strayed off course somewhere in the Mount McKinley Range.* Frozen in stunned silence, she probably dissolved in slow motion to the floor while the junior officer who delivered the message stood by helplessly. And curling herself into a ball, tucking bare legs under her night shift and enveloping her auburn head with trembling arms, I can just envision her waving him away with one flimsy flick of her wrist. I have no doubt she descended into a numbing sleep of escape and denial. Supposedly, First Lieutenant Fitzsimmons grabbed Oliver's woolen bathrobe from across a chair and draped it across her body before seeing himself out. When he returned the next day, she was still huddled beneath Oliver's robe shivering, but awake. No doubt embarrassed by her predicament, his message spilled carelessly from his lips: *They found the wreckage ma'am. Up in the clouds at eleven thousand feet. The fuselage is busted in two. Cockpit's still in tact at the peak, but the rear end slid half a mile downslope. It's buried under a drift of snow and hangin' over a glacial crevasse.* Mother could only have looked up with a single question in her vacant eyes. *No, ma'am. No survivors. Not even bodies. All eighteen of 'em are missing."*

Fitzsimmons, a shy junior officer and barely twenty-three years old, might have shifted his weight from one foot to the other, knowing he needed to do something for Mother, but what? He probably stared out the only window of the attic bedsit which happened to frame Mount McKinley like a painting. That jagged twenty thousand foot peak, small in the distance yet ferocious in its daunting dominion over the valley now held sixteen men captive in an arctic embrace for the rest of time. What had these guys done to be so brutally punished as they made their way home to loved ones? With a flat, blond light warning winter's imminence, Fitzsimmons could not have imagined any rescue or recovery of bodies occurring until next spring's thaw. He must have felt swallowed up by pity and gloom. Mother continued to lie there seemingly catatonic, making him feel, no doubt, like a voyeur. So he sidled toward the door. *The Army will be in touch, ma'am.* The vapor of his breath, cold enough to be visible, billowed into the room. So, he went over to the tiny fireplace and added newspaper for kindling and another log to the grate. Lighting the paper then stabbing the logs with a poker, he watched as a flight of sparks raced up the flue and flames crackled to life. Looking over his shoulder at Mother he probably pleaded with his eyes for her to get up. She must have blinked her assent with a tiny nod then waved him away.

Three days later Congressman and Mrs. Hart arrived in Alaska to pick up their daughter-in-law and bring her home. From the sky, an azure so radiant one could almost believe in God's mercy, Congressman Hart probably fixed on the crash site and what debris was still visible below. I can see him drawing deeply on his filterless Camel, eyes squinting against the acrid smoke curling around his face and balding head. He studied that mountain range for clues, not only not ready to give up on bringing his son's broken body home, but also hatching a plan of recovery; an expedition that would become the first of its kind both in magnitude and in peril. It was then he gave that place of saw-toothed horrors its name. Mount Deception.

Ironically, the day Jackson and Alexandra Hart escorted Mother back home to New York, the Alaskan skies were as clear and kind as ever. Spangles of light probably danced on the snow-covered tarmac while an orange sun rose above the frozen horizon setting it aflame. Snow crystals swirled about them as they walked out to the waiting plane, its engine droning with propellers feathered. The majesty of Mount McKinley with her ice-encrusted peaks bathed in stunning hues of pink, her valleys in shades of deep rose, melted upwards to a periwinkle heaven. It's as if with her beauty she were making a mockery of this most dreadful of days.

On any other day but this solemn one, Mount McKinley would have been a spectacle to photograph because seldom did she ever come out from behind her shroud of fog to smile so gloriously on mortal man. For Alexandra and Mother, one a grieving mother the other a heartbroken widow, this sunbathing mountain was a travesty of nature that day. No wonder neither woman could bear to look at her vertical peaks and undeserving crown. An unholy cemetery of jagged, rime-covered rock and bottomless chasms was up there. Wherever Oliver lay in his ice-bound grave, he was now going to be eternally entombed. A loving son and adoring husband not laid to rest, but gone forever, frozen both in time and grimace. I can hear Mother mournful, even accusatory. *Why? Why did Ollie have to enlist?* and her mother-in-law, Alexandra, replying, *He's a hero, dear. You must always cling to that.* In spite of her own grief, what an example of courage she set for her daughter-in-law, though I imagine Mother never did subscribe to that perspective. Especially since the army failed so miserably in its search and recovery. The Hart family returned home to New York without their boy.

I am puzzled by Mother never knowing why they were billeted in Fairbanks and Oliver was stationed on the Aleutian Islands during World War II. Did Oliver have anything to do with the Lend-Lease Program between the Soviets and our government? Lend Lease otherwise known as *An Act to Promote the Defense of the United States,* was a program under which the United States supplied France, the United Kingdom, the Republic of China, and the Soviet Union with food, oil, and materiel.

It began in 1941 ending in August 1945. This included our lending warships, planes, and munitions in return for leases on Allied army and naval bases for our military operations during the war.

Delivery to the Soviet Union was by way of Arctic convoys and though the Arctic route was the shortest and most direct means for lend-lease aid to the USSR, it was also the most dangerous. Due to weather and the presence of the Japanese hidden among the Aleuts on the Aleutian Islands, transport of materiel was under constant threat. Some 3,964,000 tons of goods were shipped by the Arctic route; 7% of it lost, 93% arriving safely. This constituted 23% of the total aid to the USSR during the war.

Franklin D. Roosevelt compared, a bit simplistically if you ask me, his Lend Lease plan to one neighbor's lending another a garden hose to put out a fire. "What do I do in such a crisis? I don't say, 'Neighbor, my garden hose cost me $15; you must pay me $15 for it.' I don't want $15. I want my garden hose back after the fire is over." To my way of thinking, that can only really apply to ships and aircraft. After all, food, bullets, and oil once *borrowed* are used up, are they not?

Joseph Stalin is quoted saying at the Tehran Conference in 1943, "Without American production, the Allies could never have won the war." What he meant, but would never admit publicly is that without the U.S. the Soviet Union would never have been able to beat back the Nazis.

Maybe Oliver played an important role in Alaska's strategic defense position against Japan, commonly known as the Aleutian Islands Campaign, or *forgotten battle*. A small Japanese force had occupied the islands of Attu and Kiska early on. It's where their remoteness and the challenges of weather and topography delayed U.S. forces in ejecting them for over a year. These islands held enormous tactical value due to their ability to control Pacific transportation routes. America was not about to let them go. Furthermore, America did not want to see aerial assaults being launched from that position against the lower forty-eight. According to U.S. General Billy Mitchell who stated to Congress as early as 1935, "I believe that in the future, whoever holds Alaska will hold the world. I think it is the most important strategic place in the world."

What about Oliver's duty having something to do with the Manhattan Project? This a research and ultimate development of nuclear weapons which were dropped on Hiroshima and Nagasaki forcing an end to the war with Japan. It can only be conjecture on my part that Axis spies were getting ever closer to obtaining information during the fall of 1944. Perhaps, too close. Under the auspices of moving men on furlough could Oliver's transport really have been carrying a pouch of highly classified information? As conspiracy theorists would have it this might have led to the transport's deliberate demise in order to cover up the possibility of national secrets of the highest classification being exposed. Didn't Mother wonder why, after the crash, Jackson tagged that formerly unnamed peak *Mount Deception*? The Army knew what happened that day, but they weren't talking.

Sadly, all the families of the dead soldiers were kept in the dark. A war was on, so of course, no information was going to be leaked. That, though, didn't make it any easier for the loved ones who needed closure. Even Mother, whose congressman-father-in-law had the clearance to inquire, wasn't given any special privileges. I, on the other hand, would have wanted answers yesterday and doggedly harassed every single soldier or civilian who'd pick up the phone at HQ, the War Department or the newly constructed Pentagon. I would have hounded Congressman Hart, as daunting an endeavor that would be. In all fairness, though, *ladies* just didn't make nuisances of themselves in those days; *women* today, however, would. I guess I wouldn't have been much of a *lady* then; too assertive and outspoken. Anyway, Jackson was not a man one browbeat; not if you valued his respect and/or good graces. He could be very stern, unrelenting if he so chose. He only imparted what he felt was necessary. Nevertheless, he did eventually come through with information, and the families were eternally grateful.

Just two short months after the accident, Mr. Hart wrote:

November 16, 1944
To the Next-of-Kin of the C-47 September 18th Crash:

I have received the following additional information concerning the crash of the C-47 plane on September 18th. This is written from memory some twelve hours later.

The plane left Anchorage in the early morning - somewhere between 6 and 8 A.M. The flight normally would have required about 2 hours. It was a transport plane operated for the government by one of the well-known commercial lines and was piloted by an experienced commercial pilot. As is customary on such routine transport flights, parachutes were probably not carried.

Within a few minutes after the takeoff, the pilot reported by radio that he was over Talkeetna, an emergency landing field on the regular route. Shortly thereafter he radioed for permission to increase his altitude to 9,000 feet on account of fog or mist. This was granted by radio from Anchorage, and the pilot, in his acknowledgment, predicted that he would pass over Summit, another emergency field, within a normal number of additional minutes. This was the last radio message from the plane.

Within two hours the field at Fairbanks had reported the plane overdue. Immediately the commanding general of the area directed that the army's great resources be devoted to finding the plane. Many searching planes set out that very day, Monday. Tuesday flights were impossible because of bad weather. Wednesday the search was resumed and on Thursday, the 21st, the wreckage was discovered from the air. Photographs were taken. Enlargements showed no signs of life. Doctors, medical supplies, food, etc. were immediately made ready for parachuting to the site of the wreck. Meanwhile, however, further photographic enlargements disclosed conclusively that there were no indications of survivors. Since the parachute descent would have involved great danger due to the nature of the terrain and violent winds, it was decided not to risk additional lives.

The plane first struck a ridge of Mount Baker within about a hundred feet of the top. It rebounded from the precipitous side of the ridge and fell some 1,500 feet to come to rest on a steep snow field. The location is between Eldridge and Muldrow glaciers at an altitude of some 9,000 feet. The immediate vicinity has never been charted. It shows blank on the most detailed maps of the United States Geological Survey. The temperature was between 10 and 15 degrees below zero Fahrenheit.

The wreckage shows clearly in the enlarged photograph. There was no fire. Wings remain almost intact. The fuselage tore loose and lies almost parallel and close to the wings. About a quarter of the front end of the fuselage is shorn off at an angle toward the rear.

Experts believe there was no foreknowledge of impending disaster else there would have been additional radio messages, or else the pilot would have turned about and returned to Anchorage. They also believe that death was instantaneous. The angle of shearing of the fuselage may indicate that the pilot, an instant before the plane struck, may have seen the ridge before him and have attempted to pull the plane up.

The Honorable Jackson Hathaway Hart
United States House of Representatives

Congressman Hart invited all those who lost a loved one on that doomed furlough to come to New York for a detailed, off-the-record explanation. Paying for their round trip travel and a one-night stay in a hotel near LaGuardia Airfield, he treated them to a discussion given by the man whom Hart had hired at his own expense to mount a second and more thorough recovery expedition. Since the military's mission was found wanting and the families were desperate for closure, Jackson

Hart wouldn't dodge providing them what he was so privileged to have acquired for himself. Crowding the room rented at Laguardia Airfield to capacity, seventy-five men and women came to hear the truth from the leader of what was then the most arduous and dangerous glacier search and rescue ever attempted. No lives were lost, thank goodness, but none of the soldiers were found either. The only things retrieved from the crash site were a deck of playing cards strewn in the snow, an unopened bottle of Jack Daniels, Wrigley chewing gum, furlough papers and several photographs. Oliver's army cover, identified by the photo of Mother tucked inside, was discovered buried beneath ten feet of snow.

Imagine my surprise when some seventy years later I discover a whole host of websites covering this particular catastrophe in 1944. If it weren't for the internet and my random curiosity, I would never have seen the photographs or read all the literature written about the crash or the recovery mission. I cannot begin to describe how surreal it was to read a chapter of my mother's life as an actual documented and published event. As if reading his obituary, I fell instantly into a kind of mourning for a man I never met, but always felt so close to because he lived on in Mother's heart. Just before shutting down my computer, one last article caught my eye. It was a jacket cover of a recently published mystery novel surrounding the very crash in which Oliver died. The author, Jim Proebstle, provided his email address and heaven only knows what ever possessed me to shoot him an email, but I did.

Ten minutes later he is on the other end of my telephone line. After we get past the usual pleasantries of making each other's acquaintance, he remarks, "I wish I'd known of your mother's existence when I was writing my manuscript." And my reply is apologetic. She would not have been able to contribute. She was kept in the dark as she was too distraught.

"That grieves me terribly," he replies solemnly. "The pilot of that airplane was my uncle."

I am speechless and begin to cry. Not just for the re-opening of an old wound which left Mother so permanently altered, and affected our family dynamics going forward, but for Jim, too, whose uncle not only died in that crash but who also brought a regrettable ignominy to his own name and family. Jim explains how hard it has been for both his family and that of the pilot's because no one ever talked about it. He and his cousin, Jack, the pilot's son, spent years collecting all the data surrounding that fatal flight because they, too, needed closure and couldn't achieve it without knowing all there was to know. It's a means for catharsis, possibly even redemption, Jim acknowledges, that the two cousins collected so much information over the course of their lifetimes. And it's by fluke that Jim, a budding author in his fifties, decides to base his second novel on this particular historical event as it provided too good a backdrop for a World War II mystery.

The following day, not only did I order Jim's book from Amazon, but I received this email from Jim's cousin, the pilot's son:

Dear Alex:

Your emails have been forwarded to me by Jim Proebstle, author of Fatal Incident. I am the son of the pilot, Capt. Roy Proebstle and since 2005 the archivist for most of the materials connected with the crash. I have many photographs taken at the time of the crash and at the time of the recovery effort in November. I also have the crash report, letters and correspondence with Congressman Jackson Hart, father of Oliver Hart. I made an attempt to make a contact list of the relatives of the crash victims. The Joint Prisoners of War and Missing in Action Accounting Command (JPAC) is ultimately responsible for the recovery and has the contact list on file for possible Mitochondrial DNA identification purposes of the remains. Prior to his death in 2007, Brad Washburn (a glaciologist and member of the recovery expedition) advised that the plane would soon be emerging from the Eldridge Glacier and that immediate attempts should be made to locate the plane. Since then, many attempts have been made to interest JPAC and others to search for the plane, with no success. Our hope is that some day the remains of the crew and passengers will be recovered for proper burial in their home towns.

Jack Proebstl (Jim's cousin)

After Oliver died, the Harts embraced Mother as their own. Overnight, she morphed from daughter-in-law to unofficially adopted daughter, becoming a permanent member of the Hart family. So much so, that when Mother eventually remarried in 1948, Jackson and Alexandra accepted Luke Saunders as their son-in-law. How bittersweet and welcoming of the Harts. When adopted into the fold four years later, I acquired the best Grammy and Gramps a girl could ever hope for. It was a remarkably loving turnaround for Mother and me!

COUP DE FOUDRE

My mother, Jackie, and my father, Luke met on board a navy transport vessel in May of '45. They were both on their way to Le Havre from New York. She to Cannes on the French Riviera where she was to serve as hostess with the Rest and Recreation branch of the American Red Cross. And he detailed to Eisenhower's Allied Expeditionary Force for the final push into Berlin.

As the story goes, it was love at first sight. When the ship slowed to two knots entering Le Havre, it was night time. Finally, the nauseating pitch and roll across the Atlantic were over. And mercifully, they'd not encountered any U-Boots, thanks to the convoy method employed by allied ships crossing the Atlantic between America and Europe. Jackie and Luke were huddled at the railing so engrossed in each other, I imagine they didn't notice a thin ribbon of light twinkling along the Normandy coastline. Instead, Luke lit Jackie's Lucky Strike, cupping the flickering flame with tapered fingers, his head bent close to hers. She examined the tip briefly before inhaling deeply, then tossed her head backward and exhaled slowly. He lit one for himself, squinting through the smoke engulfing them both. His blue eyes narrowed as he stared at the port city of Le Havre. Something didn't look right. Perhaps, it crossed his mind that the blackout had been lifted, but I imagine his trademark cynicism prevailed and he thought instead, *Nah, no such luck.* Overhead, bossy seagulls wheeled and dove in raucous protest as the ship slid by their nests atop buoys and pylons. Salt water slapped the hull in gentle timing as it cut across the harbor without a wake.

Jackie must have shivered because Luke snatched an Army issue blanket from one of the wooden deck chairs and wrapped it around her shoulders.

"Wanna borrow my long johns?" he asked with a twinkle in his eye.

She shook her head and smiled wanly, doe eyes round and glistening. "I'm so afraid."

Holding her close, he said, "Don't be. We've got those Nazi bastards on the run, so it won't be long now."

Suddenly the ship's horn blew a series of loud and long and very deep blasts. Cheers were ringing out along the beach as did a chorus of klaxons from French trucks parked along the quay. Strains of La Marseillaise playing on accordions could be heard coming from every direction. Couples danced. Dogs barked. Boys splashed into the harbor with whoops of joy while girls, lifting their skirts unabashedly, twirled across cobblestoned streets. The red, white and blue of Allied flags waved in great sweeps of glory.

"It's over!" a sailor on board shouted. "The Krauts have surrendered!"

I think this must be what happened next: Daddy turns to Mother, clutches her face in both hands, then shouts, *Marry me!* And he kisses her long and slow underneath a sky as soft as velvet; a sky filled with a treasure box of stars.

After VE Day Mother and Daddy had a long courtship, no doubt out of respect for Oliver, for whose memory Mother needed to mourn and properly commemorate. So, they didn't marry until 1948. Wishing to protect and honor the Harts by keeping her marriage to Daddy a modest affair with only two witnesses, Mother chose a little chapel on Montmartre in Paris; far away from New York and any vestiges of her past and/or previous nuptials. When they returned to the US a year later, Daddy entered Georgetown Law School and Mother went to work for Congressman Hart.

At this juncture, I was not yet even a twinkle in anyone's eye.

THE RANCH

Echo Lake Ranch, or "Hart's Madness" as it was called over a century ago, lies ninety-eight miles west of Laramie and borders the Medicine Bow National Forest to the east near a small village by the name of Saratoga. At the time of its purchase by my great-grandfather, Carlton Hart (Jackson's father), a sum of $10,000 was paid for two thousand, forty acres of vacant nothingness. The property was a wasteland of fall-down and unwanted timber scattered in random piles like pick-up-sticks. Abandoned by loggers for miles in every direction much of Carbon County was for sale. This was where Carlton Hart saw an opportunity. And three generations later it is where I began spending much of my time growing up when not in school or traveling with my parents.

Despite the clear-cut of a barren, even hostile panorama, Carlton saw the land's potential for cultivation as farmland and grazing. The property afforded plenty of water. Echo River meandered lazily in big serpentine curves through the property on its way to the North Platte River. And at the foot of Echo Mountain lay two lakes: twenty-acre Echo Lake and eighty-five-acre Greta a mile away. To the north and west stretched arable land for growing crops; grasslands for horse herds and cattle to graze; and tree plantations for the paper mills. While at first, it was the Jeffersonian hobby farm and business, eventually it became a playground for Carlton's descendants, his future heirs.

This was his vision and a very daring one at that. Who would have the courage to buy such a large tract of seemingly dead land even if it were cheap? What did Carlton see that others could not? Family lore would have his decision emanating from his business partner's retirement plan; that of William Wrigley, Jr. At that time, Mr. Wrigley's interest in purchasing Catalina Island off the coast of southern California inspired Carlton to look for a similar refuge, but much closer to home, which was Denver. Since he and his family were already members of the Snowy Range Golf and Angling Club and familiar with the northern Wyoming area, the land near Saratoga seemed the answer to all his prayers. After the plunder done by the railway barons in their quest for lumber with which to lay their tracks, the Hart family needed to restore the habitat of native species, such as mule deer, antelope, bobcat and red fox. Next they built a barn which housed hogs, draft, and saddle horses. They planted fields of alfalfa, potatoes, and buckwheat; cultivated a vegetable garden; started a beef herd from scratch; and stocked the lakes with rainbow trout, bass, and perch. Not until the 1930's did Carlton's three children, Chloe, Harrison and Jackson, my grandfather, build their cabins on the shores of Echo Lake.

Echo Lake Ranch was indeed recklessness at a bargain price, but a vision nonetheless. Today, it lives on in the hearts of ninety-five living progeny of Carlton Hart one hundred years later. The vision to create a sanctuary to which an ever-burgeoning family farther and farther flung apart could return was as foresighted as his going into business with William Wrigley in the first place. Echo Lake Ranch has allowed citified children of five generations to share in the farming experience milking cows and feeding pigs, gathering eggs or gaping at the miracle of life unfold when cows calve their newborn. We, children, have all worked the land, heaving bales, picking and shucking corn, weeding or making dump runs with our trash to the pit. We have played together multi-generationally on the golf course, tennis and shuffleboard courts, rode miles of horse trail by day and by moonlight, picnic-ed, water skied and fished in the wee hours of the morning when fog rolled off the lake in great curlicues of smoky magic. They were special occasions indeed when we could throw down blankets on the fairways to count the falling stars or better yet, watch the Northern Lights dance their celestial ballet above our upturned faces.

No madness this. Rather an oasis of joy and building memories.

GIDDY-UP

Scents are memories. They keep the past alive. Besides lavender, which I've always associated with my birth mother for no reason other than I must have detected it from the womb, it's the odor of a barn that takes me back to a splendid past spent with Grammy, my adoptive grandmother, and to 1956 in particular, when she first taught me how to ride.

There is nothing finer-smelling than a horse barn. The tangy fragrance of fresh bales of hay stacked to the rafters is earthiness spilling from the loft down. Mixed in with alfalfa, an aromatic molasses-based meal called sweet feed gives the barn its hints of a bakery. Who doesn't swoon over freshly baked bread? Even the pungent fumes of manure and urine creating an acidic cocktail is sweet-smelling somehow. Add to that the smell of tack - leather saddles, leather halters, bridles and reins - dusty blankets and sweaty horses themselves, you've got a pure Eau de Barn. I'd have lived in a horse's box stall if I'd been allowed.

I have Grammy to thank for introducing me to the world of horses and some of the best adventures of my childhood. Every morning of summer she greeted me at the stables with eyes profoundly blue, brimming with gladness. Under her wide-brimmed, low-crown doeskin hat with rawhide tie cinched beneath her chin, her gaze projected childlike joy. Eyes always ready for laughter, they promised mischief and the occasional departure from propriety. She wasn't just the best, most affectionate grandmother a girl could wish for, but she also made me feel total acceptance. Being in her loving and non-judgmental midst was nirvana. I did not realize until much later how at peace I was whenever in Grammy's midst. Learning how to ride under her tutelage was the highlight of my summer vacations.

When Grammy decided it was time to put me astride a horse, I was four. But before I was hoisted onto Sandy's back, I was given a tour of the mare's entire body. Held in the stable boy's arms, Grammy instructed me to first caress Sandy's velvety nostrils then run my hands along her crown and muzzle. She demonstrated how I should hold my palm open and flat when feeding Sandy an apple or cube of sugar. This was followed by stroking her coarse-haired withers, knobby spine and wide rump. Then being lowered, still in the stable boy's arms and tipped almost upside-down, I was encouraged to run my fingers down the back of her legs. First the gaskin, then the hock, cannon, fetlock, and pastern ending with her hoof, which I rapped with my knuckles. I was very sternly warned never to walk too closely behind a horse's hind quarters as there could be a nasty kick in the offing. As far as I was concerned, Sandy was the prettiest mare in the barn, maybe even in the whole wide world. Never mind she was really the oldest, fattest and slowest nag on the ranch.

Sandy pitches her head and swings round to look at me, her long forelock draped across one big, brown, cataract-damaged eye.

"Is she safe?" I squeak.

"Of course," my grandmother replies. "While you hold the reins like a big girl, I'll be at the other end of a lead rope. That sound good?"

"What if…"

"No what if's. Sandy is so gentle, you'll be able to take a nap. I suggest you sightsee, though."

Of course at age four, and probably for several more years, I made little note of my surroundings too enthralled was I to be astride Sandy's back. And it wasn't 'til I was much older did I actually learn the names of the parts of a horse's anatomy. So, when I was just a beginner, I listened to her sneeze and snuffle. I stood up in my stirrups, as instructed to do, whenever she tinkled or pooped. And I laughed hysterically whenever she stopped to shimmy some invisible itch away. I smoothed her silken mane, leaned forward in my saddle and whispered in her ear, then stroked her neck and sang nursery rhymes under my breath.

Grammy led countless rides across Echo Lake Ranch, each of them scenic, and had I paid attention I'd have noticed that under Wyoming's blue skies dotted with big, cotton-ball clouds, heaven seemed to bend down to hold us in her embrace. We left the barn on dew-soaked mornings and headed for the Camp B Road, my grandmother astride her black mare, Sky Baby. How I marveled at her gleaming liquid-looking coat, white blaze in the shape of a star and long satiny tail sweeping the trail. Grammy usually suggested we head out to our tree plantations at the base of the Snowy Range. This was a longer ride, taking us through several stands of scrub oak on a narrow trail of s-curves, crossing a dusty county road and negotiating several saddle gates. We entered fields studded with orange hawkweed, purple thistle, and goldenrod, the fragrances of wildflowers almost stinging my eyes. The logging roads allowed us to ride side-by-side as we passed one plantation after another, the trees standing erect and proud, looking every bit like squadrons of soldiers at attention on their parade grounds. Beneath the Snowy Range cranes congregated in pairs, and when they rose from the ground, startled by our intrusion, their enormous shadows crawled across us. They looked as prehistoric as the primordial sounds they made and I was certain they were either a cousin to dragons or dinosaurs. Where a ditch swollen with rain water stood, the grass, willowy-tall and lush, was frosted with a profusion of daisies. Even at an early age, I knew not to disturb their beauty.

Grammy often suggested, we go to the Cathedral and *see if we can catch sight of a woodland sprite or one of Uncle Slim's gnomes.* Uncle Slim was my grandfather's nickname garnered from his days in the navy. Nearby was the U.S. Swamp, a marshy place where most of the trees were dead or dying. Many leaned over, dripping with Spanish moss and reaching with finger-like branches to snag the hair of little girls on horseback. The atmosphere was of the afterlife, perhaps a fitting graveyard for the Cathedral next door where the trees on either side of the road rose up so high they met in the middle to create a leafy arched roof. Huge hemlocks towered over tumbled, moss-covered boulders which centuries earlier had cascaded down Echo Mountain. I imagined God throwing a tantrum or Mother Nature wielding a punishing wand given such a catastrophic mess of boulder and fallen tree. The ferns were so fat and tall their fronds whiffled like the wings of an albatross whenever the wind rushed into the forest. In the

Cathedral where it was always so reverently quiet and peaceful, streamlets meandered down the slope in a gentle tinkling. They glistened wherever the sun's rays pierced a hole through the canopy. Filaments of spider webs stretched across low branches catching the light and shining briefly like threads of spun gold. Cushions of moss grew between rocks, giant bed pillows where Gramps' gnomes could lie down for an afternoon nap. Red polka-dotted toadstools big enough for me to sit on clung in groups of three or five at the base of the lodgepole and ponderosa bordering the Cathedral's aisle. I'd squint to see if any fairies were playing underneath their rooftops. I swear they were peeking back at me.

For many years, Grammy and I rode over miles and miles of ELR trails. A grandmother and her granddaughter coming together by chance, who shared a name, *Alexandra*, and even the birth sign, Aquarius. Little was said whenever we rode, as traveling through nature was an excursion of magic, necessitating silence. Grammy showed by her serene example how to appreciate the wonders of field and woodland, mountain and river or lake, flora and fauna. I soaked it all up like a sponge. Whether it was the aroma of wildflowers we could not see or the frogs croaking *clunk-clunk* amongst the lily pads on Greta Lake or just sitting in a sunbeam while our horses drank, I loved each of these simple delights. Crossing a summer hillside covered in ripening wild blackberries and stopping to pick them while remaining in our saddles was always an unexpected treat. Even watching the swallows dive-bombing and dimpling the lily-padded surface of Bear Paw was a spectacle for which we had front row seats. We caught sight of raccoons with their bandit faces clinging to poplars, stacked atop one another in a row, or porcupines and their families waddling in and out of the overgrowth playing peek-a-boo. White-tail deer twitched their tails in warning or bounded ahead of us, sailing over hedges, disappearing into thickets. Bears which were, seldom seen when I was a child, lumbered across our path every now and then, luckily at a distance.

When I look back now, I absolutely do owe my love for riding to Grammy. All those rides covering miles and miles of trail and varying Western terrain are indelibly stamped into my memory. Yet, I can't help but wonder if my deep affection for agriculture and the wilderness wasn't somehow already in my blood.

LEMON MERINGUE

I ran away when I was five and a half. I was caught licking the meringue from Mother's freshly baked lemon pie; a pie she made from scratch for a dinner party my parents were hosting that night. It was early Saturday morning and Mother and Daddy were still in bed when I wandered downstairs ready for breakfast and discovered the pie. It was hiding under a plastic dome against the backsplash just a tad out of reach. So, I pulled a chair over to the counter, climbed up, and with bare feet dangling in space, balanced on my belly and reached for the prize. You might think this a painful position, but I was cushioned in my favorite velour bathrobe speckled with pink bunny rabbits and white lambies. Besides, I discovered pay dirt so didn't mind the discomfort. Just hanging off the Formica counter, dipping two fingers at a time into a deliciously gooey, lemony center, then licking them with mm's and ah's, I was oblivious to all else. What with the citrus tang so sweet and sour, soft and smooth and I so delirious, I never heard Mother's slippered approach into the kitchen.

Mother interrupted my feast with an *Oh*, then a pregnant pause followed by *Al-ex-an-dra*, and another lengthy pause, drum roll please, and an emphasis on the two syllables of my last name, Saunders!

Yup, that shaming, I-am-so-disappointed-in-you gig again. I jerked my head up, wisps of hair clinging to sticky meringued cheeks, banged my head on the cabinet above with a dull thud, then flipped around so quickly I toppled off the counter completely bypassing my makeshift step stool, the chair. After she was certain I hadn't broken any bones, Mother led me by one arm to the foot of the stairs and pointed in the direction of my room. Her message was pretty clear. No breakfast, no lunch and no dinner for the rest of the day, young lady! It didn't matter, really. I was stuffed. What mattered was the lecture I received a couple of hours later.

Mother finds me on the floor in front of a set of shelves where all my toys and books are stored. I am deeply engrossed in organizing the books in descending order of size all facing in one direction. She pulls up a wicker footstool and asks for my attention.

"Pie is not a breakfast food," she announces.

"But I was hungry."

"No, you weren't. You were greedy."

"What does 'greedy' mean?"

"It means you're a little piggy."

My eyes immediately well up with tears. Embarrassed I probably blush four shades of crimson.

"The pediatrician, that's your baby doctor, says you will always have a weight problem. Your father and I don't want you to grow up fat, so we are obliged to monitor everything you eat."

"I'm not a baby."

"Alex, pay attention. Your doctor has warned us that you will always be heavy. Too many sweets and bread is not good for you. Certainly, eating dessert at seven in the morning is highly inappropriate."

"What's 'inpopiate' mean?"

"Not acceptable." Mother stands and smooths her robe. "You'll spend the rest of the day in your room. No lunch or dinner today."

No doubt I stared after her departing backside and stuck out my tongue. It was a habit I'd learned recently in school. Not pretty, I know but perhaps justified in this particular case. No question, I was stunned by the deprivation of my breakfast Cheerios, lunch-time bologna sandwich and glass of milk and that helping of Mother's party Beef Stroganoff she'd promised. I was yet to be struck until much later in life by the absurdity of this punishment, not to mention all the subsequent unintended consequences of Mother's and Daddy's handling of my so-called weight issues. Suffice it to say as the morning shadows stretched across the bedroom rug, I hatched plans for my escape from home.

Having watched enough tv episodes of Our Gang, I knew that if you were going to run away, you needed a long pole and a bandana in which to stash your belongings. The bundle should be tied in a knot at the end of a stick, then carried across one shoulder. As there were no poles or sticks in my bedroom, I used a tension curtain rod, easily wrested from the wall above my window. And having no kerchief or bandana, I used a t-shirt instead. It wasn't hard figuring out what to bring. I packed a pair of panties, socks and an undershirt, my teddy bear, and my favorite story books, Madeleine and Goodnight Moon. I thought about taking the photograph of Mother, Daddy and me standing in front of the Washington Monument, but decided against it at the last minute. Didn't need to be reminded of home or them.

It was mid afternoon when I tiptoed down the stairs and out the front door. My bundle fell off twice as I made my way to the curb, which necessitated my having to sit down on the walkway's hot bricks and retie the ornery wad. Through angry tears I finally got it fastened by using a barrette yanked from my hair. When I got to the street, I looked first left then right and froze. Where to go? Where was anything anyway? I didn't know my way around northwest Washington DC. Mother and Daddy did all the driving. I just sat in the back seat and stared out the window. So I sank down onto the curb and stared at the blacktop.

Across the street at the Dillons', empty wooden bird feeders with corrugated roofs swung from low branches in the Magnolia trees framing their house. An autumn-flowering cherry tree was in full bloom, its pink and white blossoms dancing in the breeze. Through a window, I could see Mrs. Dillon with purple sponge curlers in her blond hair talking on the phone. She paced barefoot around her kitchen at the end of a long telephone cord. Dr. Lewis, not my baby doctor, was fixing his screen door one house up. He had nails protruding from his mouth and a hammer in one hand. I think he might have been swearing through his clenched lips because the sounds were sharp and guttural. Around the corner, I heard Danny screaming at his mom that he'd pee wherever he felt like it. I was quite fascinated how a boy could relieve himself just about anywhere thanks to having the right equipment. Frequently, I asked him to show me, but when Mother caught him demonstrating his technique in our back yard against the ivy-covered brick wall, she forbid me to play with him anymore. Years later, I was told he was not right in the head. He seemed fine to me at the time. In fact, he made me laugh he was so much fun, but what did I know?

Around five thirty when daylight is almost finished, the wind riles the leaves and those that fall with each gust, skitter across the lawns of Manning Place. I watch them cartwheel up our street across the shadows of trees which are now stretching to eerie, distorted lengths. Low in the sky, a sickle moon lies on its side, offering little light. I huddle with knees drawn up to my chest and chin tucked into the collar of my sweatshirt. *Why hasn't anyone come out to get me* I wonder? *Has anyone even noticed I'm gone?* I shiver.

With that, I jump up and walk back up the driveway to very slowly circle the house. My footfall on the gravel makes crunching noises as I pass by the kitchen window where Mother is fussing over h'ors d'oeuvres. I think she had carrot sticks on one side of the plate and celery sticks with peanut butter on the other. I bang the gate when I wander by the library where Daddy is reading his Wall Street Journal. I make five languid loops around the house, all to no avail. *Isn't anyone going to stop me?*

"Hi, Mom!" I call as I come around for the fifth time.

"Oh! What are you doing out there?"

"Running away."

"Did you pack your toothbrush?" That has me flummoxed. "I'll run upstairs and get it for you," she shouts over her shoulder as she runs from the kitchen. I wait for an eternity, figuring when she returns she'll be full of forgiveness, but when she materializes with only my toothbrush and toothpaste wrapped in a small hand towel, I bolt.

"Don't forget to write!"

I return to my post at the end of the driveway and slump back down on the curb. Hugging my bundle, it having fallen yet again from the curtain rod, I try to gulp back my sobs. All around me lights in our neighbors' houses twinkle in a pattern of white, though through my tears they are nothing but blurry dots spanning the darkness. I am seized with hiccups, stuck with nowhere to go, and the realization that my mother apparently does not love me anymore.

No sooner have I this horrifying thought, than Mother and Daddy sit down on the curb, flanking my shivering body with their warm ones. Leaning in and bowing her head to touch the top of mine, Mother whispers, "I think maybe you should re-think this."

"Okay."

Daddy drapes his arm lightly across my slouched shoulders. "Little girls shouldn't travel after dark. Get it?"

I look up into his face, my lashes spiky with tears and mumble, "Got it."

"Good," they exclaim in unison.

As it so happens, I did wind up with half a tuna fish sandwich and a glass of skim milk before being sent to bed.

CHOSEN

I was five when I found out I was adopted. I remember that night because it began with a star-flooded sky. I was sitting in Mother's lap with my back to her chest, my pajama-ed legs dangling on either side of her. We were in front of a pre-bedtime fire watching the flames dart up the chimney in a happy riot of crackling yellow and orange.

"Where do babies come from?" I ask. I was looking for the birds-and-the-bees story, not for what came next.

"You're a chosen baby, and that, little girl, makes you extra special." I must have turned around to look at her because I remember how the moonlight poured through the window highlighting her face. She looked odd, as I recall. I can guess why now, but not then.

"How come I'm chosen?" For some peculiar reason, I remember noticing the little bird feeder with its windows and shutters hanging from a branch of our old cherry tree.

"I picked you out of a nursery of babies. And it was these strawberry blond curls that caught my eye." Mother coils one around her finger, letting it go to spring back. "When I picked you up, you grabbed this little finger right here." She wiggles it in front of my face and adds, "You squeezed it so tightly, I just knew you were the one for me."

I take her finger but am distracted. Through the lacy etchings of frost on the window panes, I see icicles glittering on limbs of dogwood. An unblemished carpet of white lies over the lawn, catching the moonlight and making it sparkle. It's like magic outside, but inside my thoughts are suddenly flying out in all directions and I'm frightened.

"But I thought, um, I had to come out of you," I point to her tummy. "What if my real mother comes back for me?"

"Your birth mother couldn't keep you. I'm your mother now" She tightens her embrace.

"Didn't she love me? If you picked me it means she un-picked me, doesn't it?" The corners of my mouth turn down and my lips tremble.

"I don't know why she couldn't keep you, Honey, but I'm so happy she didn't because now you're mine and I love you very, very much!"

Outside, the bird feeder is swaying as sheets of snow begin falling in a slant. The stars are gone, and in front of us, the fire has turned into a bed of ash with embers barely glowing.

I think I must have gone very still, because from that moment on I swear I felt my real mama hover beside me. She was like a spirit, who from that day forward never really left my side.

"Let's get you to bed," Mother murmurs in my ear. I remember she carried me upstairs and tucked me in with an extra long hug. I also remember how after she shut the door a sliver of light ran beneath it like a ribbon. What a surreal thing to have kept in my mind's eye.

So began a lifetime of missing Mama. It was like living with a hole inside me. I often ached with the hurt of not belonging, of feeling lost. Even in a crowded room, I could feel lonely. Over the years my curiosity about Mama never waned, probably because we shared an undeniable link of body and spirit.

That star-studded night ended with a white-out of snow falling gray/white and spooky. It was the first time Mother forgot our bedtime ritual of praying *Now I lay me down to sleep*. It also marked the beginning of my ambivalence toward winter, the emotions this season stirs about Mother if I want to be honest. Yet it also became the first day of my search to find Mama.

Of course, I never admitted any such thing to Mother. It would have crushed her. Knowing her now as I do, I imagine she returned to her bedroom with a face ravaged by tears of anguish. While I cannot question her level of concern for my confusion, I do know she is prone to self-doubt and neediness. It is most likely she feared I'd pull away from her; be more interested in the mystery of what I couldn't see or have and bored with what was in front of me. I cannot fault her for feeling that way. Rejection is probably the number one fear of every adopting parent. It certainly is for adoptees.

Over the years it became apparent that my adoption was more about Mother than about me. It's been tied up with the tragedy of losing her own mother at an early age, her infertility; and her desire for a perfect, magazine-cover family. I doubt she has the first clue of what it's like being adopted. She never asked me once, so how would she know? Perhaps, she was too afraid. At the time, I was obviously too little to get caught up in what was going through my mother's mind. I had a lot on my plate: the fear Mama might come and take me away for one; secondly, the fear Mother might un-choose me, too. What had I done to deserve being rejected was a prevailing concern. I needed to know what it was, so I wouldn't do it again and risk losing everything.

All I really wanted then was for Mother to love me, keep me close. I clung to her words *you were chosen* and *you are special*. They chased each other across my mind for two-thirds of my life. I even believed it when Mother told me she selected me from a brood of bawling babies. After all, the fairy tale was enchanting and I its leading character. I don't think it was until I was thirty or so that it even occurred to me how an adoption is achieved. It's an arduous process of testing and matching and bureaucratic protocol done by social workers of every variety. There's no choosing to be had.

I was torn between wanting to know the mother who belonged to me and wanting to belong to the mother who wasn't mine. The second-guessing of all the what-ifs or could-have-beens came later. In the meantime, I settled for acceptance or at least the pursuit of it. I suffered a wound on the day of my birth, so I was in constant search of the emotional Band Aids of belonging and approval. I lived with what you might call a kind of melancholy for which there was really no cure. Over time, though, it shrank to a manageable size. I got on with the business of living.

"Two Mommies would be really complicated. I might have to say which one is prettier or smarter. What if someday, they made me pick one of them? That would be scary."

CONFUSING, INDEED

It was a blustery day when Grammy and I boarded the train in Denver bound for the ranch in southern Wyoming. As we settled into our seats, the train's whistle pierced the silence. It was a woeful sound as I remember, making me cringe a little. Grammy pulled me close and I all too happy to snuggle, remember resting my cheek against her cashmere sweater. She was so soft. When skirts of smoke billowed past our window obscuring my view of the families lingering on the platform, I lost sight of them making their farewells. But I knew there were lots of long hugs, tears, and smiles, even laughter. It looked nice, real nice. I envied it.

"The train seems alive, doesn't it?" Grammy whispers into my ear, sensing my disquiet and wanting to distract me. I nod my agreement. The train chuffs out the station at a slow pace, people outside on the platform keeping pace with those on board. Then it begins clickety clacking through the suburban towns of Thornton, Brighton, Lafayette and Fort Collins where houses become farms and front yards morph into fields. Eventually, we are streaking across flat farmland where red barns rise up against a cerulean sky and sunflowers face the sun in thoughtful, silent prayer. Ox-eye daisies dance in the wind. I grow calmer out here in the countryside. This feels better. It feels like home.

"I love you Grammy," I remember blurting, thus startling her from her reverie. "I'm really glad you're my grandmother."

"Me, too. Me, too, Sweetie." she kisses the top of my head.

"Of course, I love Mommy and Daddy, but you're my favorite grown-up."

"Do you ever think about your other mommy?" Obviously, Grammy is seizing an opportunity, I only realize now. She must have been real nervous embarking on the subject of my adoption, not knowing or even being prepared for the answer.

"Nope." The lie was meant to hide my disloyalty. "Why would I want two mommies? That would be very confusing." And that was a truth which really frightened me in those days.

"Young lady, I think you're right," Grammy says. "Very confusing, indeed!

"I feel really alone in a crowded room where everyone,
but me, seems connected. I know I'm not one of them.
So I retreat to my room to organize my books and toys,
or some even smaller place, like an attic where it's dark
and silent. The tippy-top branches of our old eucalyptus
tree are pretty good, too, cuz no one ever thinks to look
for me up there. That tree hides me from view. The more
remote, the better. At ages five, eight or ten I don't
know what this feeling is all about, but one day I'll know
I developed some pretty good defense mechanisms."

UNDER CHLOE'S BRIDGE

I must have been feeling really brave that afternoon, or maybe I was just bored. I was five or six that summer, and the urge to explore came over me like a rake handle slapping me right between the eyes. You know, when you're oblivious enough to step on one left lying around on the ground?

I simply took off and followed a deer trail through a grove of poplar until I reached the edge of Echo River. Its shore line was hemmed with giant ferns as high as my shoulders, their fronds wide and arching. Wild Queen Anne's lace poked their snowy heads above tall grasses and spindly reeds. Pillow-soft cushions of moss were so inviting I even thought about lying down for a nap, but I'd given those up for Lent. Instead, I started to yank off my socks and sneakers hopping up and down first on one foot then the other. Though the water was so icy cold it bit into my bare feet when I stepped in, I let the sandy muck squish between my toes. With each step taken, the squelching sounds were so loud and so rude I lost myself in a fit of giggles. Of course, I lost my balance, too, and fell hard on my bottom right underneath Chloe's stone bridge.

I remember just sitting there in liquid amber, legs splayed out in front of me, not dazed by any sort of injury, but transfixed by the sensation of moving water. I hadn't yet learned how to swim and baths were a chore I hated. So I caressed the water with the palms of my hands back and forth, fascinated with the texture. It felt as smooth and soft as velvet. And it gurgled when it slipped through the slimy rocks tripping over polished stones. As I sat there, no doubt numb from the waist down, a blossom floated by and under the bridge. It disappeared around a bend, and out of sight.

I have no idea what possessed me to wander down to the river, which was forbidden to do alone. Why I actually parked my butt in the middle of so freezing a bath tub, I'll never know, but it was the best thing I'd ever done. I went there as often as I could get away unnoticed and reveled in my newfound sanctuary, a place I could call my own and where no one would ever think to look for me. To this day, I still hide among the Queen Anne's lace to contemplate life's ups and downs. I like the sound of bees buzzing in the shadows. Watching squadrons of minnows dart in cloud formation is mesmerizing. Most of all, though, I wait for another blossom to glide downstream. Was it a sign? It sort of felt like one.

BLOWING BUBBLES

It wasn't much past five thirty in the morning when my Aunt Ann shook me awake. I still remember how she yanked the draperies open and started barking orders like a drill sergeant.

"Up and at 'em! Chop chop, kiddo!"

The first bronze glimmer of dawn is poking through the woods, making a tight thread of a line across the horizon. This is going to be my first swimming lesson. I don't know whether to be excited-afraid and burrow deeper under the covers or excited-happy and leap from my top bunk.

Aunt Ann hands me my swimsuit. "C'mon, Sport. Today's your big day. I'm gonna make you an Olympian, got it?" Hearing that, I throw the covers off, grab my suit, and run for the bathroom.

"No need for such modesty. We're girls, here."

"Gotta tinkle!"

As we tromp along the trail toward Hart Lodge dock, dawn is breaking. Once the sun rises higher, the looming tree shadows lose their mystery, so I stop worrying what wild animal might be lurking around every corner. This is, according to Gramps, the time when bears come down to the water's edge for a breakfast drink. By the time we make our way onto the dock the sun is shining down on Echo Mountain, turning her forested hillside first mauve then dusty rose. The lake is sheer glass, not even a ripple disturbs its surface. Yet here and there, battalions of gnats swarm over the water's veneer, and I wonder why they want to tempt fate. Don't they realize fish and frogs lurk just below? Gramps has taught me that one, too.

"Let's get in the water, Sport. C'mon. Down the steps you go."

I gawp at her standing hip-deep in the water. I'm pretty sure there is muck oozing between her toes.

"You'll be fine. The first lesson is just standing here, so you can get comfortable."

"But…"

"No 'but's. While you stand here," and she slaps the water, "I'm gonna talk and you're gonna listen." Aunt Ann caresses the water with the palms of her hands and waits patiently as I descend the stairs one tentative pudgy footstep at a time.

"That's great! Look at you. In the water in no time. Hah!"

"It's icky," Suddenly, something slithers around my ankle. "No-o-o-o!" Hopping around, and of course, losing my balance, I face plant in the water.

"It's just a silly old weed." Though I must have looked mighty doubtful, she perseveres. "Let's splash the water and see who can get wetter. Ready? Go!"

Once I'm laughing again, she suggests, "See if you can put your face in the water and blow bubbles. When you run out of air, stand back up and breathe normally."

I do as she says but wait so long that when I stand back up I'm gasping for air.

"Okay, let's slow it down a bit. You're doin' great, kiddo, but I want you to blow bubbles, not slobber all over yourself. Count to five in your head and then stand back up. You shouldn't be out of breath. Here, lemme show you." Aunt Ann's face disappears, and the bubbles she makes are truly impressive. They sound like a motorcycle engine, but I think that's because she's put a little whine in there somehow. She makes me do this several more times until I get the hang of it.

"Now. Let's try something else. Take a breath, hold it and breathe out through your nose."

I gulp in air to the point my cheeks puff out like a blowfish and blow. Air escapes like a tire blowout from my mouth. "Try again, only keep your lips tightly closed and gently push the air out through your nostrils. Watch me."

Several tries later, I get the hang of it and as a reward, Aunt Ann pulls me into a hug and twirls me around and around.

"You're a genius, kiddo! How does it feel to be such a smarty pants?"

"Pretty good. What's next?"

"Now you're gonna practice doin' that same thing under water." My jaw drops and my eyes bulge, which causes her to laugh. "I'll be holding you the whole time, okay?"

I remember I wasn't too sure about that at all but must have agreed.

"I'll be right here the whole time. You can trust me, Lexie. I won't let anything happen to you."

And that's when I took my first plunge. At first, when I couldn't figure out how to drive the air through my nostrils, I panicked and raised my head spluttering. Aunt Ann, who was holding my hands, just nodded her encouragement with a broad smile. So I sucked in a bunch more air and went back below, this time determined. And what do you know? I made the bubbles rise to the surface! It was such fun seeing globules of air dance in front of my face on their way to the top I rose and dropped down over and over again. She stopped me before I hyperventilated.

"Look at you!" my aunt hooted. "I've created a bubble-monster!" When her voice skittered across the lake and bounced back at us, we both started to laugh. How I remember as if it were yesterday leaping into her embrace with my arms around her neck, and she bouncing me up and down and all around.

When we climbed back up to the dock, I copied my aunt by wrapping a towel around my shoulders. She stood hugging herself in the terry cloth warmth, so I did too. I remember us both teasing each other over our goose bumps and blue lips as we stood there, our legs shaking.

"Can we do this tomorrow?"

"Of course. The next step will be to get you comfortable floating on your back and your tummy."

"Do I make like a snow angel?"

"Wow! There you go again bein' a Miss Smartypants! That's exactly how it's done!"

I beam up at her. She always makes me feel so good. "And the doggy paddle? When do I get to do that?"

"Soon, kiddo. Right after you master the art of floating. That a deal?"

"Deal!"

Aunt Ann had a way with kids. She knew how to boost morale, encourage without criticism and make most things fun, even when they were challenging. I was glad she was tasked with teaching me how to swim as was Grammy with teaching me how to ride. Had Mother or Daddy been the ones, there would have been tears and upset. I can't explain why, exactly. Perhaps, they were too preoccupied with appearances, unable to handle the imperfections which occur along the road to eventual success. I don't know. They were good at other things, such as their grooming and fashion; setting the perfect table and entertaining; being well-read and able to argue politics or discuss current events. They both shared having unsophisticated roots and dreaming of a better life. Together, they were diamonds in the rough and glittered with a certain kind of promise.

DON'T EVER DO THAT AGAIN

Daddy stands at the window and lights yet another cigarette. He stares through a swirl of gray smoke, his electric blue eyes narrowed, his lips pinched in a tight line. His face is blurred by the smoke, but I know it would be unwise to interrupt his thoughts. He is tense; very tense. And so our sleeper compartment of the Pullman car feels like a grenade with its pin already pulled. So, I remain on my upper bunk, trying to look through the fumes at the same landscape Daddy is watching but not really seeing.

Outside, the start of day rushing by us is serene. Blankets of lush alfalfa undulate to an unseen rhythm as we race up to New York City. Rows of sunflowers turn their faces toward a radiant sunrise as we charge through Pennsylvania farmland dotted with barns and livestock. These fields give way to glossy stretches of mown lawns in front of colonial-style houses, azalea bushes in splashes of bright pink or purple, red swing sets and basketball hoops. My attention is captured by the alluring sliver of lavender at the edge of our horizon, followed by salmon pink then yellow, and azure. Such a glorious sunrise makes everything golden, and bands of sunlight reach through our window and into our compartment. As we clickety-clack our way toward Mother, that sky is the color of hope. I am so excited to have her back home.

Even though the sun is pouring in, there is darkness in our cabin. Darkness in Daddy's silent brooding; a hush of loss hanging in the air, though at the time I wouldn't have been able to identify it as such. His mood frightens me, so I keep clear with only my pajama-ed legs dangling over the side. We remain like that for a while until the mournful wail of an oncoming train passes us just inches from Daddy's face leaning on the cold glass of our compartment. It knocks him out of his reverie and he jumps back. He faces the tiny mirror over the brass sink and arranges his necktie in grim silence. Soon we begin to chug slower and slower north into the city's looming outskirts and Penn Station.

"New York City!" The conductor blows his shrill little whistle and bangs on each door as he struts down the length of the car.

"Hurry up and get dressed," my father says in a flat tone.

"Can you pass me my things?"

"'Please'."

"Sorry. Please… with cheese," I add, instantly regretting it.

"Enough."

When ready, I hop down from the bunk dressed, but hardly pulled together.

"C'mom. Your buttons are uneven. And put a comb through your hair."

Why is he barking so? I foolishly proffer my hairbrush and a rubber band. "Can you do me a side ponytail?"

"Damnit! Seven years old and you can't do your own hair?"

Immediately, I burst into tears. "Mommy does it. Or Isabel when Mommy isn't home."

"Well, you'll have to go without today. I don't mess with barrettes and ribbons."

"But I was hoping to be pretty for Mommy."

"You're whining."

The train, trailing soot and smoke, squeals to a sudden and belching stop, which causes me to fall. I cry harder now, not because I'm physically hurt, but because I'm insulted by being dumped to the floor. I feel ashamed.

"You look fine, Honey," he relents. "C'mere, lemme fix these buttons." Sheepishly, I stand in front of him, not daring to look into his face when he kneels in front of me to rearrange my lopsided blouse.

Throughout my childhood, Daddy and I rarely clicked. We were like two dancers whose steps were alien to one another. Our tune was always off key, our rhythms out of sync. If I wanted to goof, he was never in the mood. When he wanted to tease I didn't get it and felt slighted. His expression when in repose often looked angry, almost intimidating. Too bad, since he was such a handsome man. When he smiled, he was gorgeous. I'll never forget that day on the train. It's when I first realized he'd given up on being my father. Maybe, he'd never really even begun. Was it because I wasn't his biological offspring? He'd clearly didn't sense my needs and he was clueless about nurturing my development. *Build my self-esteem? What's that?* Of course in fairness, self-esteem was not the be-all and end-all it is today. In other words, in those days you had to earn it, not just receive it. Nevertheless, he didn't seem to want to impart words of wisdom. He just thought his example was good enough, which actually it was. Maybe he thought one should figure things out on one's own, like he had. His mother and father had instilled a work ethic so intense there wasn't time left in the day for anything else but six hours of sleep, so he didn't grow up with a lot of talk or input. But I was needy; not that I knew it at the time. And I was too sensitive for my own good. I was easily hurt and uncertain; no doubt another symptom of adoption, having been yanked from the mother ship and cast into outer space. I needed far more reassurance than my tall, robust self belied. No one ever suspected my insecurities because I was so mature-looking. My hyperactive willingness to please, while deemed a good thing, didn't do me any good. This meant burying personal objections. This was a flaw plaguing me throughout my childhood and well into adulthood. Anyway, I often felt like a stranger in Daddy's midst, lonely even when seated right next to him. I hate to say it, but I frequently felt unloved or unwanted.

Apparently, Mother wasn't the only one who felt unloved and unwanted. She started telling me about hers and Daddy's marriage woes when I was quite young. The story was always the same. Daddy was ungrateful for the help she had given him when he was attending law school and working full time clerking for a judge. She had attended his classes, taken copious notes so he could sit his exams and eventually pass the Bar. Supposedly, Daddy frequently talked about all the *blond, buxom bombshells* he had dated before meeting her; comparing her with them in an unfavorable light; complaining she was too uptight and prudish. (She was a petite, small-breasted brunette who insisted on twin beds). He spent his weekends playing thirty-six holes of golf at the Congressional Club, often returning home late, sometimes even a little loaded. He worked most Sundays way past midnight. So, she felt unappreciated, unloved and belittled by his chauvinism. I would listen in sympathy, though at first much of what she said I didn't really understand. There's no question, though, that this story told me so many times over the years gave rise to an antipathy for Daddy, bringing me ever-closer to Mother, taking her side and wanting to champion her cause. Was this by her deliberate design? I wondered about that more and more as the years went by.

All of this back story is to explain why she left on a three-month cruise. She told Daddy she needed a separation; time to evaluate their marriage. So, she accompanied her former in-laws, Oliver's parents on their annual cruise to the Mediterranean. Her sister-in-law, my Aunt Ann, was also on that trip. Both women, ironically, were rethinking their marriages. So what better way was there to contemplate divorce than out on the ocean under starlit skies of indigo, putting in at exotic ports along the Amalfi Coast, touring the Greek Islands of Crete and Santorini, or cruising through the Bosporus Straits where East meets West, followed by Morocco, Algeria and Egypt? Mother told Daddy she would come home with her answer. This explained Daddy's anxiety the day we went up to New York on the overnighter to fetch her. He didn't know whether she was coming home to stay or leave.

Luxury Liner Row, aka Port Authority Passenger Ship Terminal, sits on the Hudson River between West 46th and West 54th Streets. Piers 88, 89 and 90 lie four hundred feet apart and extend into the river more than eleven hundred feet. The US Army Corps of Engineers, who controlled the water-front dimensions at the time, refused to extend the pier-head line far into the river, so the city extended the pier by cutting away at the land instead. I remember stepping from the Yellow Cab and simply gaping at the three ocean liners moored abreast each other. They loomed out of the water as tall as any apartment building on the West Side. Dumbfounded by their size, I wondered how anything that enormous could even float?

The terminal was very busy as the SS America, Mother's ship, had just put into port and tied off. I could tell no passengers were disembarking yet because the gangway had yet to be lowered. The holds were open, though, and cargo was being unloaded by large cranes swinging back and forth. As the giant mechanical arms grabbed palettes and placed them on waiting flatbed trucks, motors continued to run while exhaust billowed from their tailpipes. Inspectors walking around each truck carried a clipboard with bills of lading flapping in the wind. The officials shouted in accents I'd never heard before and they gesticulated constantly. Seagulls wheeled and dropped, calling to each other in shrill tones, eerie to my ears. Daddy moved us along quickly. Flags from nations all around the world encircled the terminal in bright cheerful hues. They slapped in the early morning breeze, adding to the already loud cacophony of port-of-call activity.

With one hand tented across his eyes, Daddy stares up at the ocean liner. "C'mon!" he urges, extending his other hand to me. We make our way through the sea of porters, longshoremen, carts and limousines only to land in a long queue for boarding the cruise ship at the end of a rickety-looking ramp. I look up to the decks where passengers in coats and hats are crowded along the railing waving. Daddy scans the faces of each person in the crowd, searching for Mother. I do, too, but the sun makes me sneeze. I keep thinking we should remain at the terminal, instead of in this line, but Daddy seems very anxious to embark. *What if Mommy gets off while we get on?* I know to keep my mouth shut.

We wait for over an hour. I watch curlicues of silvery smoke twisting from the smokestacks drift across the river to New Jersey. Daddy competes with those funnels, exhaling at least half a pack while we stand in line. Shifting our weight from one foot to another, staring up at the rails and willing the gangway to lower doesn't seem to make any difference. Nor does my father's grumblings. An annoying ship's bell keeps ringing over a loudspeaker every fifteen minutes, but I have no idea what that means and don't dare ask. A tick tock of anticipation thrums in my chest. Fish smells and bilge water make me want to hold my nose, but I refrain, knowing a reprimand is in the offing. So, I pick and flick the lint off my sleeve and play with a pulled thread on my sweater instead. Mother is up there somewhere. So close, yet still so far.

"You nervous or somethin'? Stop your fidgeting," Daddy snaps as smoke pours from his nostrils.

Mother was gone for three months and I missed her so terribly, I was sick to my stomach for much of that time. Staying home from school became routine; it was a pattern of one day in class, another at home; or two days nauseous and achy, then back to school again. Isabel and Boots, my grandparents' domestic help, were tasked with my care while Mother was gone. They did everything they could to compensate for her absence, but to little avail. Daddy, who was home the entire time, or should I say in D.C., never appeared while Mother was gone. I'm not sure he slept at the house because I never saw him. I presume he went to work and played golf on weekends, but I'll never know why he didn't eat his meals with us or read his Sunday paper out on the terrace with his coffee and Lucky Strikes. All I know is that while my mother was gone my whole world was turned upside down. I was confused and afraid. Every day and every night.

The ship's horn suddenly blows a loud and long and deep blast, signaling the lowering of not one but two bridges; one for going aboard and the other for disembarking. Daddy tosses his cigarette to the ground and crushes it with his loafer-ed foot. The seersucker jacket he has slung over his shoulder under a hot noon-day sun is now back on and buttoned at his slim waist. He straightens his tie, runs long tapered fingers through his hair and reaches for my hand.

"Show time!"

I slide my hand into Daddy's and hope he won't let go as we fly up the bridge, run down one deck and up another, dodging deck chairs and luggage, hopping even tripping over bulkheads. There's a reason they call those infernal things *knee knockers*. My mind is racing, too. *Will she be happy to see me? Will she still love me? Have I said or done something to make her mad? Why did she leave me behind? How come no phone call or even just an itty-bitty little postcard?* Our search for Mother on board that ship is utterly madcap as we rush to midships straight into the Grand Lobby. And suddenly, there she is. Standing in the middle of an array of matching suitcases like a movie star.

When Daddy comes to a sudden stop, I slam into the back of him. He is very still. Clinging to his khaki pants and peering around his legs, my heart flips and somersaults, and straight away I feel very shy.

I stare at Mother. She looks different somehow. For a moment I'm not even sure I recognize her, it's been so long. Has she cut her hair? She is smiling through her tears and clutching a handkerchief to her mouth. I hesitate because a tornado of emotions is playing across her features; ones I'm unable to read. I probably forgot how. Anyway, some kind of silent exchange occurs between my mother and father, because instead of approaching, she kneels right where she is and extends wide her open arms. She's waiting for me to make the first move.

I look up at Daddy. "Go on."

With that, my heart explodes inside my chest and I fly to her. "Mommy!" I scream, hurling myself into her arms. I wrap my arms around her neck as tightly as my young limbs can muster and sob into her neck. She, too, squeezes really hard. I'll never forget that hug. I am bent so far backward I cannot breathe, but we hold each other for a long, long time. When she pulls away to look closely at me, she croons, "I'm home now. I've come back because of you, Sweetie. Because of you."

Those were such welcome words, you have no idea. In an instant, all my fears evaporated. I glowed to know I meant so much to her. Such a relief. We adoptees' often subconsciously fear rejection. And while there is no blame to toss, it's just a fact that children like me, who are separated at birth from our natural mothers suffer an incomprehensible loss. Our bond with the mother in whose womb our life experiences began is prematurely and abruptly severed. As a result, we tend to be very fearful of it happening again. I think I was one of them, though I didn't know it at the time. I just knew I was very, very happy Mother was home!

THE PENNY GAME

When I was seven, I earned a seat at my grandparents' dining room table at Chuck House up at the Ranch. Gramps's ingenious way of teaching me my table manners so I wouldn't be banished back to the Kiddie Table was the Penny Game. Thanks to him, I mastered Emily Post's top twelve table manners from the Rules of Etiquette after just a few meals. Under Gramps' watchful eye and patient tutelage, he used pennies as a reward. The rules were as follows:

1. Chew with your mouth closed.
2. Do not talk with your mouth full.
3. Don't use your utensils like a shovel or stab your food.
4. Don't pick your teeth at the table.
5. Remember to use your napkin.
6. Wait until you're done chewing to sip or swallow a drink.
7. Do not gasp after taking a sip.
8. Cut only one piece of food at a time.
9. Sit up straight and don't place your elbows on the table while eating.
10. Instead of reaching across the table for something, ask for it to be passed.
11. Do not speak unless spoken to.
12. Do not interrupt.

Every day, Gramps came to the head of the table with a pocket full of bright copper pennies. He stacked them next to his water glass in several towers of varying heights like poker chips on a gambling table. Whether we dined in sunshine or candlelight, they sparkled prettily. Before each meal began, he slid five shiny coins across the mahogany table to where I sat on his right. This spot was also known as Starvation Corner as it was the last place to be served by Cook's pretty little waitress.

"These are for you, Lexie. You may keep them if you perform well today."

Wow, what a gold mine!

"You might earn more from this stash if you use good manners. You also might lose some from your pile if I see you performing poorly." I blink. "It's up to you."

So at every breakfast, I ask for the milk to be passed even though it sits on the lazy Susan. *Bingo!* Same goes with the jelly or the butter or the sugar bowl. *Jackpot times three!* I use fifteen sips to drink my orange juice from a small juice glass when it only takes nine to finish because it reveals I have mastered the art of not gasping. One cent per gaspless sip is financial independence! At lunch, I cut chipped beef on toast into the tiniest bites, always placing my knife on the rim of my plate and switching the fork from my left to my right hand. Tedious, but paydirt for each morsel! When I chug-a-lug my water after downing two scoops of ice cream with chocolate sauce on top, my pennies start to disappear. Sometimes I forget. Delirium is to blame, but Gramps brooks no excuses. Dinners are the hardest because he's more engrossed with adult conversation and misses many of my stellar moments. He doesn't seem to miss the missteps, though. And so I learn.

And so, too, I felt loved. Attention from so stern and busy a man was as good as any hug or kiss. The humor in his eyes revealed his belief in me. That I could master Emily Post's Rules of Etiquette and be a star in his eyes was a big deal. He intimidated lots of people. Not me for some strange reason.

INVISIBLE IS GOOD

"Only one 7-Up, Alexandra. There's a lot of sugar in soft drinks and I'd recommend you unlearn the taste for them."

"Oh, c'mon Mother! Pretty please? Two isn't gonna hurt."

"I don't think you understand how important it is for a girl to keep her figure."

"Mom, I'm nine. Why would I care?"

"When I was your age, I was just a wisp of a thing. It was the Depression years and we had nothing to eat."

"Not that again," I stomp my foot.

"Young lady, sit and …

Listen. For me, there were perks associated with not eating, or in your case being careful about what you eat. When you are pretty you not only attract lots of young men but you also enjoy the superior position of being selective of who to date. Men of means were my ticket out and had I not had my slender figure I doubt I'd be where I am today. In your case when the time comes, you will want that same opportunity; not because you'll need to be lifted out of poverty like me, but because you'll want someone compatible with the lifestyle to which you've been accustomed. Men with money are more fun. They provide far more opportunity than a fellow with no means. You don't want to sit on a porch rocker all your life, do you? There's travel, fine dining, the theater… Well-to-do men own sports coupes and have the means to show you a good time. The guys I dated took me to clubs, parties, tea dances, football games, and shows on Broadway. Those boys were entirely unaffected by the Depression, which was pretty darn nice.*

"What's this got to do with drinking two 7-Up's?"

"My story has a lot to do with it. Men like pretty girls, not fat ones."

I must have screwed up my face. "Don't turn your nose up at me, young lady. It so happens I don't want you to be like a girl I once knew. She was a wall flower who sat through parties never once invited onto the dance floor. She might as well have been invisible."

"Invisible is good," I mutter, but Mother is on another trip down memory lane.

I wore the latest in fashion. Seconds, of course, because that's all I could afford. Or I sewed my own clothes when I wasn't in school or working. My favorite was the bias-cut for dresses. And, ooh, those darling little bolero jackets that matched were the rage. In those days the emphasis was on broad, padded shoulders because it made a lady's hips look slim. Halter necklines were another of my favorites because it showed off your shoulders if they were worthy. Mine were. The very best, though, were high-necked, backless evening gowns with long slinky sleeves. Can you say, 'gor-gee-ous'?"

"Can I go out to the pool now?"

"Alexandra, you know the pediatrician said you'd always have a weight problem. I've told you this countless times. It's my job to make sure you only put the right food and right amount in your tummy. I shouldn't even be allowing you one 7-Up."

"Mom, I've heard this bazillion times already, It's getting dark. I really want to go out and play in the pool before you drag me in for dinner. You know, one of those meals I'm not allowed to eat too much of."

She didn't stop me when I fled outside, the screen door slapping shut behind me. As I crossed the yard at a run, pulling off my t-shirt and tossing it over a chaise longue, I pretended not to hear Mother calling after me. I dove into the pool at the shallow end, slicing the water like a knife. I stayed under for as long as I could, undulating mermaid-style with legs together as if they were my tail. Not until my lungs were exploding did I surface, hopeful Mother would not have followed me. I remember folding my arms on the side of the pool and resting my chin on top of my hands, staring out at the Island of Catalina. That evening it was as clear as a bell, the sun setting over a placid Pacific Ocean. The lights of Los Angeles in the foreground were beginning to twinkle, car headlights along the tangle of freeways but a streak of luminescence. A giant orange moon peeked its head above the horizon to the east surprising me by its sheer size suspended there so weightlessly.

I was angry. *Yes, I know, Mother,* I remember thinking. *You were gorgeous, smart and popular. Still are. You were the bee's knees. Still are. So, la-d-da! But you got born that way. I didn't. I'm not you, so stop trying to make me into you. Is it because I embarrass you? Well, tough toenails! I can't help how I look. I'll never be teeny weeny like you. Get over it, Mother, and let me be me!*

THE RUSSIANS ARE COMING

You can say my grandfather was ahead of his time, although really, given the intensifying strain between communist Russia and our country, known as the Cold War during the '50's and '60's, maybe calling him a "prepper" is unfair. Gramps's basement was his bomb shelter. In the cellar under the Chuck House kitchen and dining room, there were several rooms dedicated to an enormous cache of food and supplies. I asked Gramps if he would give me a tour since I wasn't allowed to go down there by myself. He obliged by taking my hand in his and leading the tour down a steep flight of stairs.

Before we even get to the bottom of the steps, I can feel the temperature drop ten degrees. Goosebumps spring onto my bare arms. And though the floor is cement, the air holds a dampness smelling faintly of dirt and mildew with a hint of mothballs for camouflage. The walls of the cellar are cinder block, whitewashed to make things seem cheery. Our footsteps and voices echo and the place feels more like a prison. Only one window offers any light over the laundry sink. There is an ironing board, drying racks for hand wash and a clothesline on which some of Gramps's shirts hang on their hangers, all facing the same direction like soldiers in parade formation. On the walls there are mops and brooms neatly fixed into clamps in descending order of length. From this center area, several rooms gape from open doorways like the dark maws of monsters.

I shiver in the gloom and am grateful when Gramps yanks on a little string attached to a light bulb dangling from the ceiling. This room is lined with shelves of canned veggies and fruit, dried beans and herbs, and MRE's (meals ready to eat, pre-cooked and pre-packaged for military personnel). Another room boasts four white chest freezers packed with meats, poultry, and fish.

"Why do you have so much food down here?" I ask wide-eyed. I might have even been salivating.

"Because the Russians are coming."

"Are they gonna be here soon?"

"Probably sooner."

There are fold-away cots, pillows, and blankets stored in what is called the Tin Room because the walls, ceiling, and floor are paneled by sheets of tin to keep the likes of moths and silverfish from eating everything. Another room is modified to be a walk-in safe with long guns, pistols and ammo, bankrolls of silver coin, Grammy's jewelry and bottles of Russian vodka and tins of Beluga caviar.

"Why aren't these bottles in the bar?"

"Because until the Ruskies get the heck out of Eastern Europe, I'm not consuming their products! But I don't expect you to understand, so let's leave that discussion for when you're older. Okay, l'il Lexie?" I nod. "Let's just say you'll never go hungry down here," he says smiling down at my upturned face.

"Why do you have so many light bulbs and batteries?" I ask.

"In case we run out, Lexie. In case we run out."

When the tour is over and we are back in the sunlight, I go sit on the front door step and wrap my arms around my knees.

"Not coming inside?" Gramps asks as he pulls open the screen door to the main house.

"Nope."

"Suit yourself, kiddo. I'm going to catch a nap before your grandmother gets back."

"I'm gonna wait for the Russians."

CONFOUND IT!

Chuck House etiquette at Echo Lake Ranch was rigorously upheld by my grandfather. Summoned by a gong for breakfast at eight o'clock sharp and lunch at noon was a solemn tradition, amusing nonetheless as the schedule was indelibly imprinted into our DNA. Happy Hour began at five forty-five, so if you wanted two drinks, which was frowned upon by Gramps, it was best to be on time, because forty-five minutes later, alcohol never followed the drinker to the table. That was considered uncouth.

There were countless rules: no pajamas, bathrobes or towel-wrapped heads at the table; no wet hair or curlers either. Collared shirts were *de rigeur*. And then there was crying. This was the most offensive crime, punishable by expulsion from the dining room should by the count of ten, tears still be flowing. It only happened to me once, which proved the effectiveness of his rule.

Gramps is at the Queen Anne sideboard, mixing a Caesar dressing in a wooden bowl. From the oak paneled wall, a portrait of Thomas Thomson is staring austerely down upon Gramps's balding head as he mashes anchovies with garlic into a paste followed by a vigorous whisking of egg yolks, lemon juice, Dijon mustard and two splashes of olive oil. A contented smile is inching its way across his wrinkled cheeks. This is a Chuck House specialty, reserved for only the most favored guests. And today, the guest is Judge Arnold.

"Judge, why do you call people spear-chuckers?" I ask innocently. At age twelve I'm legitimately curious. I have no idea to whom he is referring, but I'm wondering how a court judge can reveal his bias. He is my Uncle Ralph, so I feel safe asking the question.

Gramps's serving tongs clatter to the parquet floor and a hush descends around the table. My cousin shakes his head at me and mouths, *Now, you've done it!* Grammy giggles and the judge reaches for his Camels.

Stupidly, I persist. "And what's a *kike*?"

Gramps erupts. "Confound it!" Gramps's wrath is nothing anyone ever wants to encounter. Since his favor is so glorious, losing it is devastating.

Of course, I begin to cry. Great convulsive gulps burble up in between my sobs and the tears are flowing as though a dam has burst. Impossible to corral any of it and knowing I'm about to be expelled, I never even hear Gramps start to count. When he reaches ten and bellows, *OUT!* I search the table for sympathy. My cousin is doubled over laughing. Grammy is staring into her vichyssoise, but Mother? She is crying, too! Gramps points to the door. "You, too, Jackie! Both of you, out you go. Now!"

Isabelle, the cook swore she was acting on the QT when she brought lunch trays up thirty minutes later. Mother and I were commiserating on the lower bunk, with a blanket wrapped around our shoulders. To this day I bet Gramps authorized the meals being sent up. I'm sure he took pity, especially since it was the Judge's foul language during past meals that had prompted my questions. No doubt, my crying was Gramps's best excuse to get me out of the room. And since he knew Mother was not amused by Uncle Ralph's word choice either, he was happy to chase her from the dining room too. Yes, Gramps was strict. He liked order. Tears he couldn't abide, probably because they were so messy. But he was never unfair. If he said this was the way it should be, there was simply no point in arguing.

SHHHH... DON'T TELL...

If I tell you my secret, you can't ever tell anybody, especially my parents. They'd kill me if they knew I told you this. Are you ready? I have a brother. We were separated when our real parents died in a car crash. There was no one to take care of us, so the social workers split us up. Different foster families took us in and mine moved me from Chicago to Virginia, D.C., L.A. and Switzerland before coming here, to England. I don't know what happened to my brother. He could be dead, too, or maybe he's still in the Midwest somewhere. His name is Jamie. He has green eyes like me, and he is really tall and skinny. I miss his lopsided smile and those stupid knock-knock jokes he used to tell.

That's what I told friends up until I was fourteen. Not sure why I did this, except for attention. I must have been pretty adrift in those days; not at all certain where I belonged or fit in. Telling people I was chosen didn't seem to capture people's attention like it used to. Maybe, I was in want of sympathy. I'm embarrassed to admit I did this, but I'm sure there's an explanation to be had by some shrink or other.

Even though I conjured up this whole story out of thin air, I was certain I did have a brother; not a make-believe one. Oh sure, I was a lonely only, in need of an invisible friend or something juicy like that for the likes of shrinks to analyze, but it's as if I knew it to be true.

Don't feel sorry for me. I just got on with life the best I knew how. Maybe, I actually do have a brother. Ghosts of one's past are known to follow just a few steps behind, aren't they?

THE REINS OF DESTINY

In June the courtyard of box stalls at Morton Down, Daddy's stud farm, always teemed with a great show of flowers. Between each of the twelve horse stalls, vines of yellow roses crept upwards to the eaves, joining with each other in one long braid of blooms. A wide path of pea gravel surrounded the quadrangle of closely mown grass, in the middle of which Daddy often exercised his yearlings. Iris, gladiola and hollyhocks competed for recognition in the beds along the front of our stone manor house while elm trees lined the drive running from the courtyard out to the country lane. Seven of Daddy's Thoroughbreds stood at the openings to their stalls, one or two cribbing the softwood, wearing it down to a polished carving. The others nodded their heads up and down, nickering and pawing the ground. All were demonstrating the nervous energy so typical of race horses.

I remember the day when Mother and I sat side by side on a stone wall watching Daddy lunge one of his thoroughbred one-year-olds in this front paddock. The filly's dam was in a pasture behind us cantering back and forth along the fence line, skidding to a stop and pivoting to start her tantrum all over again. Clearly, she was unhappy to be separated from her foal.

"You seem pretty preoccupied. Something on your mind?" my mother asks, eyes forward.

"No," I lie. The yearling seems so willing to obey Daddy's commands at the end of her leash. Her hooves churn the sandy dirt as she lopes around and around, nice and steady.

Mother watches the training through oversized Jackie O. sunglasses, with eyes still forward. "Good," she replies. "Too much introspection never does a girl any good."

"I know."

"When I was growing up it seemed pointless to ask the why of things." She looks over her shoulder at the frantic mare then back again at Daddy and his agreeable little yearling.

"I can't help wondering…" I stop, knowing I can't really say what's on my mind because it will hurt Mother's feelings. My head is a jumble of wondering why I was cast aside by my birth mother, worrying that were I to complain about it out loud I might break my mother's heart. I recall watching the filly's hooves churn the soft dirt, noticing how willing she was; content at the end of her tether, obeying what was being asked of her. I wanted to do the same; be a good and obedient daughter, comply with my parents' expectations and fit in. I wanted to be the answer to all of Mother's prayers. After all, she suffered so much. Yet, I think now I didn't understand the burden I was trying so hard to shoulder.

As if knowing intuitively where I might be going, Mother cuts me off. "Life can be so much simpler if you just accept your destiny, Lexie. Hurt and all." She smooths the front of her quilted Burberry jacket against any unwanted wrinkles, imagined or real, and then crosses her arms across her chest. She is the quintessential picture of stoic.

A dog barks in the distance. Another not far away woofs its reply. *They're connected* I think. *They're talking to each other, not at each other.*

When I notice Sneakers, the barn cat asleep under a wheelbarrow of still-warm manure, it occurs to me *He's content. Why the heck can't I be?*

"No life is perfect, dear." Mother has managed to read my mind again, so pats my knee, continuing to focus on the lunging.

Daddy continues making soft clicking noises in the paddock while the foal lopes in circles around and around. Mother waits. She must know I am about to ooze more teenage melancholy so interrupts my brooding.

"Come inside and help me set the table for luncheon."

Does she know what I'm struggling with? Is this suggestion a means for me to avoid too much introspection? She's prone to giving advice about too much self-absorption, so much so it's as if she doth protest too much.

I wouldn't have thought so at the time, but now I can see she's waged her own war with it. I hop off the wall and tag behind her, any chance to tell her how often I feel alone, even in a crowd, gone up in smoke.

Instead, I listen as she reminds me of her own suffering as if to say whatever I'm trying to cope with is completely trivial by comparison.

Mother was barely sixteen years old when tragedy struck again. Doctors discovered cysts on both her ovaries. Medical practices were neither as sophisticated nor technologically enlightened as they are today, so her only option was to undergo surgery to remove them. She never expected to wake up to the news that both ovaries were removed. I've always envisioned her lying there dazed and dwarfed by the enormity of it all. Not just the cold, antiseptic ward surrounding her, but the dreadful news as well, strangling a young woman's hopes and dreams in a viselike grip. She was robbed of her fertility. Whether it was stolen by a man in a white coat with a speculum and a fistula, the wiles of Mother Nature or the mysterious ways of God no one can say, but this had to be devastating.

Mother's was a story I would hear for the rest of my life many, many times over. It would morph as I got older and it would persistently affect me throughout my life, eventually handicapping my outlook about my own adoption. So as usual, I brush my woes under the proverbial rug because they are indeed insignificant compared to what Mother endured and change tack.

"I just want us to be close. You know, best friends."

"I'm not your 'friend'." Her voice has dropped an octave. "I am your Mother. There's a difference, dear."

Soon, that summer came to an end and the roses grew leggy, petunias tattered and eaten by hedgehogs. Elms shed their yellow leaves. while the skies over the Cotswolds turned gray to match my adolescent mood. Signifying that nothing would change during the drab monotony of an English winter, the rains came and washed away my hopes to communicate with Mother. There'd be no remedies for my unease; not for now. For the rest of that year, I struggled to corral my emotions like the mare in the pasture cut off from her baby. I vowed to better attach myself to Mother and be there for her…as a daughter, of course, not a *friend*.

The chosen child may drive you wild
but that is not her aim
her suffering bleeds intensely
as she soaks up all your pain
she asks you just to love her
yourselves and others too
to cast off your entanglements
and let her come to you ...
(Charles Moore)

"Who am I? I'm not London or New York even though
that's the veneer shellacked all over me. I'm Laura
Ingalls Wilder out on the prairie or the Girl of the
Limberlost. At least that's what I see whenever I
look in the mirror and stare at my adolescent self. I
can pout, grimace or smile, but whose life am I living?
Why don't I fit in? Am I even who I think I am?

FAT FARM

It was getting late. Even though I was tired from hiking miles of trail running along the edge of the North Downs, I was determined to stay in spite of encroaching twilight. I didn't want to miss seeing night capture day, a phenomenon perfectly displayed if one were positioned high on the south-facing White Cliffs of Dover. Having trained down from London, I promised myself I'd catch the 9:45 train back to Charing Cross. It would be past midnight when I returned home, but I didn't care if Mother and Daddy were worried. In fact, I think I wanted them to be.

I visited Dover when I was eleven and was beguiled by the mysticism hanging in the air. A castle, wide open moors, and towering cliffs had a way of making magic in a little girl's imagination and I wanted to recapture that drama. In particular, the cliffs suited my mood. I wanted, no needed, to be thoroughly swept away.

What does a sixteen-year-old girl feel? She feels anything and everything, all of it at once and most of it very confusing. For sure, each emotional sensation is experienced to the nth degree. She goes from zero to sixty in a nano second and doesn't even realize she's there until the implosion begins and it's too late to dial it back to a slow simmer. Throw being adopted into this mix and she's more screwed up than a soup sandwich!

According to Mother and Daddy, I was fat. Five foot eleven, and I was tipping the scales at a whopping one hundred and forty pounds. I was a *fat girl. Wow!* They sat me down that morning to have a heart-to-heart because *we care so very much for your well-being and happiness.* They wanted to sign me up for a three-week inpatient stay at an exclusive Fat Farm in Surrey. I should be pleased to know the actress, Hayley Mills, recommended it highly.

"Are you for real? I'm five foot eleven! If I weighed any less I'd be lying below the frost line." I receive a warning scowl. "I'm a competitive swimmer! How the hell do you expect me to win the 100 meter freestyle subsisting on nuts and yogurt?"

"Language!" my father growls. Another warning grimace from Mother, this one leaving deeper furrows.

"What's wrong with you?" I whine as tears threaten to fall.

"Nothing is wrong with *us*." Big emphasis on '*us*'.

"You forget, which is kind, I s'pose, but I'm not sprung from your, um, you know, loins. I'm not an ectomorph like the two of you string beans. Mom, I'm six inches taller than you. Why would you expect me to weigh the same as your petite self?"

"You have a problem, dear. You should be grateful that Daddy and I want to help."

"Help?" I squawk. "With my height, it's not possible to be like you. Who'd want to be like you, anyway?"

"Young lady, do not speak to your mother that way."

"Yes, I have wide hips, but so what? Nobody's perfect" I was crying now. "It's not like I weigh two hundred and can't fit through the door! All you've ever cared about are appearances. Well, I'm not built like you. And I'm certainly not vain like the two of you, either!"

"That's enough!" Daddy stands up and towers over me, arms akimbo.

And then I explode. "When did *you* ever, ever ask to have a 'heart-to-heart' to discuss my progress in school, or where I might want to go to college? Or what about this one? How I feel about being adopted? You don't want to have a 'heart-to-heart' about that one, do you?" They both stare at me stunned. Then Daddy clears his throat; a signal he is beyond angry.

"You're not my father, so don't speak to me! What do you know or care anyway?" I scream pointing a finger at him. "You're just a fitness freak afraid of a heart attack! And you, Mother, only care about what other people think. Maybe it bothers you I don't look like you and therefore you have to explain why. Have you ever told anybody you couldn't have children of your own? I'm betting not!" Before either one of them can answer, I snatch my trench coat from the closet, grab my wallet and run from the house. I have no idea Dover's my destination until I'm at Charing Cross train station buying a ticket for the ten o'clock express.

When I wandered around Dover Castle that afternoon, I thought about Julius Caesar, who was the first to come to England in 55 BC, but it was here in Dover where less than one hundred years later the Romans came ashore for the second time in AD 43. This time they actually conquered *Britannia* and ruled for several centuries until the fall of the Roman Empire circa 450. If I held my breath and cocked an ear, I could hear echoes of those invaders bellowing as they pillaged this serenely pastoral landscape inhabited by a pagan people ill-equipped to defend themselves. I envisioned sylvan sprites scurrying into the forests to burrow underground or into hollowed trees in an effort to flee the marauders. After the Romans left, it was Christian traders who brought their religion to England's shores. They borrowed pagan traditions and rituals in an effort to persuade illiterate peasants to believe in, if not fear, their God. Thus the Celts were suborned into practicing a religion fabricated solely for the benefit of the clergy and were deliberately kept ignorant and fearful, too. Consequently, the British were caught for centuries between a mercurial and erratic monarchy and a suffocating, if not punitive theocracy. Those were issues I wrestled with then.

High atop Dover's white cliffs, the townsfolk used to cringe watching aerial dogfights between Nazi Luftwaffe and the British Royal Air Force during the Battle of Britain in 1940. What a vantage point and oh, those whining engines as aircraft dove and careened across the skies above the English Channel. They disappeared into big, puffy clouds and reappeared, the formerly chased now the chaser. Guns would crack rat-a-tat-tat only to be suddenly silenced as the vanquished screamed headlong toward the sea and sank beneath her chilly white caps. The RAF was an exceptionally brave lot, single-handedly preventing Hitler from softening any more English targets than those already devastating London during the Blitz. Hitler's planned invasion never occurred.

Most moving to me was the Dunkirk evacuation, planned and

launched from within a hidden bunker in these very cliffs. As if I were actually there, I could and do still see that day clearly. It moves me to tears. Code-named Operation Dynamo, also known as the Miracle of Dunkirk, this was the amazing rescue of thousands of Allied soldiers from the beaches and harbor of Dunkirk, France between May 27th and June 4th, 1940. Our men were backed up to the sea with nowhere to go, held by an impenetrable line of Nazi forces. But an armada set sail from Great Britain comprising motorboats, sloops, fishing boats, yachts, ferries, barges and every other variety of boat imaginable. They poured out of the Thames River and ports lining the English Channel to make their way across the Channel to rescue the beleaguered men. Guided by the smoke and flames filling the sky above Dunkirk, the ragtag rescue fleet, comprised of regular civilians - men and women - pushed its way through a rigorous German defense and choppy waters to the stranded troops. The rescuers found the beaches clogged with soldiers. Some clamored along piers to reach the rescue boats, others waded out from shore to waters nearly over their heads. All the while the beach was under attack from German artillery, bombers and fighter planes. The British thought they would be lucky to rescue 40,000. In the end, approximately 340,000 British, French and Belgian fighters were brought to safety on Britain's shores. Even after twenty-five years since that prolonged siege occurred on the war-torn coast of France, I could hear the reverberating whoops of joy as mothers and fathers, sisters and brothers, sons and daughters embraced their wounded and starving compatriots.

After a few miles along the cliff trail, I find a relatively protected spot by a couple of lichen-covered rocks and wedge myself between them, sitting down on thick cushions of damp moss and pebbles of flint. I let my legs dangle over the edge of the cliff. Very foolish, because beneath my legs a striking facade of chalk falls three hundred and fifty feet to an increasingly grumpy English Channel. This virtually vertical escarpment melts straight upward from the sea as if to touch heaven and then fall precipitously back. The cliffs form a jagged hem of bright white, skirting eight miles of England's southeastern coast of pasture and flat moors. They are distinctly visible from France or to any sailor put to sea miles away. Years later the White Cliffs of Dover are even recognizable from a satellite circling the globe in outer space.

I notice the horizon is taking on a yellow tinge, a sign a storm is brewing. Gusts whip my hair into a salty mess of tangles crisscrossing my face and clinging to my eyelashes. My cheeks sting from all the salt spray in the air. And all five foot eleven and whopping one hundred and forty pounds of me is actually jostled by the wind's gathering temper. The wind's turmoil matches my inner conflict; one of feeling quite rudderless, blown about by an angst I can't name. The wind lifts my blouse, too, and it unwinds the school scarf around my neck, which Jeremy gave me shortly after we started dating. But I catch the black and white stripes of Saint Paul's School for Boys before they can sail away. This should be my cue to get up and leave, but I ignore the warning signs. Instead, I belt my trench coat even tighter around my waist, shove my hands deeper into my pockets and hunker closer to the ground. With chin tucked low, I look out at a sea as gray as metal. It is pretty difficult to differentiate the skyline from the watery expanse. A flat steely distance of open water and sky blend so seamlessly, there looks to be an endless void. Unexpectedly, I feel very small and insignificant. Mother Nature is clearly greater and more powerful than I. She might not even notice, much less care what I am thinking of doing. As darkness floods my domed ceiling, I can feel her encircling me in her arms. Or is it God? He might be watching over me, too. Whether it's Mother Nature or God holding on to me, the Cliffs beckon.

I remember the last time when I'd come out to the cliffs, my mood was much different. Then I had laughed as I watched night crawl across the sky. It was as if Night were sneaking up on Day. A mischievous darkness intent on snuffing the sun's light in some sort of cloak and dagger sport. Would she actually succeed in capturing the sun or just nip at his heels as he slipped out of sight in pursuit of her? Or was it the sun taunting her with a game of tag? Whatever, I was so delighted by the spectacle of this sunset I had vowed to come back.

One by one, spangles of the sun's rays stretching over the water dance offstage, leaving an undulating surface of smooth, flexible slate. On the beach below, the waves aren't lazily washing backward and forwards with soft slapping sounds anymore. They are beginning to crash against the buffed and polished face, leaving in their wake giant bucket-loads of spray and great clouds of yellowed foam and sickly bubbles. This is how it always is where the Channel meets the North Sea during inclement weather. It's what happens when history's ghosts decide to come out to play. And this evening I have a front row seat.

Though the sun is gone and the moon is rising, there is still light enough to see robins hopping about on the grass. They hesitate and cock their heads listening for worms. When they find any, they fly across the downs to where a thin line of elm trees border the cliff road. I picture nests of baby birds, nestling among broken bits of blue egg shell, their necks craning above the rim of their nests with mouths wide open greedily grabbing whatever their mamas have to offer. I think maybe, I'm like those baby robins, greedy for every morsel.

A few dragonflies flutter and linger, their blue tinted wings so beautiful it never occurs to me to duck or flinch. I even allow one to rest within the crook of my arm so as to offer a respite from the wind steering her off course. Clouds begin to roll toward me, bringing with them fog. It bleeds across the beach and creeps up the cliff to engulf me in its vapor. For some reason, I neither care nor move.

I close my eyes to the panorama laid out in front of me and wait. In time, the anthem of the sea calls to me. Her gentle lyrics whisper I have every right to object to my parent's plan. They have been thoughtless. Besides, my weight seems such a petty issue compared to all the other stuff that needs attention. I look down at the frothy sea and am gratified for her permission to feel what I'm feeling. *I clearly come from bigger stock, most likely German or Slavic.* And though I am slim I do possess a larger frame with a bosom not easily concealed. Can I help being a tall blond, taking on the voluptuous curves of womanhood? Is it my fault I'm no longer colt-like and gamine? Did my looks threaten Mother in some way? Such a shame the trend is for a Twiggy-like look all stick limbs, flat chest, and narrow boy's hips. I do not spring from that mold. I suspect I'm being groomed for a coming out party in the not-too-distant future with English débutantes and eligible titled boys. Fat is so not done.

Far more weighty a concern is my mixed emotions surrounding my being adopted. I've been silently grieving. Something is wrong and that's Mama is missing. Perhaps, Mother does know exactly what's troubling me but doesn't want me to give it lip service. If the topic of adoption or the whereabouts of Mama is never addressed, perhaps it could all just go away. *Poof!* But why isn't it okay to accept that my life is indeed shaped by my adoption? Why pretend? Can I tell Mother that? Might she grieve with me? Share, even shoulder, some of my hurt? Or would she take my suffering personally to heart and ask me why she isn't good enough? I already know the answer to that question. She would never tolerate competing with my birth mother for either my attention or affection. I come to the conclusion that to have any kind of meaningful future, one must give up any hope of ever changing the past. Does that mean forget about being adopted and convince myself my life is normal? But then I figure it's hard recognizing what's abnormal about one's life if the abnormal is already the norm. *Bloody hell!* I, who so like order, hurl an anguished howl of objection into the murk.

That night I did realize for the first time that it was okay to recognize my circumstances were indeed unusual. I think I also came to understand that I was like a bird with clipped wings. All I could really grasp at that time was the notion I was missing something; something very important, such as the ability to fly. It scared me because I saw myself handicapped when no one else could see a limb missing. I wasn't bleeding or covered in oozing boils. There was just a vague, yet persistent sense of loss. Somehow I felt deprived, which felt morally wrong because in so many ways my life was blessed. I was not an orphan. My parents loved me as best they knew how. We lived comfortably in tony Knightsbridge. I was receiving a private education from prestigious Hathaway School for Girls; had a boyfriend who was cuckoo about me; and was able to travel throughout western Europe on holidays to such places as Majorca, Portugal, Italy, and Greece. Nevertheless, I woke up and went to bed every day feeling fat, ugly and unlovable. Faint feelings of rejection, of not belonging were shadows that followed me even into a dark closet. Whatever it was, it caused me to be unsure of who I was, clueless of who or what I wanted to be. It was maddening not to be able to share my feelings with others because I knew no one would understand. How could they? Asking for sympathy when the surface of my life appeared so perfect would be asking too much; particularly of Mother and Daddy, who had created an ideal life. Sadly, they were the ones whose understanding I most craved.

That night I remember feeling as though there were a hole in my heart. And with the fog closing in around me, I felt very lost. The waves tossed in a chaos of salt and foam three hundred and fifty feet below. A howling wind pummeled me frontally as I stood at the edge of the cliffs. The gale's insistent hum rang in my ears, but I couldn't resist listening. As haunting and discordant as the vibrations of wind and sea were, it was like my lullaby that night. All I wanted to do was sleep. Forever.

HIDE YOUR BREEDING

A huge stone fireplace dominates the central wall of the Cuckoo's Nest, our cabin in Wyoming. On either side are two pairs of windows each with six panes of glass divided by leaded mullions. Beneath each pair of windows is a cushioned bench with a collection of brightly Indian patterned pillows. The view is of Echo Lake, a shimmering oasis surrounded by aspen and golden willow, which in early fall release a palette of yellows and oranges so brilliant it bedazzles one's soul. In front of the fireplace are two oversized armchairs and ottomans separated by an end table. A lamp, its base made from a deer's antler and the shade fashioned from deer hide puts out an amber glow on this rainy afternoon. Piles of unread magazines and copies of *Reader's Digest* litter the polished wood floor of wide plank cherry. It gleams from a recent coat of beeswax and is slippery under stockinged feet. Rain raps at the windowpanes and the sky is like a sheet of metal, sitting low over the lake. Mother's head is bent over a painted canvas, her fingers needlepointing a sleeping lioness. She's clearly in another one of her reflective moods, so I stare into the flames waiting. I know not to interrupt her as she launches into one of her stories all of which I've heard many times before.

I'll be honest. By the time I was nineteen I discovered that being Catholic was not only causing me to live a lie, but it was also becoming increasingly inconvenient. That sounds sacrilegious, I know, but to my mind, I suffered too many heartaches and I was sort of done with God. I couldn't help but repeatedly ask myself if there truly were a God, how could He want to punish me? And so many times? Surely, I didn't deserve this much loss! After all, I was good and kind and always devout. How could I continue believing in a God who would bring me so much suffering? So I left the Church.

Anyway, growing up Catholic in the 1920's, 30's and 40's was almost as socially prohibitive as being Jewish. Did you know that? Many to this day don't even realize this was the case. Catholics were barred as frequently and callously as Jews from joining prestigious country clubs or ladies' groups solely because of their religion. Anti-Catholics, including the Ku Klux Klan, believed that Catholicism was incompatible with democracy. Even parochial schools encouraged separatism and kept Catholics from becoming loyal Americans. Catholics responded to such prejudice by persistently asserting their rights as American citizens. They argued they were truer patriots since they believed in the right to the freedom of religion. It was hard to be a practicing Catholic. I didn't like being in a spotlight of controversy.

Lightning suddenly zigzags across the sky and for a moment everything in the cabin stands out in electrified definition. I remember actually thinking God didn't like hearing Mother say that last bit. Anyway, bringing the Ku Klux Klan into her story always gets my attention and that time, it particularly rattled. I've always had these gruesome visuals of Blacks or Catholics hanging from tree branches with potato sacks over their heads, their legs twitching in macabre throes of some horrifying death while urine runs down their legs and into their socks. This time I heard her story one too many times and wanted her to stop.

"You do know, don't you that it was the Democrats who largely made up the Ku Klux Klan, don't you?"

With a shaking of her head as if still incensed and not in the least bit bothered by my observation, she continues. *In 1925 the right to open parochial schools was upheld much to the chagrin of the Ku Klux Klan. And in 1928 Al Smith became the first Catholic presidential nominee. That galvanized the Lutheran, Baptist, and Fundamental churches into hostile opposition. The fear was that instead of representing the American people, Smith might only listen to the Pope or the dictates from the Vatican. It wasn't until World War II religious tolerance for Catholics began. When the horrors of the Holocaust became common knowledge, few with a conscience could pursue religious bias with any justification anymore. Religious bias' potential for pure depravity was revealed by the Nazis and has been vigorously repudiated ever since. Thanks to the returning American soldiers of mixed race, creed and color they explained that fighting alongside one another leveled the playing, or in that case, battlefield. Under extreme circumstances, our boys on the ground, in the air or on the sea relied on each other regardless of religion or ethnicity. In many ways it is they who reshaped American society, extinguishing the biases within an ever-growing melting pot. But that of course, came a decade or so too late to be of any use to me.*

The damage had already been done. I hated the pressures of that debate because being singled out as a Catholic and obliged to stand up for a faith that had so let me down made me feel like a hypocrite. And ostracism was acutely mortifying. Can you imagine never being able to belong or fit in? Simply because you were of a particular religion, over which you didn't even have any responsibility? It wasn't my fault I was born and raised a Catholic. Understand, though, I wasn't about to let my dreams be controlled by an adherence to religion. So I formally excommunicated myself from the Catholic Church and joined the ranks of the Episcopalians. For what it's worth, I've never looked back.

She sure knew her facts about the plight of Catholics and after hearing this story so many times I couldn't help but wonder if perhaps, in the words of Shakespeare, she *doth protested too much?* Doubt seemed to be nibbling at the edges of her conscience. Not surprising, really, as guilt runs thick through the veins of Catholics. At least, that's what I've been told. Nevertheless, I do realize that for her to have had any kind of brighter future and the chance to realize her dreams, it meant giving up on her past and her religion. That's how she felt, anyway, even if it did mean dealing with the guilt of it all.

This is when she asks out of the blue, "Why do you persist in wearing that crucifix around your neck?" She looks up from her needlework and gives me a long hard look.

Sensing a challenge, I don't really have any solid riposte at the ready, so I answer her question with one of my own. "Does it bother you?"

She purses her lips into a thin line of disapproval and arches an eyebrow.

"I'm on a journey in knowing God, " I declare. "And while I haven't figured out yet whether He exists, I still feel like I'm a Christian and shouldn't be ashamed to wear a symbol as testament."

"Those are lofty words coming from someone so young."

"Not meant to offend, Mother."

"I don't like it."

"Well, I do."

"If I were you," she cautions, "I'd hide your breeding."

I'm up on my feet in a heartbeat. "What's that s'posed to mean?"

She never answers my question, or in all fairness, I don't hang around to hear one. I grab my book and head to my bunk at the other end of the cabin.

All afternoon the storm continued to grind its teeth. So did I. I've often thought back to this episode and wondered if she knew something about my heritage she wasn't willing to share. My adoption story was pretty much off limits, so I knew nothing about my ancestry, my heritage. Nothing. Was I a Catholic by birth? Did a love of God run through my veins?

EASIER SAID THAN DONE

I remember it wasn't until close to midnight when we exited the Royal Opera House at Covent Garden hand in hand, strains of Wagner still echoing in our heads. As the crowd melted away from the front entrance and into waiting taxi cabs, Jeremy and I remained on the steps. A velvety darkness enveloped us like a cloak. I remember his suggesting we walk home, but not until we'd seen all of Covent Garden. How can I ever forget our first kiss?

Once a meeting place in the 1700's come red light district in the 1800's, it's 1968 when we cross the famous piazza, as the English like to call it, and head for the Floral Hall and Jubilee Market. Gas lamps light our way along the cobblestone street, blue flames flickering as I recall, casting long shadows which creep up the terraced buildings forming a square all around us. When we pass three men bundled in threadbare coats, caps pulled low over their ears standing around a drum warming their hands over a fire, Jeremy tightens his hold around my waist. Flames pop, followed by flights of sparks soaring into the night. The only conversation between these men seems to be their vapored breaths billowing in the cold air. Is this what homelessness looks like I remember wondering? Underneath the portico at the entrance to the market, an old woman is bent over as if burdened by many sorrows. The linked beads of her spine are visible through a makeshift gunny sack coat. I drop a few shillings in her outstretched palm.

All of a sudden the empty square behind us is clogged with trucks. Women are pushing carts of pink peonies, crimson dahlias, and yellow jonquils. Men pull wheelbarrows full of potatoes, onions, cabbage, apples, and squash. Girls younger than I, stagger under the weight of cases of strawberries stacked high on their heads or cartons of gooseberries, crates of peaches and apricots in their arms. Everyone is crowding into the great atrium toward their designated stalls. The midnight rush into the iron-framed hall, two stories high with a domed ceiling of glass running its full length, is impressive, to say the least. As is the noise of bargaining coming from shop owners and restaurateurs who bicker with the growers over price per pound. In the middle of all this commotion, a mother and her pimple-faced son have set up a fryer and are hawking battered fish 'n chips, served in cones of greasy newspaper print. The odor is foul to my nose, but then to tell you the truth I've never liked fish. In no time the floors are covered with refuse trampled into a slimy, pulpy muck of squashed tomatoes, lettuce leaves, pomegranate seeds and crushed blooms.

When a perfect lilac blossom lands gently at our feet, Jeremy picks it up and presents it to me with a bashful flourish. *First love* is what I think he says but I am so stunned when he takes me in his arms I cannot be certain that's what he, in fact, does say. His breath feels warm on my eyelashes as we embrace without any qualms in so public a place. I think a few chaps whistle.

"Let's go, " Jeremy whispers. "Your parents will be cross with me for keeping you out so late."

"I doubt it," I remember muttering.

"What does that mean?" Jeremy stops and turns to face me.

"Well, I'm not actually sure. I think maybe they are more interested in being a couple than being my parents. They don't seem to be too interested in much of what I do. There's a disconnect."

Jeremy is silent for a long while, as I recall, and then he offers *we tend to wish being loved the way we would love and so perhaps you aren't recognizing their brand.* If I were with him today, at this older and wiser stage of life, I'd probably agree and hazard, *maybe you're right. It's wrong to judge another by one's own standards; just let 'em be.* And his reply would surely be, *Probably easier said than done, but give it a try?*

As we make our way back toward the West End, the sun begins its ascent behind us. Dawn gilds the streets with a warm glow and a crisp London sky radiates with soft blues and pinks. Jeremy and I proceed toward Knightsbridge in comfortable silence, I pensive, almost brooding.

I didn't talk much about my adoption in those days; not like I did when in grade school, bragging to everyone who'd listen that I was *chosen*, carefully handpicked from a nursery of babies; the lucky one. Poor Mother; I'd drag my friends into the kitchen or wherever she was at that moment and demand she confirm my assertion of being *handpicked*. I wonder what she thought about that or if it bothered her entire neighborhoods knew about my not being her natural child. People wondering what went wrong. Who's fault was it that my parents couldn't have children, Mother's or Daddy's? Yes, I lied about having a brother for a while, but when Mother and Daddy and the headmistress of my school, Bridget Merriweather, caught on, I dropped this ploy for getting attention. Nevertheless, somewhere in the recesses of my mind I was convinced I had a brother.

So, if I weren't talking about adoption that much did it mean I was growing up? Looking back with 20/20 hindsight, I was definitely nowhere near any sort of maturity. I was nothing but a sheltered girl, whose very existence depended on her parents' love and acceptance. While they kept me preserved in a bubble of comfort and structure, there was a growing awareness, on my part anyway, that a true connection was lacking. It made me afraid not having a bond; scared rejection might come again. Yet I was just as afraid of my own pulling away. How imperative was it to be connected to something or someone if it didn't feel right? It's hard to explain because I don't wish to throw around blame. Fortunately, an extremely rigorous curriculum at a proper English girls' day school, studying for 'O' Level exams and eventually three 'A' Levels in foreign language and literature didn't yield much time for solving this dilemma. Being in love for the first time was a glorious distraction, and acting as Swim Captain and Vice Head Girl of my school put the what-ifs or could-have-beens on the back burner. Mother would have been happy about that, I'm sure.

To shed some light on how weird my family life could be, a typical weekday went like this: I, in my uniform of crimson and navy, at a small table in the center of the kitchen eating a poached egg on toast prepared by Elda, our Italian housekeeper; Daddy in the dining room at the head of a long refectory table stationed behind his pink newspaper, the Financial Times, sipping a cup of coffee between spoonfuls of warm oatmeal; and Mother upstairs in bed, propped against five or six pillows reading the Tatler magazine with a tray across her lap cradling a pot of tea, flakey croissants, pats of unsalted butter and strawberry jam for her breakfast.

Jeremy was good to me; attentive, caring and sensitive about my adoption. He genuinely wanted to soften the hurt he imagined I felt. And yes, he was very aware of how my parents lived for each other, suggesting I not take it so personally. That's why he thought I should try to understand their kind of love. *To each his own. Try to accept it.* But what I was missing was my parents' interest. There was very little affirmation for how hard I studied; the good grades I received, the work I did as a Task Force volunteer, befriending the elderly and shut-ins. Never being thin enough was the only message I heard, and I railed against their preoccupation with appearances over accomplishments. Why was I not good enough? What would it take to impress them? Did they not realize by carping on my very appearance it highlighted the difference between us and how I didn't fit in? I came to loathe all things superficial. Social climbing, the débutante circuit, the who's who bored me intuitively. I wanted no part of that scene. I wanted to roll in the mud. Preferably somewhere in America's heartland.

Mother once asked if I were *grateful* for being adopted to which I innocently asked *more so than would be the norm for someone not adopted?*

She said, "Why, of course!"

And I told her that if I were to be grateful more than any other child, regardless of the circumstances surrounding his or her birth, it would be like asking me to be constantly aware of my adopted status; of not belonging; of wearing a label and being different.

I remember asking her almost too boldly, "Is that what you want?" She backed down. And of course, I did, too, for fear of hurting her feelings. Admitting I was appreciative for all my parents had done for me was the right thing to do. Just not more than any other child would be for whatever they had been given, all things being relative. It's a matter of perspective, I guess. One that still to this day is very difficult to convey, especially when all anyone has to do is look at my trappings and ask themselves *what more could she possibly want?* My mama is what I wanted, but I wasn't willing to own up to it yet. I was too busy being compliant and working within the confines of the only family I knew. It never occurred to me to assert myself. It only mattered I not make waves or render Mother unhappy.

When we lived in London, first in front of Harrods in a six-story terrace house, then later behind it after Daddy bought Morton Down and all they really needed in the city was a pied à terre, Mother and Daddy busied themselves climbing the social ladder, meeting the crème de la crème, planning their thoroughbred stud farm in the Cotswolds, and generally reaching for the stars. They were both diamonds in the rough, one from a fly-over state and the other from Brooklyn, both conquering poverty or rather leaving it behind, was what they had in common. Not to forget they were both gorgeous people with Hollywood glamor and elegant poise. I did not fault them for any one bit of it, though it did seem to exclude me. You know, *two's company and three's a crowd?* They seemed to be growing closer, though, and I was glad of it; particularly for Mother's sake, as she had always painted herself quite the victim. Losing her own mother; losing her ability to have children; losing her first love; Daddy comparing her to *pretty, bosomy blondes.* Now they were building something together which mattered a great deal to both of them; they were sharing a dream. Daddy said from the time he was fourteen living on a farm in Colorado that he planned on *getting out of Dodge* as soon as possible, getting his law degree and raising race horses when he grew up. He was making his life happen; not the other way around, life happening to him. I was proud of my father for being so motivated and consequently successful; a truly self-made man, attaining, what I would come to learn much later, as the *American Dream.* Mother was becoming such an Anglophile and loving every moment of the ride. This new twosome was fine except for when my bedroom was converted into a dining room while I was away at college. Mother simply packed up my things and gave them to charity, re-papered the walls and installed new furnishings. Apparently, the city flat needed a dining room, though it didn't jive with how she and Daddy dined out most nights. When I came home from college each summer, I slept on the living room sofa.

Before college, my forty-minute bus ride to and from high school was used to think about life, its inconsistencies, and its meaning. If lucky, I'd find a seat in the front row upstairs on Number 73, if I recall, and there I'd block out the commuters and ponder right from wrong, what it would be like to smoke, or have sex, run away, find my birth parents. The panoramic view of such sights along the way included Hyde Park Corner with its sweeping roundabout; followed by the Hilton Hotel where Howard Hughes was reputed to be holed up drinking his own urine and letting his nails grow into grotesque talons; Speakers' Corner at Marble Arch, where hippies stood on soapboxes denouncing the Vietnam War, capitalism and all things American; Marks & Spencer and Selfridges, two of London's most popular department stores; and the whole length of Sherlock Holmes' famous Baker Street. I'd make note of all that was red in this bustling city: telephone booths, public letterboxes, double decker buses, umbrellas and handbags with matching pumps, neck scarves, and Burberry trench coats. I'd ask myself what was I made of and decided I must be of German stock because the language came to me so easily it must have been in my veins primordially. I also seemed to share the physical characteristics of a *fräulein* - big breasts, wide hips, blond and tall. I remember being certain I wasn't Scandinavian, which would have been the more obvious guess. Anyway, I'd tell anyone who asked, *I'm German*.

Dear Jeremy. He was my port in a storm. I shall always be grateful for the romance he brought into my life. I've saved all his letters. He wrote at least two a week for the year we dated between my sixteenth and seventeenth birthdays. Filling the pages in his illegible scrawl with melodramatic professions of undying love and plans for our future, he pretty much swept me off my feet. Those letters are safely tucked away somewhere now, tied with a strand of rawhide along with that very lilac bloom he presented to me at Covent Garden in 1968.

"Mother is my mother. She is the one who has raised me. The one who has fed and clothed me and sent me to good schools. Mama gave me up. What's done is done. I'm not mad at her. In fact, I feel sorry for Mama. I wish I could tell her I'm okay."

SUMMONED

One night long after we had pushed our chairs away from the dinner table and gone back to the main house for a little puzzling and a rubber of bridge, Gramps sent for me in his library. We had all been getting ready to retire for the evening, so a summons at this hour was not only a first of its kind but also a bit daunting. When I think about it today, I'm guessing he knew he didn't have much time left in this world and had a few things he wished to impart. This exchange occurred about five days before he died:

"Alexandra," he waves me to the ottoman in front of him. "I understand you are heading off to Skidmore College next fall."

"Yes," I barely eke out.

"Speak up, young lady."

"Sorry," I mutter.

"That's not much better. What do you plan on studying?"

"Foreign Languages." Grammy, Mother, and Daddy are all standing behind his wheel chair just outside his peripheral vision. They look like a Greek chorus nodding their heads in unison.

"And what languages would those be?"

"German and French. I'm already fluent in both, but…"

"'German'?" he asks in what sounds like a hiss. The Greek chorus gasps collectively, and I feel like my cheeks are on fire.

"Why German?" I've stepped on a landmine.

"I'm hoping to become an interpreter or a translator…"

"Young lady, do you know what the difference is?"

"An interpreter translates orally. So maybe I can work at the U.N.

or in an embassy. A translator translates the written word." The Greek chorus nods in unison.

"Again, why German?" Gramps is fixated and I have to find a means to step off this mine before we are all blown to bits.

"Well, ever since WWII and all those German scientists emigrating and coming here to our country, there's a huge need for people to translate their theories and theorems." My blather tumbles from my lips loud enough this time for him to hear. "I'd have learned Russian for the same reason, but decided that might be going too far."

Daddy beams his approval and nods in my direction.

"You're right about that, young lady. Well then. I have every reason to believe you will do a very fine job whether it's at the United Nations or in a rocket lab. Just remember this: never waver in your pride of America. There's no other country in the world with our level of strength or nobility. There's none other with our capacity for charity and sacrifice, be it American lives or treasure. National freedom is key. Individual freedom, too. Got that?" He reaches across the space between us to pat me on my knee. "Now be a good girl and get to bed, Lexie."

Gramps wasn't about doling out superfluous praise, so his encouragement that night made me feel ten feet tall. His compliments, if and when they came my way, were sincere. I would never forget his faith in me.

Looking into his rheumy eyes, I bend to squeeze his gnarled hand and kiss his shrunken cheek. I don't know it's the last time.

I'M IN!

Every day after school, we sit together on the sofa of floral pink and green chintz and a glazed finish, with a tea tray set on a low glass table in front of us. I pour first a spot of milk into each teacup and then the tea, which has steeped for ten minutes under a very silly Union Jack tea cozy I gave her for her birthday. One lump of sugar and I pass Mother her cup. As usual, she takes it from me absentmindedly. Outside, lights are coming on and Harrods is silhouetted against a pink sky. I am eager to talk about my acceptance letter to Skidmore College, but instead of our making plans, she wants to tell her college story again. Thinking it better she wander back in time than focus on my future, which means my leaving home, I let her ramble.

I must confess I did excel at school. I've told you I was a straight-A student, right? I won many awards in every subject except for History, but let's not dwell on that shall we? You might think I'm bragging but every year of high school your grandfather as it would turn out, who was Superintendent of Schools for all five New York City's boroughs under Mayor LaGuardia, awarded me with certificates of merit and excellence.

He was so distinguished with that white carnation affixed to the lapel of his pin-striped suit and a gold fob stretched across his waistcoat. I was always so shy when approaching the stage to receive his congratulations. I'd never met so grand a gentleman. With a handshake and a quick curtsy, I'd scurry back to my seat never daring to look past his bow tie. I'd just grab that scroll tied with forest green ribbon and rush from the stage all flushed and flustered. Who'd have thought that not so many years later he would be my father-in-law, your grandfather? Do you know what he said when Oliver introduced me to him? 'I know you, young lady. You're the brunette who won all those awards in High School.'"

I shake my head in fake incredulity. I'm not mocking her, but playing along as if I've never heard this story before. I do remember, though, I resolved to research what it means when someone lives in the past.

I wound up earning a full scholarship to New York School of Interior Design. It's famous you know. Very exclusive. Very hard to get into. Unfortunately, neither my father nor my aunt would help pay for my books, art supplies or room and board. That's all the help I needed and they couldn't or wouldn't do it. I was devastated. You have no idea how it broke my heart. As a result, I was forced to accept a scholarship at a lesser known, certainly less prestigious school in Brooklyn. It was a no-name school then, called Brooklyn College, and if it weren't for Oliver coming into my life I might have died of boredom!

In the slanting sunlight coming through the tall french doors of our living room on Trevor Square, I watch Mother's face as she spins her tale. I honestly don't think she has any idea she's dancing all over my big moment. There I sit in my Hathaway School for Girls navy and maroon uniform with the acceptance letter in my hand, and a ripped envelope lying on the floor with forms and campus literature, and all she can talk about is her college disappointments. I can't help wondering why my life is constantly being invaded by her past. Mother's stories, like this one or the ones about losing Oliver and her mother, repeated over and over, have silenced me all my life.

SHOP TILL WE DROP

In typical Ann Hart fashion, my aunt announced at breakfast that tomorrow she and I were going to the big city and buy clothes for college.

"All young ladies need a wardrobe when they head off to college." Her eyes danced mischievously, and quite frankly I thought she was kidding.

If there were one thing you could pillory Aunt Ann about it was her clothes sense. She had absolutely none. This was a woman who lived in baggy jeans, rumpled western shirts with snap buttons and frumpy cardigans. Cowboy boots and Birkenstocks, were her only footwear. And to confuse me even more, I couldn't fathom what big city she had in mind. We were in the middle of rural nowhere in the middle of rural Wyoming. At least that's what I was ungenerously thinking having grown up in Zürich and London. Don't misunderstand, I loved country life with all my heart, but it just wasn't where one went for fashion. And Aunt Ann with her plain-faced dowdiness could hardly know what girly things might be suitable. I guess I was accustomed to Mother's fashion sense.

"Are we going all the way to Denver?" That was the only logical big city I could think of. There would be personal shoppers there to assist.

"Yessiree!" She beamed like the man in the moon.

The next morning, sequins of sunlight dancing on Denver's skyline greet us as we make our way into the city. Cottony clouds dot the light blue sky, a welcome sight upon which to focus as the urban blight of the newly completed I 25 corridor is noisome in not only its odors but its sights as well. It feels like we are running a gauntlet through a maze of railroad tracks and warehouses. I am quiet as we make our progress through traffic over to 1st Avenue. This after my aunt and I have shared our first adult conversation during the four-hour drive down from the ranch.

"This is Gramps's last summer isn't it?" I say softly.

"I think so, Lexie. It'll be curtains if he falls again.

"Will you miss him?" I ask.

"Of course," whispers Aunt Ann, staring straight ahead. A veil of tears shimmers on the surface of her bright blue eyes. "What about you, kiddo? You'll miss him, too, won't you?"

"He means the world to me. Even though he's stern and strict and seemingly unapproachable, I have never been scared of him. You know he scares most of our cousins…"

"That's because he rarely twinkles for any of them the way he does for you." My aunt reaches across the front seat to pat my knee.

"Well, he twinkles for you, too." I shift my weight and face her as best I can given the constraints of my seat belt. "Say, do you s'pose it's because we are both adopted and he feels sorry for us?"

"Wow! That came out of nowhere."

"Well, we both come from The Cradle and he has loved us as if we were his own offspring. Even though we don't share blood, his love is the closest thing to unconditional love I've ever known."

"You're so right, but I don't think it stems from pity. My aunt throws a quick glance my way. "How'd you get so perceptive?"

"I watch people."

"Uh huh."

"Aunt Ann, what's it been like for you being adopted?"

There is a long silence and I know well enough to not fill the void with prattle lest she balks. "It's been easy," she says with a degree of caution coursing beneath her words. "I'm grateful for the comforts and opportunities." She glances my way again. "You should be, too."

"Of course, I'm grateful. I meant how has it been for you emotionally?"

"If you mean, have I ever looked for my natural parents, the answer is NO!" That comes across as pretty defensive, so I decide to drop it. She persists, though. "Have you ever looked?"

"No."

"Do you think you might some day?"

"No. Do you?"

"Never! Why wouldn't you look?"

"I dunno." I stare out at the flat blue distance of the open sky. No more corn fields or acres of alfalfa stretch on both sides of the road. Rather housing construction and road work mar our 360-degree view. I say nothing.

"'I dunno' is not an answer."

"Do you feel special?" I ask ignoring her mimicry.

"Nope."

"Who needs two sets of parents anyway? It'd be awfully confusing."

"It would," she agrees, "besides, your mother would be jealous as all get out if she knew you were ever looking for your birth mother."

"Well, that's another helluva reason not to look," I remark. "I have no interest in hurting her any more than she already does."

"Hmm. Some day, you might think about what's right for you and not your mother."

"What does that mean?" I ask. But all I get for an answer is, "You're a good daughter, Lexie. I admire your loyalty."

"Were you told you were chosen? I was, but I don't believe it."

"Oh, that old saw where the parents go up and down an aisle of cribs on either side, looking for their favorite baby?"

"You got that spiel too?" She nods all-knowingly.

"What do you think happened?" As is her wont, she deflects the question and instead prompts me.

"I think the agency matched my profile with Mother's and Daddy's and thus a fit was born. Pretty clinical, really."

"I think you've hit the nail on the head, Dearie. Ready to shop 'til you drop?"

The Denver, famous for its Thanksgiving parade and arch-rivalry with Macy's, stands like a fortress alongside Cherry Creek. With its chamfered corner, bright neon sign and the cursive script letters T-h-e-D-e-n-v-e-r ten feet tall atop the six stories of shopping paradise, it occupies the area of at least two or three city blocks. One look at it and I believe this might very well be a mecca of goodies after all.

Aunt Ann squeezes her boat of a car into a parking space between a cute little red Mustang and a vintage baby blue Thunderbird.

"Let's hit it, kiddo! Last one to the entrance is a dirty rotten egg!" Of course, I let her win, because that's what nieces do. So I wait until she is half way across the lot before sliding sideways out the passenger door, careful not to scratch the T-Bird.

Stepping into the elevator, a grizzly old caramel-colored man with hollow cheeks and deep sunken eyes the shade of chocolate asks us which floor. I stare at the board above the sliding doors trying to read the names of all the departments: Boulevard Dresses; Better Dresses; Town and Country Casuals; Women's World; Daytime; Circa Now Shop; Better Coats; Spectator Sportswear; Fashion Shoes; Shoe Place; Wigs. Good grief!

"Third floor." Aunt Ann shrugs her shoulders and mugs. How I love my aunt, whose moon face is always in motion. So, too, her body, cloddish and jerky; a virtual clown most days. With her cap of closely cropped prematurely white hair and ruddy complexion, Aunt Ann loves to make people laugh. She doesn't take herself too seriously, or at least it seems as such, so she is easy to be around. Opening up on a personal level, though, is not her forte. As I experienced during our drive, it is obvious humor keeps nosy parkers at bay. A good defense mechanism I find useful later.

All before lunchtime, I try on thirty cocktail dresses: off-the-shoulder pieces, strap-y black numéros that don't do me any favors, flouncy florals, lacy baby-doll things that make my five foot eleven body look utterly foolish - scores of slacks, most of which cannot go past my square hips, matching cashmere sweater sets, scads of skirts - corduroy, woolen, A-line - two pair of culottes, which were the most becoming, casual jackets of every style and fabric, and heavy winter coats of any length and color. While I struggle in and out of clothes, most of which do not like me, Aunt Ann sits on the edge of a sofa outside the dressing room, leaning forward and scanning the Wall Street Journal held between her open knees. She waits for my next appearance with every slap of newsprint. I emerge from behind the curtain with a flamboyant flair. No model I, though maybe a wannabe, the pantomime lasts all morning. With a slink, a slide and a sidle down the imaginary catwalk, I sashay with hips thrown forward rolling first this way, baa-boom, and then the other, baa-boom, in front of her appraising eyes. We giggle, she sometimes nodding enthusiastically or at others simply scrunching up her nose in distaste while returning to her paper.

"I'm done," I finally announce. "What now?"

"Good. I'm starved. Let's ask this nice young lady here to ring us up, get everything wrapped up…"

"B-b-b-but," I stutter.

"No, kiddo. I'm not buyin' all of it… just what I think you should have for the cocktail parties or dinners out, football games and ice cream socials. It's over there in that pile." I glance at the mountain of clothes she's pointing to and burst into tears.

"Oh, stop that nonsense. Aunt Ann fakes a frown. "Shoes after lunch." With that, she turns to our grinning salesgirl, who's just made the commission of a lifetime and says, "Please have these things waiting for us in the shoe department in an hour. I want to make sure her footwear coordinates with her wardrobe. I'd never hear the end of it from her mother if I screwed this up."

"Aunt Ann, that's not true," I protest.

"Oh, yes it is, Dearie. And you know it." She reaches up to push a strand of my hair behind my ear. "Surely, she tells you you are pretty?"

I shake my head *no*.

"What's wrong with that woman? Really?"

"Let's not go there. Not now." I so need affirmation like air or water I ache for more, but as much as Mother has wounded me over the years with all her fussing about looks instead of what I might offer from within, as a person, I can't bear anyone else's criticism of her. That's my domain. So, I link arms with Aunt Ann and pull her along. We walk in tandem to the escalator as if our inside legs are tied together in a three-legged race. People stare at us, but they are smiling, too.

We both order cheese burgers, medium rare; she with a side of onion rings while I forgo the urge to devour an order of fries. Aunt Ann snarfs down a strawberry milkshake while I sip a TaB, my foul-tasting concession to reduced calorie intake. We chat amiably, gossiping about the cousins and planning our next horseback ride under a full harvest moon. It is a day I will treasure all my life; not just because of her generosity of spirit and coin, but because of the time we spent together during this first milestone. Neither of us says it, but we both know Mother is not here for this occasion. Aunt Ann is.

At five thirty, we limp back to the car and practically fall in. Before Aunt Ann can throw the car into reverse, she remarks out of the blue, "I owe you an apology for pouncing on you earlier. You didn't deserve that. I was out of line." *Wow, 'I am sorry' has never crossed Mother's lips.*

Mother is everything Aunt Ann is not: slim, pretty, fashionable, the list goes on. I know Aunt Ann is jealous of Mother, but what she doesn't realize is that Mother is jealous of her for being an effective, capable, hands-on type of Gal Friday. They really are two great halves to one great whole. The trouble is I've always been sandwiched between them. I've had to remind each of them why I value them both.

"It's okay, really. And for what it's worth, I'm happy. I don't need to look for my birth mother. I honestly think that people who do must be very miserable and in need of a replacement."

"So you've thought about it that much, have you?"

"Sure. Haven't you?" I dare not look at her, my question is so intrusive.

"Me? No, not really." Reluctantly, I take her at her word.

"When you think about it, I'm the lucky one," I say. "Ever since I understood the whole thing about the birds and the bees and my adoption, I have felt nothing but sympathy for my birth mother. How difficult it must have been for her to give up her infant. The sacrifice she made for my sake, though..."

"You have a good heart, Alex. I hope no one ever breaks it." She reaches across the seat to hug me, a gesture of physical affection she rarely gives. When she pulls away, she is already changing the subject again.

"You know, your grandfather was my life raft while I was growing up. He's been as true as the North Star. There could never be any other father for me."

"He's been my anchor, too. I shall remember him for as long as forever."

"We're lucky women, you and I. We know we weren't really chosen. That's a goofy fairy tale to make us feel better, but we are special, nonetheless." And with no warning, she says, "Wanna take the wheel home? Shopping wipes me out."

"Sure!" She runs around the front and I the back, a game of Chinese fire drill, to switch seats.

"Wake me up when we're there," she chortles reclining the leather seat all the way back to a near horizontal position.

I'm not out of the parking lot before she's snuffling like a contented calf.

GRAMPS

When Gramps died later that summer of 1970, having succumbed to a long battle with arteriosclerosis, which I have since learned is a euphemism for Alzheimer's, and complications stemming from a fall, he was seventy-eight. Though I was eighteen, and I thought old enough to be permitted by his bedside, my Aunt Ann forbade me. She wanted me to remember him when he was at his best; not the crumpled vestiges of his former self, fighting for air as his lungs filled with fluid. I resented it at the time, but am grateful now that I have no memories of his drained features or the crippled way he looked during his final hours. I was allowed to keep vigil outside his bedroom door the night he lay dying, so I did, hugging a pillow on the floor.

The following day, as Boots and Isabel raced through the house vacuuming, dusting and removing all items that might remind us of him, I fled. I hated to watch all my memories of him being boxed up and carted out the door: his wheelchair with lambskin armrests and seat cushion; his frayed tartan bathrobe, still redolent with his essence; spectacles and reading materials; the hand tooled bowl of Wrigley's Doublemint Gum; all the Parr puzzles; his onyx backgammon and ivory chess sets; and mahogany cribbage board given to him by Mayor La Guardia. I escaped outside to sit on the stone terrace wall and gaze across Echo Lake. It was such a surreal morning flooded with tears and fears for what was yet to come. The silence surrounding all that hustle and bustle made me feel like I was caught in a black hole. I remained there for a long time, lost in contemplation.

While staid and proper, Gramps had a playful side. For us kids'
amusement, he climbed aboard a bicycle's handlebars and pedaled it
backwards around the tennis court. This while wearing a seersucker
jacket with a carnation in the lapel and a bowtie around his neck. He
played an expert game of jacks on the floor of his living room, having
peeled back the carpet much to my grandmother's dismay. When I was
seven years old, he started me on dominoes, which quickly progressed
to backgammon, even encouraging me to bet with the $5 he proffered to
get me started.

"What if I lose?" I bleated.

"Lose?" He arched his eyebrow.

"I don't want to lose my money."

"Lexie, it's not your money, now is it?"

It always took me a minute to work out this logic, and then we would
play. Invariably, he won his money back and never ever did he let me win. I
was almost always intimidated by the seriousness of our games. Certainly
frustrated by every loss, I loved nevertheless the hour we spent huddled
over the table in the picture window overlooking Echo Lake. Those so-
called nap periods of my summer vacation were just the best. Today, I'm
grateful there were no freebies when it came to winning. He taught me the
value of something earned, not given. He never stooped to my level. I had
to reach for his. Today, kids get a medal or a ribbon just for showing up!

Gramps wrote ditties such as the lyrics to our Ranch farewell song:

> The cows and calves in the pasture,
> the trees along the trail,
> the horses you have cantered on,
> the wild flowers in the dell.
> They'll miss your good fellowship
> They'll want you to return again.
> Come back to ELR where your welcome is high
> Goodbye!

He loved games, puzzles, conundrums, riddles, and wagers. One was
to offer anyone $10 if he or she could ride a bike sitting on the seat (not

standing) while pedaling all the way to the top of a very steep road from Chloe's bridge. These were the days when a regular bike had no gears. I didn't earn the prize until I was fifteen. A favorite quote he'd challenge others to repeat after only hearing it once was:

"Good evening, madam,"
to Eve said Adam.
"Good evening, sir,"
to him said she.

He kept a games folder, containing a description of contract bridge, directions on how to make and throw boomerangs, play a Dutch game called Bikini, and a magazine article on how to play a more modern version of croquet. He kept score sheets of the summer's bridge tournament tacked to the pantry wall. He maintained records in a leather bound book of every fish he caught in Echo Lake, Greta and Echo River. He kept a log of every animal sighted on the property along with the date and location. It was rumored but never proven, that he kept snakes in a dark and dank pit under the terrace. All of us cousins were told to stay away. So we did just that with nary a complaint.

Gramps' career was admirable. He was President of his senior class at Dartmouth College in 1913. First working for the William Wrigley & Co., starting in their receiving room as a laborer, then entrusted with the mixing of secret ingredients in the flavor vault and finally making it upstairs to a variety of departments. In 1917, after America entered World War I, he attended Naval Aviation School and was commissioned as an Ensign in the Naval Reserve Flying Corps Aerographic division. This involved charting weather conditions which might have an impact on aviation safety. While serving, he was engaged to my grandmother, Alexandra Schuyler. He moved over to the Dreyfus Company on Staten Island in 1919. There, he was quickly tasked with assuming control of the company after the sudden death of his boss, Dr. Dreyfus. Subsequent years were spent searching for sources of gutta percha (gum) all across Asia, South America, and Africa. He drew up contracts for the purchase and manufacturing of chewing gum. Gramps retired from "working for others," and became Superintendent of the Board of Education for New York City's five boroughs under Mayor LaGuardia during the 30's. He even wrote a book on Sex Ed, which is hysterical, because if you knew him, this was such a contradiction. He was the epitome of prim propriety and modesty! Gramps was elected for two terms to the U.S. House of Representatives between 1944 to 1949. While on Capitol Hill, he did everything he could to undo, undermine and squelch any and all aspects of FDR's New Deal. Gramps saw the writing on the wall. He knew that eventually, the government would run out of other people's money to pay for entitlements to folks with a sob story. He knew that it was not the government's job to give handouts. Where was that written in the U.S. Constitution? In retirement, Gramps founded the Staten Island Zoo, stocking it exclusively with American species. He even collared an injured bear in Wyoming, named it Saratoga, and dragged it all the way back east.

Sitting on the terrace, feeling as if caught in a vacuum, I watched millions of diamond-like gems dance across the lake as the sun played across its glassy surface. Such a pretty sight on so terrible a day, but then maybe this was how the road to heaven ought to look. I felt numb and in a daze, struggling to understand what his death might mean. To whom would I turn for encouragement or a game of backgammon? How would I know the right from wrong in politics? Who would fill the void of making me feel special? Who could ever replicate the games and pranks and admonitions? Would anyone else ever call me Lexie? As Gramps's body was taken from the house and my grandmother remained shuttered in her room with the shades pulled, I forced away those self-absorbed thoughts and focused on his favorite pastime.

Gramps loved to fish. Echo Lake was where the heavens reached down to hold him in her gentle embrace. It was where he sought renewal and was always restored. Almost every morning, in the blue hour that was dawn, a mist would rise from the lake, a sheer, flat surface as clear as unbroken glass. Fog swirled in gentle puffs. Constantly in motion, the brume lifted, fell or suddenly dispersed like Indian spirits being chased away by his white-man presence. Save for the drip drip drip of his paddle as it lifted from the water to reach for the next stroke, his wooden canoe slid across the lake without a sound. The low flat hull seemed to slice the water and part the vapor like a knife. Knowing him, I'm sure he imagined this was how the Cheyenne and Arapahoe fished these waters a century ago and was contented in the emulation of their example. Soon, a mesh of stars in a dome of inky indigo was extinguished one by one as the sun began to paint the sky with amber daylight.

I remember watching him from the terrace one crisp fall day when in a week he'd be returning to the hurly burly of New York City. He drifted with rod and reel parked across the gunwales and a thermos mug of steaming brandied coffee cupped in his hands. All around him, a woodland caught between autumnal life and death tumbled down in wild silence. A vibrant palette of primary colors and evergreen were reflected at the water's edge. Images were doubled - one real the other a mirrored duplicate in which he was actually floating. Graceful hemlocks tucked in a cool cove, seemed to bow as he slipped by. Sylphlike tamaracks competed with quaking aspens. Fluorescent yellow heart-shaped leaves shimmered against blue-green tufts of short needles in a dance celebrating the new day. When he paddled back to the boat house, he passed under a willow whose elongated branches and feathery leaves caressed his whiskered cheeks. With a sudden splash, an otter often dove from its hiding place among moss-covered rocks. Half-eaten perch and bass lay rotting, the putrid stench making Gramps cover his mouth and nose with a handkerchief. Nevertheless, his suspicion proved correct *Mr. Otter* might be there made him laugh heartily. Echoes of joy ricocheted across the lake.

Echo Lake was definitely Gramps' sanctuary. After a semester of bloviating congressmen or an ideologue for a President (FDR), how could he not seek solitary comforts in the wilds of southern Wyoming? His old, wicker creel might be empty by the end of some mornings, but that was never the point of his outings.

During my grandfather's memorial at Echo Lodge, the linesman was working on the ranch's phone service a mile away. Two days after the service the linesman told my grandmother that some prankster kept calling and saying it was the White House. The linesman hung up, but the White House kept calling back. As it so happened, it was indeed the

White House. President Richard Nixon called to offer his condolences to Grammy. Nixon and my grandfather had served together on the Maritime Committee. Besides, Jackson Hart had been a former Congressman, so protocol dictated this personal touch from a sitting president. You could say that right up to the end if it involved my grandfather, then along with great respect, mischief often came, too.

TWENTY DOLLAR BILL

Our Yellow Cab pulls up to the curb in front of 666 5th Avenue between East 52nd and 53rd in Midtown Manhattan. Always vivid in its colors, clamor and odors, New York City this evening is a humid eighty-three degrees; not at all unusual for the first week of September when the northeast still swelters under its last dog days of summer. Aunt Ann and I quickly duck into a unique T-shaped atrium walk-through where sparkling glass storefronts showcase a book store, Al Italia Airlines and clothing boutiques. Via a non-stop elevator all the way to the top, we head to the penthouse, otherwise known as the Top of the Six's Restaurant. Aunt Ann has promised me a special last supper before escorting me to Upstate New York and my start at Skidmore College.

The mâitre d' leads us to our table, laid with starched white linens and silverware three deep on either side of the charger. A two-story-high picture window affords diners stunning panoramic views of Central Park to the north and a setting sun over the Hudson River to our west. Shafts of cascading light tumble into the oak-paneled dining room, making prisms on the walls dance as light refracts off crystal goblets at each place setting. It is truly magical, and I am dumbstruck by the unexpected beauty of the city outside. So accustomed am I to the noise of hawkers hawking and cab drivers honking and people's dour faces and black garb found at street level, I am transfixed by this high-rise view of New York. Far removed from what could often be characterized as sour and foul, New York's incredible skyline of varied architecture is clearly on display.

"If you don't close your mouth all your teeth'll fall out."

"Aunt Ann, I'm speechless."

"So I see. C'mon, sit down and try to remember the manners Gramps taught you."

"Aunt Ann," I whisper leaning across the table, "this is incredible!"

"That's why I brought you here."

As waiters bring our shrimp cocktail and refill our water goblets, Aunt Ann pummels me with questions about boys, my possible major and whether or not I think I might get homesick. When the waiter brings us our *amuse bouches*, I am rescued from her incessant, though well-intentioned barrage. As it is explained by our waiter, here is an unexpected bite-sized h'ors d'oeuvre, not ordered by us, but a gift from the chef as a sampling of his culinary expertise free of charge. As they are placed in front of us, two itty bitty parmesan pannacotta, a cold Italian custard, glistens golden. My mouth waters as I gently prod mine with the spoon handed to me. It shimmies in response.

"What fun! I've never eaten an *amuse bouche* before. Have you?"

"It's de rigeur," my aunt says in the very worst accent imaginable, "by all the fancy restaurants in New York."

"I never encountered this in England."

"Of course, you didn't." She wipes the corners of her mouth. "English food is disgusting."

"Touché," I concede in my best upper crust English accent. "And might I add this custard has been ever-so terribly terribly amusing!"

A mere sliver of a moon hangs suspended above the rooftops over the East River. The city is ablaze with lights against a black sky.

After our Dover Sole, we sink spoons into a delicious *mousse au chocolat* and swoon with pleasure. Throughout dinner, Aunt Ann's face has glowed within a halo of candlelight, and now she looks as though she has one more important pearl of wisdom to impart.

"I want you to take this $20 bill and tuck it into the back of your wallet. Do not, I repeat, do not ever spend it. It's for emergencies only." She hands me the crisp note. "Take it, Honey. You never know when you might find yourself in a difficult situation and need a ride home."

I look a little quizzical. "I see I need to be a little more explicit," she sighs. "Let's say you're out with a fella who's had too much to drink or is getting a little too frisky. You decide you wanna go home, but he's not the one who should be doin' the driving or goin' home with you..." I nod. "Good. I see the lightbulb's come on."

Needless to say, I am touched. How is it she always seems to be looking out for me? Whether it is swimming or driving lessons, remedial math or supervising my summer reading, she has always been there nudging me along in a supportive manner; not in an accusing or sarcastic way that might damage my ego. How does she know I need to be handled this way? I am so very grateful for her attention and thoughtfulness.

It was a clear night when we stepped out onto 5th Avenue. The sidewalks were almost empty, streets free of cabs hurtling south to downtown Lower Manhattan. Gone were the food trucks and pretzel vendors. So, too, the black market handbag peddlers with their card tables laden with all things ersatz: quilted pleather Chanel's with their faux gold chain straps, Gucci wannabe's and Versace clones all lined up in neat rows; fakes hot off the presses, but tempting nevertheless. I remember feeling giddy from too much wine (legal drinking age in New York was eighteen in those days) or more likely just the night-before-heading-to-college jitters.

We spent the night at the Women's National Republican Club on 51st Street, a block away from the Three Sixes. It was the oldest private club for Republican women in the United States, and Grammy was one of its founding lifetime members. It was founded by Henrietta Wells Livermore in 1921, spawned by the women's suffrage movement, which led to the nineteenth amendment and women's right to vote. The club, housed in a Neo-Georgian style building constructed on the former site of Andrew Carnegie's home, was decorated in soft shades of cream and butter, accents of blue, upholstered sofas and armchairs and reproduction Queen Anne case goods. The building was listed on the National Register of Historic Places, and to this day it continues to host Republican events and admit men only as daytime guests. I was given a room of my own, sumptuously trimmed in rose and ivy chintz both on its walls and its furnishings in the middle of which was a canopy bed. Cozy and fit for Sleeping Beauty, I slept not a wink.

While Aunt Ann drove through the Catskills I caught up on all the literature for freshmen I'd been sent.

"Listen to this. Skidmore College was founded by the daughter of a wealthy coal merchant and widow of publishing heir, J. Blair Scribner. Lucy Scribner, who was a frail lady, arrived in Saratoga Springs to take its healing waters in 1900. Though she fell in love with the resort town's charms and decided to stay, she didn't approve of the flamboyant lifestyle of the rich and famous. Silly parties, gambling and thoroughbred horse races were the privileged activities of the social élite attending Saratoga's famous August Season. Mrs. Scribner was a religious and shy woman, who disapproved of frivolity, so in light of the foolishness she observed every year, she invested her wealth on something worthwhile, namely a school for young women where they could learn skills making them self-supporting and not dependent."

"Good for her. My kinda no-nonsense gal."

It was two o'clock by the time Aunt Ann swung the rental car on to Union Avenue, the main artery running through the heart of Saratoga Springs' historic district. A storybook campus of Victorian-era houses surrounded by sweeps of mown grass was delightful, yet I was suddenly terrified. The street was at least fifty feet wide with a median strip lined with trees running from Congress Park in the center of town all the way through the Saratoga Race Track to the east and the interstate beyond. On either side of the boulevard was an array of mansions, almost all of them Skidmore dorms. I spotted a High Victorian Gothic with dormered mansard roof and iron cresting. Were it not for all the girls sitting on the front steps drinking cokes and laughing, I might have thought this house haunted. A Greek Revival, characterized by its columns and triangular pediment, loomed imposing and incongruous. I took an immediate dislike to it. Happily, Aunt Ann rolled past that one. Turns out it was the home of Skidmore's president, Dr. Palamountain. Several Queen Ann's with wrap around porches, projecting gables and a turret or two stood in a row. These dorms looked homier, maybe even jolly. Stained glass transoms glinted rainbow colors in the mid afternoon sun. And scores of girls gathered out front greeting each other as they unloaded luggage from their parents' cars. A Colonial Revival marked by its curved windows, railings and hipped roof looked inviting because it was so traditional and was something to which I was most accustomed. But smack dab in the middle of the avenue was a contemporary block of a building painted bubblegum pink. It sported three rows of vacant casement windows and commercial-looking glass doors. Known as the Pink Monstrosity, this would be my freshman dining hall. I was still looking over my shoulder at that hideous building when Aunt Ann came to a stop.

"Here you be, Lexie! 125 Union Avenue. Your home for the next four years!" I duck my head out the window and assess my dorm. The building is massive but homey. Charming yellow clapboard siding, tall double-hung windows and gangly wrought iron fire escapes give the place an informal, don't-take-me-too-seriously look. It feels intimate with two stories of screened-in porch and white wicker rockers scattered every which way. This is Van Deusen; formerly owned by Samuel River and considered but a small summer cottage. Once it was home to the owner of America's most famous thoroughbred, Man o' War. Keep in mind summer cottages, as they were called, are actually McMansions for the super wealthy, and this so-called cottage slept fifty.

"Are you going to get out or do I have to drag you out by your pantyhose?" asks Aunt Ann, who is standing on the sidewalk and poking her head in the passenger-side window.

"Uh, how 'bout a few more minutes to just take it all in..."

"Nope." When she opens the passenger door and waits with all the pantomimed flourish of a chauffeur doffing his cap, I move quickly, embarrassed someone might see. Immediately, I hear the strains of Janis Joplin's Piece of My Heart blare throaty and raw from an upstairs window. It melds with Chicago's more melodic Make Me Smile from a downstairs dorm room where the window is held open by a pair of chrome stereo speakers.

My aunt hands me my Tourister train case, picks up my bigger suitcases, matching of course, and clomps up the steps. When we enter the vestibule to check in at the front desk, Led Zeppelin's Whole Lotta Love grinds out its insistence in souped up bass. With such a hip amalgam of late sixties sound colliding in one place, I suddenly feel very at home. To my way of thinking at the time, it was *goodbye London's West End la-de-da and hello America's down-to-earth unpretentiousness.* Since then whenever I hear those songs, a flood of happy memories rushes in, reminding me how good it feels to be free of society's silly comme-il-faut.

My future room mate appears on the stairs. She's dressed in a denim mini skirt, purple plastic flip-flops and a lacy see-through T-shirt. She isn't wearing a bra, which oddly, as I recall, really impressed me. Sporting octagonal wire-rimmed glasses, she looks like something straight out of Alice B. Toklas' kitchen. What an incongruous pair we're going to make, I remember thinking and for the first time that day I smile a real smile, not a fake one born from manners. As I soak in this visage of 60's funk, she stares at me, probably wondering from what planet I come. There I am in my navy blue dress and matching hose with coordinating purse and pumps. She must think me utterly ridiculous.

"I'm gonna say 'goodbye', kiddo." Aunt Ann is still standing by the door, flanked by my suitcases. I remember how I ran back to her and hugged her with everything I had.

"Thank you, Aunt Ann, for bringing me to college. I could never ever have come all this way by myself."

"I know," she whispers. "It's not right you start this journey alone."

I walk her out to the car and kiss her doughy cheek, then watch her Cadillac until it has melted away, red tail lights growing smaller and smaller. When I go back inside Lise Nilsen, my rocker-chick, Swedish-bombshell-babe of a room mate is waiting with a broad, toothy grin.

"What-say?" she queries in some sort of slang I don't understand. Is this an invitation for me to speak? Then looking me up and down, she gently probes, "You for real?"

That day, when Aunt Ann and I said our farewells, each of us looked into the other's eyes and shared an unspoken understanding. Mother was not there.

THANK YOU

Graduation Day at Goucher College was a fairly short ceremony. Thank goodness, since that morning it was brutally hot and stinky-humid. Except for the long-winded diatribe from our hippie valedictorian who spouted platitudes like *be fearless in the pursuit of what sets your soul on fire* and *let each of your adventures begin* I listened to every word. My college graduation was going to be an ugly memory unfolding with no photographs to show for it. Just as well since we didn't need to draw attention to the fact that Mother and Daddy weren't there.

About two hundred and seventy-five of us walked from Van Meter Hall out onto the grassy quadrangle followed by a trio of bagpipers. Their haunting strains pulled at my heartstrings, stirring the deepest of visceral emotions. My classmates felt it, too, but their tears were for a touchstone of achievement, a benchmark of adulthood. Mine came with the realization that my parents and I clearly lived in parallel worlds, our paths rarely connecting anymore. It hurt. I was scarcely cheered by the riot of wild flowers tied with wispy strands of raffia anchored at each row of wooden folding chairs. I was in a foul temper when I took my seat with the others in the first ten rows on either side of the aisle.

Before I sat, though, I got a quick glimpse of Grammy in the middle of a sea of strangers. Despite her diminutive stature, she was easy to spot as her soft cloud of blue-tinted hair caught the light. When she smiled at me, her blue eyes were brimming with tears. She dabbed at them with a lace-trimmed handkerchief and nodded her head in affirmation. She was dressed in a suit the color of sea foam and attached to her left lapel was a pink corsage. A poodle brooch glinted on her right shoulder. Grammy was far more elegant than the restive parents and siblings waiting for the convocation to begin, but she was a beautiful vision of a bygone era and I loved her for it. I smiled wanly and gave her the 'V' for victory sign.

Squinting into the sunlight while tiny white blossoms floated in the air like bits of cotton, we all perspired through two speeches, a hymn and finally the commencement exercise. Once the diplomas were handed out and we as a class were declared graduates, all of us girls tossed our mortarboards high into the air. Cameras clicked, laughter rang out and girls ran in search of parents for their hugs and congratulations. When I finally located Grammy standing under a sycamore out of harm's way of the crush, she said, "I am so proud of you, dear." Taken quite by surprise, I didn't know until just then how a word like *proud* could feel. For the first time, I understood love in a way I hadn't ever before. And when she held me close, hers was such a loving embrace. I felt like I was cocooned in a soft blanket.

That should have been a day for joy. Having come so far preparing for the greater world as an adult, there was good cause for jubilation. Yet I was not exultant; not like the rest of my classmates all acting like they'd won the lottery. Here was yet another right of passage for me, and neither Mother nor Daddy was there to memorialize it. Perhaps they were unable to forgive me for transferring out of Skidmore and moving down to Baltimore to be closer to Annapolis and my fiancé, David. They never said and I never asked. The real reason for my sudden departure from Skidmore was because a professor tried to fail me after I rejected his sexual advances. I was too ashamed to tell anyone. Perhaps, my parents' schedule was more likely the culprit. Getting to Echo Lake Ranch in July, the Saratoga Races in August and back to more ranch time in September was how they liked to spend their summers. My graduation in May brought them over from England too early, thus making their vacation in America too long. My graduation must have been inconvenient, but try as I have to understand, I have never been able to forgive them this.

No question it was at this juncture an emotional distance began to spread between us. Like spilled ink, leaving in its wake an indelible stain no amount of scrubbing could ever erase, this omission of theirs caused me to look at my parents with fresh eyes. I was deeply offended by their decision. Yet quickly I covered the wound with a bandage of acceptance, never once telling them how much I really smarted from this insult. After the scar developed, I realized scars are just another kind of memory. So, I stashed this and others like it, in a lockbox and shoved them all to the back of a closet shelf. I will confess, though, that even after that and other disappointments I still craved Mother's approval. Just her interest alone would have sufficed.

Why is it certain memories can never be erased? They live inside festering like boils. Why didn't I tell my parents that I was hurt? Did I think I actually deserved such treatment? Was I too afraid to complain for fear of rejection or criticism I was but an ingrate? What would it have accomplished in the long run? Instead, I chose to look upon that day as every cloud has its silver lining and that was Grammy's being there. She bothered to be chauffeured down from New York and back just to be in the audience for my moment; my biggest milestone. This generous gift of her time and interest were what love was all about. From that day forward I could neither imagine living without this kind of love nor not giving it back to others.

BEFORE I KNEW HIM

Daddy's sixtieth is tomorrow. And though I've got everything ready, I have just one more thing to do and that's to write a speech. When I sit down at my father's Partner's desk, slanting rays of late afternoon sunlight are pouring in the window. Daddy's chocolate Lab, Jasper, joins me by curling up in the leg opening and dropping his head on my foot with a loud sigh. It's as if he's saying: I nap, you write.

Daddy landed in Normandy the very same day the Germans surrendered. So instead of joining Eisenhower's Expeditionary Forces as originally ordered, he was attached to the Blue Spaders of the 1st Infantry Division, chosen to secure the Nuremberg war crimes trials. Mother was wont to comment that Brass wanted to show the world the face of our American esprit de corps and *your father was selected because he was so handsome.* I prefer to think there was more than just good looks involved, such as his being an excellent marksman, but far be it from me to argue. In that musty and cavernous courtroom, our boys stood guard right behind the likes of Hermann Göring. One can only guess what each of them was thinking during those proceedings. Knowing Daddy, I imagine he'd never felt so swollen with rage in his entire life. *May we live to see a more enlightened age than the one I've grown up in* became his mantra as I was growing up. Actually, I don't think Daddy ever got over what he heard during those trials, so aggrieved was he by Nazi brutality. It's pretty evident by the way he chose to conduct his life after the war as a trial attorney that he never allowed himself to imagine a life <u>not</u> shaped by the miseries of his youth.

What I see in the sepia-toned photograph of Daddy at the Nuremberg trials is a man who is decidedly a few belt holes thinner, has cheeks as smooth as a baby's bottom and is so innocent-looking one is compelled to shield him from harm instead of his being the hero, though I have no doubt he was prepared at every second. The rifle and bayonet at his uniformed shoulder belie the boy who rode his horse bareback to a one-room schoolhouse on the Colorado prairie. And what isn't visible in the photo is the Danube River outside the courtroom, meandering through the city like a ribbon, a sheer mist hovering over its satiny surface. Nor can you hear the church bells down the street summoning its German parishioners to Mass, perhaps, if they're so lucky, to their absolution.

The words *life is a mix of hardships and triumphs*, echoes in my head today. And because Daddy is a man of so few words, those, in particular, have a unique gravitas. I take a deep breath, inhaling the cigarette smoke he tries so unsuccessfully to disguise. No doubt there's an ashtray overflowing with day-old butts hiding in a drawer somewhere. Should I empty it before Mother discovers it? Na, not this time. With fingers floating over the typewriter, thinking I'll start my speech with Nuremberg being the reason he chose law as a profession, I wonder how well I can really know my father before my arrival in his world.

"They say it's hard being a lonely only. How I crave
brothers and sisters who might belong to me, look like me
or sound like me. It's bad enough
being a teenager and knowing
you don't fit in your own skin, but
having no one to call your
own stinks even more."

THERE IN THE REARVIEW MIRROR

Dartmouth College's Winter Carnival was in full swing. The ice sculpture contest held on the Green in the center of Hanover would be judged at the end of the week, so students were carving their finishing touches into such giants as Big Bird with yellow feathers and all, Gulliver, Jimmy Carter and Mr. T., replete with his signature gold chains. Students and professors crisscrossing the snow-covered square were hustling to and from class, or into the Hanover Inn for a cup of their famous hot chocolate. Traffic was stalled to let them pass. This was a common occurrence every weekday at fifty-five minutes past the hour, and I thought it charming. It was always fun to people-watch and today, what with sub-zero temps, everyone's breath was smoking in the frigid air making them appear ghoulish. So, too, were the cars' exhaust pipes blowing smoke. Snow was spilling from the sky and it lay without melting on the heads and shoulders of the passersby. The mood in the streets was festive. After all, America just won Olympic gold.

Dubbed "Miracle on Ice." Team USA was comprised of amateur and collegiate ice hockey players who defeated the Soviet Union's national team during the 1980 Winter Olympics in Lake Placid, New York. During the game, the crowd went crazy while chants, "USA! USA! USA!" ricocheted off the rafters. Fans waved posters and American flags and when it was all over there wasn't a dry eye in the stadium or anywhere in America for that matter. The team went on to beat Finland winning Olympic Gold.

What was so stunning was the American team was not expected

to win as they had not only lost to the Soviets in an exhibition game several weeks earlier, but the Soviet Union had won gold six of the seven previous Olympic games. Everyone knew the Soviet team was made up of professionals, so for our boys, and I do mean boys, to trounce the Russian Bear was truly a miracle. After the team won in a nail-biter and the players and crowds were running all over the ice, Coach Herb Brooks disappeared into the locker room for a private cry. Later, when the team joined him, they broke into a chorus of God Bless America. Two weeks later on the cover of the March 3, 1980 issue of Sports Illustrated no caption or headline appeared under the photograph of Team USA. As one of the players remarked, "It didn't need it. Everyone in America knew what happened."

Emotions were running high that winter, and more than a hockey game was at stake that day. America's psyche was bruised. Iranian rebels held Americans hostage in the U.S. Embassy in Tehran. The Soviet Union invaded Afghanistan just two months earlier. The Cold War simmered, and the U.S. economy sputtered while interest rates were climbing, eventually by summer hitting an astronomical 21%. President Jimmy Carter was on his way to becoming famous for being America's worst president of record, while Ronald Reagan would soon be our nation's fortieth and, in my opinion, one of her greatest.

I was at the wheel in our old Volvo, when I had my epiphany. Well, it wasn't a religious manifestation, but more of an unexpected insight; a revelation that took me by surprise. We were at a crosswalk bathed by a welcome sunbeam while snow crystals sifted through the sunlight. Behind me, my two toddlers, Sophie (2 1/2) and Emma (1 1/2) were sitting in their car seats mesmerized by the snow globe aura around our car. When I glanced in the rearview mirror I was struck by a mother's pride in her little darlings. Cerulean eyes shone brightly, their expressions both curious. Blotches of red from the dry arctic air stained their fair cheeks as if a painter had dabbed each one with a flourish of his brush. Tendrils of yellow blond escaped from their woolen hats to frame the dearest of faces. When I glanced away to put the car into gear, I did a double-take. Looking at them gave me such an eerie feeling. It was as if I were suddenly meeting myself as a lost soul. I remember thinking, wow, my daughters are the only two blood relatives I know! One moment I felt so alone and the next gratified to have them in my company. With that, I couldn't help but wonder all the way to the Co-op, who else might be out there.

Did my biological mother ever marry the man who fathered me or somebody else? Did I have any sisters or brothers? Where did they live? Had our paths ever crossed without my knowing? Did they know about me or was I a secret? If I met my mother on the street, would I instantly recognize her? I was all a-tingle, and very excited by this unexpected awareness. How had I managed to not have these thoughts before now? Perhaps, I'd never given myself permission is why.

When I got home, I was on a mission, but first I had to put the girls down for their naps. They seemed particularly fussy that afternoon, so it took forever for them to settle. I blamed it on the chill having made its way through all the layers of their clothing while we were out doing errands. More likely a reason was the agitation radiating from my own pores, which as I rehearsed what I was about to do must have hung in the air like a dust devil.

Finally, I was able to sit at the kitchen table, an old yellow Formica dinosaur pockmarked and on its last legs. I dialed the number to The Cradle in Evanston, Illinois.

"Good afternoon, this is Angie at The Cradle. How may I direct your call?" She sounds so kind I almost hang up. Lying to such a sweet-sounding person doesn't seem right.

"Yes, um, I'm a sociology major at Dartmouth College. And, um, I'm doing research for a term paper on the laws regarding closed adoptions. Uh, I've spoken with state institutions, but thought, um, speaking with a private entity and one of such renown as The Cradle, would be a, uh, a good idea."

At the time this sounds incredibly cogent, even scholarly. "Who would best, uh, be able to help me?"

"I'll put you through to Mrs. Davis. Who may I tell her is calling?"

"Jane Smith," I blurt, blushing crimson. At least I haven't said, *Jane Doe.* I remember thinking that would really be dumb.

I'll never forget that moment. It's as if it's frozen in time, befitting the weather outside. Rays of sunlight were slanting through the kitchen window to warm my shoulders and it had finally stopped snowing. Clouds were lifting to reveal a patchwork quilt of blues and pearly pinks. I could hear the clock in the living room. The tick tock of anticipation made my mouth go dry and furry.

"This is Carol Davis. How may I help you, Jane?" She sounds stern.

"Yes, ma'am." I've never ever used the word *ma'am* in my life. "I am doing a research paper..."

"Forgive me for interrupting, but Angie has filled me in." *She doesn't want to hear me fib.* "Here's what I can tell you. The laws of Illinois mandate that a closed adoption remain closed, but here at The Cradle our motto is *Supporting You Always*, so we try to satisfy an adoptee's curiosity about all things medical, hereditary and genealogical as best we can. Provided our records go no farther back than 1949 when a fire destroyed our archives. What we cannot tell an adoptee are the names of the mother and father or the circumstances under which an infant is placed." *She knows*, I thought. "All an adoptee need do is write a letter with his or her questions, mail it to us here in Evanston, and someone will reply if there's any information to share."

"Thank you," I say since that is all I can muster. I'm blushing again.

"Is there anything else I can help you with, Jane?"

"No, I don't think so. I'm, um, pretty sure that adopted people would really be glad to have that much information. I'll include this in my paper if that's okay?"

"Certainly," she replies. "Thank you for calling, dear."

Ooh, she does know I'm a phony. She's just called me dear. She's heard this line of guff a million times before and feels sorry for me. Never mind, I've taken the plunge and there is no turning back.

That night, while my husband, David, was studying, I sat down to my portable typewriter and hammered out the following letter and questions:

Mrs. David P. Chambers
25 Indian Road
Hanover, N.H. 03755

Mrs. Carol Davis   October 20, 1980
The Cradle
2049 Ridge Avenue
Evanston, Illinois 60204

Dear Mrs. Davis,

My name is Alexandra Saunders Chambers. I was born on February 2nd 1952 and placed for adoption by your agency. While I understand the documents concerning my birth are closed and must remain so, I am seeking any information you can give me. Below are my questions.

I look forward to your reply and please accept my thanks in advance.

Very Sincerely,

Alex Chambers

1. Was my mother married at the time of my birth?
2. Was my mother's pregnancy a healthy one?
3. Was I healthy at birth?
4. Is there any ancestral information?
5. Is there any medical history available?
6. How much time elapsed from birth to placement with a family?
7. Has my birth mother tried to locate me?
8. What is the physical description of my biological mother?

Two weeks later a reply arrived in the mail. I remember asking David to take the kids to Thayer Skating Pond as I wanted to open the letter in peace and quiet. I knew I was going to fall apart. David complied. When they'd left the house, I sat at that old pockmarked Formica table and just stared at the letter lying in front of me. I was too scared to open it. What if it told me nothing? What if it said something I wouldn't like? How would it feel to have answers and no more mystery? What if and what if some more? But with shaking hands, I slid a paring knife under the flap and slowly lifted the pages out. I read each page slowly. When I was done, I buried my head into my folded arms on the table and wept great heaving sobs. They rolled from me like relentless ocean waves one after another and another.

HOLY SMOKES!

The house is dark when I finally stop crying. Outside the window, I can see snow falling, whitening the driveway and coating the trees. Our kitchen window panes look like cracked pond ice, which makes me wonder where David and the girls are. The hush of the falling snow has muted everything, even the groan and clatter of the snowplow up on the street is muffled. In this hushed world, I suddenly feel very isolated and cut off. The house is so still it's as if the snowflakes have shushed the world until there is no sound at all save for my breathing. My eyes well up with tears as I read the postscript on the back of The Cradle's letter for the ninth time. There is an answer to a question I've not asked, the words a shocking revelation:

> *You do not ask for information about your biological father. At the*
> *same time I think you will be interested in knowing that he was 6 feet,*
> *3 inches in height and weighed over 200 pounds, and was of German*
> *extraction. Your birth mother told our staff member that he was a*
> *college graduate who was an architect by profession. She preferred to*
> *withhold his name so our records do not include that information.*

My not asking a single question about my birth father was pretty telling that something was rolling around in my subconscious. Otherwise, how could I have been so remiss? He honestly hadn't factored into my inquiry for one second. Yet here, were details to which I felt intrinsically connected. Wow! He was a big man; not just tall, but robust. I clearly inherited his physique; he was the reason for my size. Miraculously, I suddenly felt connected. Oh, how great it felt to have my weight explained. Excused too, as if I needed a pardon, but growing up with Mother and Daddy I was always so ashamed of how I looked. I didn't fit their body profile at all. How fantastic to know I wasn't any more an aberration living amongst svelte ectomorphs than a redhead sprung from recessive genes. He was of German origins. No wonder I excelled at that language, fluent *auf deutsch* by the time I was seventeen. German came to me so easily, as if already coursing in my very blood and bones. And oh my gosh, he was an architect; a reason for my spacial IQ being the highest of all my IQ's measured. This is why I gravitated toward interior design.

It was too gratifying and sad all at once. My heart felt like it would burst through the walls of my chest, so I crawled into my grief and let it cocoon around me. Despite the silence enveloping our house, the voices of a mother and father who were neither in the room nor even a phone call away echoed in my ears. Hers was a gravelly voice, with a combined inflection of practicality and amusement. His deeper and accented, perhaps a little stern. I tried to envision her face, his, too, to see their smiles, feel love in their gaze. It was like trying to conjure ghosts from the proverbial other side. I failed, no magician I, so resorted to tears again. Helplessness was not a feeling to which I was accustomed. I snatched the letter up and reread it again searching for details I might have missed and which could bring my birth parents' faces to the surface:

Your birth mother was 5 feet, 7 inches in height and ordinarily weighed 130 pounds. She had brown hair and eyes. You may be interested in knowing that she was 21 at the time of your birth and that she was a high school graduate who held a responsible secretarial job. Your birth mother was unmarried.

Of course, she was unmarried. I was born at a home for unwed mothers. *Duh!* Out of nowhere, Mother's accusing expression suddenly drifted into my mind's eye. I shook my head to clear the cobwebs so as to see Mama's face instead. While I was grateful for holding this information in my hands and the letter was definitely bringing Mama to life, I could only envision Mother.

Your biological mother's health was good. She, herself, described her medical record as excellent and she had no illness during her pregnancy.

No connection there either. I had toxemia with my first, Sophie, and gained seventy-five pounds. I'd barely lost twenty-five of it when four months later I became pregnant with Emma. Crossing back into the now familiar two-hundred-pound-plus territory was a sure thing. As a brick house, kittens loved me. They'd take refuge on my size 44 double D chest because it was a viable nesting shelf replete with beating heart for white noise. There are photographs, but I've hidden them from potential blackmailers.

Our record lists your birth mother's nationality descent as Northern European which doubtless means her ancestors came to this country from the British Isles.

So did a gazillion other Americans. Heck, those were the bulk of the people who fled King George III's England. The good folks who rebelled against his repressive taxation without representation, who turned the Redcoats on their heels and sent them back across the pond. Everybody was English before becoming American!

Why was I losing my temper? The profile of Mama given by The Cradle seemed so bland it just wasn't doing it for me. *What's wrong with me,* I wondered. *You finally have information you could only guess at up until today. Be grateful.* Just like that, Mother's face floated into my mind's eye again; not Mama's. With my hands flying up to the sides of my head I clenched my hair and screamed, "Dammit, stop!" The vision of Mother instantly went poof. With that accomplished, I began to pace the house, not turning on lights, which was highly unusual as I was prone to reaching around doorways to flip a switch before ever entering a dark room. But I was determined Mother not reappear and somehow leaving the lights off made that more feasible.

How was it I was living parallel lives? One a very noisy existence as wife, mother and daughter for all the world to see; the other life with which I was utterly unfamiliar, a wordless life, but no less real for its silence. I was conceived in the womb of one woman and raised by another who was a complete stranger to my primordial roots. Heck, even I didn't really know what they were until The Cradle supplied me with a few details. It had always been so confusing, more so when I was in elementary school because I was unaware of being confused. I just acted out in inappropriate ways. I focused on the fiction that I was chosen, even bragged about it, which I'm sure made me real popular. Later, in junior high, I fashioned a story about having a brother from whom I'd been separated when our parents were killed in a car crash. That confusion I knew was wrong, it spinning like a top, its whispering whir scraping at my ear drums and my conscience. Thoughts about my birth father were few, mainly because I thought of him as nothing more than a sperm donor on a hot date. Thoughts about my birth mother were shaped by childish fantasy, fixed in place for over twenty-five years. Now the freshly acquired information on the page clutched in my sweaty palm was challenging my imagination. Here were actual details, none of them matching my fabrications and none of them particularly striking. Dispensing with the fantasy meant giving up on the dream. I was a mess that night.

Of course, Mother was really the one leading the challenge in my mind. Thanks to her, a ball and chain of guilt anchored to my ankle stopped me in my tracks. I was betraying Mother. How could I rejoice over my freshly minted news, while I dragged my selfishness around? I was a spoiled ingrate, searching for more than I deserved, right? Besides, I couldn't keep secrets from the mother who'd raised me, but I couldn't share them with her either. She'd never understand why I needed to know who my biological mother was. She'd be hurt and probably never forgive me. Mother had already suffered so much I didn't want to add to her long list of tragedies: her mother dead when she was twelve; her first love and husband killed in a plane crash; a womb made barren by a surgeon's knife. Now a child abandoning her for another mother? I couldn't do that to her.

There is no record of your birth mother being in touch with
The Cradle since February 1952.

I figured as much. So, as I paraded around the house, drifting in and out of every room, I told myself it shouldn't matter that most of my life I felt like a child separated from her mommy in a crowded department store, standing in place as I was told to do should this ever occur, waiting for her to find me. It shouldn't matter that as an adult I still felt that way. A lonely little girl, misplaced, out of place, rooted in place and truly lost. I didn't know where to find Mama and she had yet to find me. Maybe, she didn't want to find me. Maybe, she'd put her past behind her and moved on. Who could blame her? She probably had a husband and children who knew nothing about me, her secret well hidden. I wouldn't want to disrupt her life any more than Mother's. I'd always thought it had been so brave of her to carry me to term only to give me up to another in the hope of giving me a brighter future, one with a mommy and a daddy. Ever since I'd understood what adoption meant, I'd always sympathized with Mama's anguish way more than any I might have suffered. So that night, I told myself to get over it, move on, be happy for all the good things. In a week I'd be as right as rain, or so I told myself.

I undressed in the dark and climbed into an old pair of flannel pajamas, fleece-y slippers and my husband's Naval Academy sweatshirt. Padding back downstairs, turning lights on as I went, I could hear the crunching tracks of footsteps in the snow. All of a sudden, the girls burst through the front door with snowflakes in their hair. Their cheeks were crimson with the cold and their smiles were as broad as boulevards. I sank down on the bottom stair and opened my arms. Holding them close to my aching heart, I nuzzled first one daughter then the other, inhaling each of their unique toddler-fragrances, reveling in being connected to them; rejoicing in being their mom.

"I don't think I'd be too happy if my birth mother just showed up on the doorstep. It would freak me out. What if she wanted more than I could give? Best to stick with whom you know. After all, Mother and Daddy have been good to me."

MY PERSON

Every year when I arrived for my summer vacation, Gramps was already standing on the porch of Echo Lodge. Smiling broadly, his profoundly blue eyes crinkling at the edges, he braced himself as I bounded into his arms with locomotive force. He lifted me up high, then held me close to his chest. I burrowed my little-girl face into his soft old-man's neck and inhaled the sweet tang of pipe smoke.

Today he is long gone, and I miss him terribly. He was the one constant in my life; a personality I could count on for his constancy of demeanor and strength of character. His aura resides in every corner of the lodge. Most especially, the enormous stone fireplace dominating the center wall, embers twinkling red and orange on a pile of last night's ash; of his peeling back the rugs to play a game of jacks on the wide-plank floorboards; a hand-tooled wooden bowl, round and deep, waxed to glistening and overflowing with packets of Wrigley's gum; an African Blackwood cane carved by a Maasai warrior brought back from one of his many safaris; or his vest, its fishing lures and bobbers stitched in soft threads of petit point by Mother.

His spirit skitters across Echo Lake, which stretches like polished stone, serene and gray-green. He bobs in the spangles of sun sparkling around the swimming dock where on only really hot days he took a quick dip with a straw hat perched atop his balding head. On moonlit fields, too, where if we are lucky enough to spy them, deer graze; or even with those deviant coyotes who lurk as a pack at the edge of our forests and howl into the night with heads upturned. He's everywhere: in the morning dew dripping from fern fronds, on top of polka-dotted toadstools poking through velvety layers of moss or hidden among spider webs stretched across our riding trails. I can still see him on the tennis court riding a bicycle backward atop the handle bars around and around and around.

He's on Echo Mountain, which melts upward to a sky, deep blue by day, a treasure box of stars by night. He's even in the Northern Lights' broad strokes of purple, electric green and pale yellow. His laughter hangs on the wind, riling fallen leaves into covering the trails of stinky skunk, prickly porcupine and bandit-raccoon. Echoes of his voice intoning the words, *He who loves not his country, can love nothing,* give birth to my abiding patriotism.

With Gramps gone, I can only rely on memory, envisioning him on that front porch now. Missing are his outstretched arms into which I used to rush headlong. Absent, too, is the scent of tobacco I'd give anything to inhale again. Worst of all, his embrace is no more. It is or was the only place where I could leave my little-girl heart undefended. Memories of him are all I have now, but they'll do. They'll do just fine.

LOST IN THE CITY

I might as well have been there that day. *Where in the world is Mumsy?* my mother probably asks herself over and over. Along with a few choice words of the off-color variety, my father probably mutters *It's been more than an hour and a half.* I can just see Mother and Daddy sitting upright on the edge of their matching slip-covered arm chairs under a cone of silence waiting for the doorbell or the phone to ring. In spite of the noise of trucks loading and unloading, taxis squealing to a stop, or workmen shouting from the scaffolding next door pouring into the living room, you can hear a pin drop for sure. Mumsy, or Grammy to me, has said she'll be right over, but that has been almost two hours ago and the walk between her apartment and my parents' condo is a mere six blocks. I'm guessing Daddy stares at the wall looking past the roses twining across the wallpaper in a riot of petals and thorns, his thin lips tight and in a straight line. He probably clears his throat more than a few times, this a sure sign of a temper on the boil. Mother fidgets nonstop.

We could only surmise what happened to my grandmother that day. She couldn't recall where she'd been or what had happened. Instead of taking a taxi as was more her habit since turning eighty, she decided to walk, breathe in the brisk autumn air, kick a few red and yellow leaves down Madison Avenue for auld lang syne. Trouble was, she strayed, like a boat without its sail. Poor Grammy, she lost a sense of time, perspective and sadly, even a little reasoning. When she did finally show up, she was lucid enough to get quite frustrated with my parents for making such a fuss. And the more my father bawled her out and Mother wrung her hands, the more Grammy protested against their drama by accusing them of something like *You're robbing me of my independence! Is that how you want to treat me?* Gotta hand it to Grammy. She knew how to stick up for herself, even throw around some guilt.

To this day I can only guess at what Grammy was up to on that little detour of hers. For starters, she didn't ever walk. She flit like a hummingbird. In fact, she used to jaywalk across the numbered streets, dodging yellow cabs, knowing full well it was against the law, but such fun to do anyway. Fun until the day a cab did knock her to the street, breaking her collarbone. Thinking the cabbie might sue her, she announced her husband was a US Congressman. Never mind he'd been dead for twelve years and retired from the government for more than thirty-five! She hoped that would deter the guy from pursuing her legally. He, on the other hand, hearing *Congressman* hopped in his cab and fled as soon as he'd helped her to the curb.

Anyway, I can just see Grammy dawdling under shop awnings, her nose pressed to the window, both hands cupping her face against the glare. First, she ogles crates of fresh produce through the green grocer's window, then decides to go in and wander up and down the aisles. I've done this with her in the past. She finds this shop as entertaining as an amusement park. As always, she is oblivious to her calfskin pumps becoming floured in sawdust. And strolling down an aisle, where on one side the plums are so plump she can't resist fondling them and on the other side, where the apples are so waxy they look fake, she knocks on them with her knuckles. She nicks grapes and pops them in her mouth till her cheeks bulge like a squirrel's. Rows and rows of glossy purple eggplant, spiky artichoke, leafy cabbage and runner beans with stalks all in a tangle capture her attention; only briefly, though, as there is more and more to see around every corner. She's like a bee hovering here, hovering there, then suddenly buzzing off in a new direction. In my mind's eye, Grammy bends to inhale, as is her wont, the rich perfume of pink peonies, her favorites; returns the daffodils' smiles with her own and a quick nod. When she comes upon the irises standing chin up and chest out in their buckets of galvanized steel, she salutes them. But when a fat little fellow in a striped bib apron by the name of Luigi asks if he may help her, I bet she looks down at his bald head and bursts into a fit of giggles. *No, thank you. Why on earth do you ask?*

Undoubtedly, aromas of fresh bread, croissants and pastries lure her into a bakery a few doors down. She has a weakness for baked goods. So do I for that matter, and on me, unfortunately, it shows. She eats two bites of a brioche and is finished. I snarf it all at once and ask for another. We've lunched in their tea room on many an occasion since I bought my first car, a Chevy Nova and could drive down from Saratoga to visit her on weekends. I can imagine her happily standing in a long line that day, patiently waiting her turn to order. When the nice shop girl gets around to asking, *what'll you have?* Grammy probably orders three of just about everything: crusty baguettes; flakey almond butter croissants; *milles feuilles;* bite-size orange or strawberry-flavored truffles; pear tarts; or a flourless chocolate torte. Sadly, Grammy has come out without a purse, as I later found out. So after the shopkeeper has carefully placed everything in pastry boxes lined with tissue and cinched them with the shop's signature lilac string ribbon, hands them to my grandmother only to discover there'll be no payment, she's pretty upset. I can easily see the girl escorting Grammy to the door by her elbow and nudging, maybe even pushing her out onto the sidewalk. Sans the goodies, of course.

Poor Grammy. Suddenly standing in a pool of lamplight - it's five fifteen now and growing dark- the shadows are long and intimidating. A sea of bodies, none of whom look approachable in their typically black New York City garb and their eyes barricaded behind dark glasses, rush past her. She has been tossed out of two shops and a man with a dolly has just shouted *Yo, watch it, lady!* A boisterous October wind is now barreling through the cement canyons of Manhattan and rush hour is in full swing. Suddenly, she is very alone and scared. The crisp autumnal air, no longer so pleasant, stings her cheeks and wheedles its way through the seams of her camel hair coat. I can see her gripping the edges of her collar together with one ungloved hand, the other arm hugging her middle. She must look quite forlorn when an elderly passerby asks if he can help.

"Are you lost?"

Assuming Grammy is confused, most likely suffering from early onset dementia, she probably replies in her best Emily Post: *By chance would you be so kind as to spare me ten cents? I can repay you tomorrow.*

Grammy finds a phone booth on the street corner of Lexington and E 65th (just two blocks east of my parents' flat) and dials their phone number, her memory perfectly in tact on the first try. Good thing, too, as she only has a dime.

Daddy lunges for the phone. "Mumsie, is that you?"

"Yes, dear. How did you know?"

"Jackie and I have been up and down 5th, Park and Lex; across and back every one of the sixties looking for you. Stay put and we'll come get you. Where are you?" Daddy demands.

Grammy, speaking through a handkerchief held over the telephone's mouthpiece to avoid the germs of a grubby public telephone, apparently says, "Luke, I'm lost."

Then click, she hangs up.

According to Mother, when Grammy finally showed up she flung herself on the sofa and sobbed uncontrollably. I knew Grammy to be pretty brave, so thought this doubtful, but were I to have challenged Mother on her details, she would have looked at me over the rim of her spectacles and silenced me. More likely, Grammy arrived with a cheerful *hello* as she came through the door, oblivious to the drama caused. Yes, her face was streaked with mascara, but caused by weather, not tears. I have no doubt raindrops clung to her blue-tinted hair and that she looked pretty bedraggled, but not devastated. And instead of sobbing, she might have asked *is it the cocktail hour yet?* Had I been there when all this happened I would have made her a *whiskey sour/no fruit* and made her a bowl of chicken noodle soup; certainly not scolded her for over thirty minutes. Didn't anyone realize she was suffering from dementia or early onset Alzheimer's? That getting lost is one of the key signs? I was saddened when I heard this story about Grammy and angry at my parents for making it all about their worry and not her obvious condition.

Here, I must cut my parents some slack, though. Both grew up under difficult circumstances and learned early to climb their way out of poverty and up an unforgiving social ladder. To them, appearances meant everything so they maintained a level of personal perfection which was impeccable and distinguished. Their view of life or others was derived from their own reflection in a mirror. How events occurred or the people around them behaved was taken über personally. Theirs was an inward outlook, though, not an outward one. There's no sense faulting them, I realize, and let it go. They simply cannot help it. A lifetime habit of vanity is a hard habit to break. It is what it is.

"I'm pretty sure I'm missing something
important, yet I'm not
exactly sure what. I feel so detached
all the time. Could it be
I've lost someone? Mama, perhaps? I really want to
belong but I don't see anyone to whom I want to belong.
No one really wants me to belong to them either. At least
that's what it feels like. I'm like a thing or maybe it's
more like a label. A cousin once told me I'm not a
REAL granddaughter.
Ouch!"

IT'S JUST A SILLY DREAM

Ever since receiving that letter from The Cradle Society, I've had a recurring dream, which in the morning renders me either confused and irritable or weirdly comforted by some crazy hope of one day meeting my birth mother. Almost always without fail, the dream goes something like this:

She is born of my past, rich with the scent of lavender and the music of alpine birdsong. She comes from a kingdom of kinnikinnick meadows and Indian paintbrush. Where one can touch the sky and drink from mountain streams, she whispers my name over and over again. Where she comes from, time is infinite. It echoes her patience while I remain deaf, blind and dumb.

Carved from a burl of fruitwood, her high forehead, prominent cheekbones and square jawline reveal strength. Lustrous eyes, shaped like those of a cat, are a profound green, the pupils rimmed in black ink. I drown in those lagoons when I struggle to know her mind. Long lashes demurely caress her cheeks. Hers is a generous mouth, full lips pursed in a pout. What is she thinking? Were she to have had a voice to perhaps tell me, it would be husky. My lullaby.

Her body is stuffed with lichen, pine needles and mulched leaves. She feels spongy, richly redolent of the woods, sprigs of lavender in particular. Her hair is made up of tresses of many colored ribbons cascading over shoulders down her back. Fantastic hues of scarlet, orange, lilac, yellow, aubergine, indigo, navy and royal blue, kelly and lime green, turquoise and pimento are interwoven with strings of periwinkle. Tucked among these tangled bands of decoration are an artist's paintbrushes and scraps of birch to serve as paper. Since her head is wooden and face is painted, her countenance may seem vacant, even melancholy. Yet there is liveliness whenever my imagination gives her flight. In the unfathomable depths of those eyes or the exuberance that is her mane of hair, I see a girl of vibrant spirit. It's just that in 1952 her heart has stopped beating at two sixteen.

I can see her heart. It is a delicate pendant watch, finished in gilt, Roman numerals, and blued steel hands. The circular gold case with blue enamel is back-bordered in tiny sapphires, in the middle of which is inscribed a date - 1952. From that long delicate chain around her neck, her heart also marks the time at two sixteen. Sadly, there is never any tick-tock, tick-tock, even if I do hold her up close to my ear.

I've named her Sylvia. Her bare feet are alabaster-white and dainty, the bones at the end of each willowy limb as fragile as glass. Whenever plumes of icy spray begin to swirl in dawn's indigo hour her feet begin to twitch. Soon she's skipping across an inky pool, toes barely grazing the surface. It's as if she were blown about by mercurial zephyrs into a purgatory of being neither here nor there. Feet splash like a child's until the sun slides down the sky's canvas and sinks below the horizon.

Hands chaste-white and as soft as butter are like new. The lines crisscrossing her palms in a dense weave look like lace doilies. In one hand she carries a small mirror, which she consults frequently. In it is reflected the truth she prefers seeing rather than the real one. It's where she imagines the rest of her life not being shaped by her past. Denied a voice, Sylvia's hands express her feelings. They articulate joy and anger. Open-handed, they demand explanations. Greedily, her hands might summon and just as rashly dismiss me. Fists seem to threaten ghosts, but who are they? She conveys such sorrow with her gesticulations, but I fail to understand exactly what. Slapping herself with a stinging fury she frightens me. Sylvia cries soundless sobs into those hands. But once her tapered fingers are soaked by tears, her hands capitulate.

Sylvia's shift is made of buttercups and fairy trumpets mixed with lacy maidenhair. Falling from her shoulders and flowing in soft folds, somehow it is always in bloom. She is my woodland sylph, and from a place I've always wanted to be; from where I think I may have come once upon a time. Whenever she becomes animated I sense she wants me to notice something. Is there something inside that small leather purse she wants me to discover? I've never really paid attention but dangling from a cord of ivy cinched at her waist, I bet I'd find more than just dried berries and mushrooms in this pouch. Could it be a dog-eared document and an empty envelope with today's correct postage?

I think Sylvia might be my could-have-been-mama. The mama who carried me in her womb; the one who in 1952 gave birth to me at two sixteen on a snowy morning. The mama I might have known had we not been separated. I might have lived with her in a log cabin shaded by quaking aspen and giant spruce standing guard. She's my birth mother, who courageously gave me a family when she could not; who selflessly made sure I received sound care, an education and opportunities beyond her woodland realm. She's been waiting for me to peek into that pouch in order to find her. How could I have been so blind?

I place her in a moonbeam under a velvet vault of stars. Somehow, I instinctively know my origins, so I create a vision of her as ethereal as any mirage, yet as real as the truth I don't actually know. There she is, with her purse always in full view. Whenever I conjure her up, fog snakes through the woods curling toward her ankles until it lifts her up to be freed from shackles of shame and secrecy. These are the restraints of regret I imagine she has experienced after relinquishing me. I will her to dance and search for a better present and happier future. I will her to sprint across my mind's eye so I can see her cheerful, not remorseful. I craft her into a frenetic sylvan dancer so I won't have to look the truth staring me in the face. The truth is what I want. I wish for us to be reunited. I am so afraid. Her leaving me again is unthinkable.

I am so sorry, Sylvia, it has taken me this long to peek inside your pouch. After all these years, I know it's where my original birth certificate has been kept. You tried to tell me, but I didn't or wouldn't hear. Tick tock, tick tock, tick tock. It reveals your current whereabouts, too! Tick tock tick, tick, tick, tick tock. Sylvia, is that your heart I hear? What's this empty envelope? Does it require a letter to be written and mailed? TICK, TICK, TOCK! One from me to you asking if I might come home? As the hands of the watch begin to move around the face of Sylvia's heart, the ticking grows louder and louder.

And then, it is everything I imagined. Just above the timberline her cabin really does sit nestled against an outcropping of granite. And there's the pond where rays of sun dance across sky-blue water. Islands of kinnikinnick growing in tall grass are like stepping stones leading to her cottage. Sylvia is waving to me from beneath a stand of aspen and my breath catches. I break into a run. Now her arms are swinging wide open to receive me, and finally, finally, we are touching each other for the first time. Minutes tick by as we wordlessly search for ourselves in each other's eyes. The scent of lavender floods my senses. Once inside the cabin, we sit on a worn sofa in front of the fireplace. We stare into the warmth of the fire she's laid, holding hands and listening to the flames sizzle before they race up the chimney. She presses a golden fob watch into the palm of my hand and gently closes my fingers around it. "This is for you, Honey" she whispers. I am silent, for right now no questions are necessary. We are mother and daughter together. Together at last.

LOST AGAIN

"Grammy, you should be asleep." I tiptoe into the bedroom, expecting to find my grandmother asleep, but she is wide awake staring at the ceiling.

With starched sheets tucked just beneath her chin, Grammy looks very small, her blue curls splashed against a starched linen pillow case. She is not a happy camper. I notice the baby monitor parked atop her chest of drawers and look away quickly. No sense drawing her attention to it, but she has already seen me avert my gaze. Not only is this contraption an ugly anomaly among her collection of pretty blue and white Copenhagen figurines, but it is also to her way of thinking a total insult. Despite her fragile, five foot two stature and one hundred and five pounds Grammy is no baby. Gramps was always so proud of her for never needing any coddling. *No sissy she,* he marveled as she picked up snakes with a letter opener whenever they slithered under the puzzle table.

Grammy pats the bed inviting me to sit. And when I do, her soft, wrinkles begin to scrunch into a more youthful mien. There is mischief afoot, I'm sure of it. I'm reminded of Gramps's clucks and wagging forefinger from across the dining table whenever she was about to tell an off-color joke. How I love this lady!

"How could I be asleep what with that racket downstairs? You're drinking cocktails and celebrating while all I've got is this pathetic bouillon."

I want to deny it, but she raises a hand to silence me. "Let me finish, dear. Who's the one who was lost, may I ask? Do I need to remind you that it was I out in the rain all night? I who fought off coyotes? Do you honestly think it fair I not be allowed a cocktail?"

Grammy has a point, but doctor's orders are for her to lay low until tomorrow or she can expect a return to Carbon County Hospital. She's lucky they agreed to release her at all, given she was in shock after the search team found her. According to the medics, Grammy suffered from exposure and was severely dehydrated; some even said she was lucky to still be alive. Not too many eighty-nine year-olds could have withstood an overnight in the foothills of the Snowy Range.

It was Friday morning when Grammy left the house at nine fifteen for her daily constitutional. By eleven she had not returned. At noon, my father and a posse of cousins saddled up their horses and headed out to all points on the compass. Daddy rode Lucky west, through the Saw Mill Yard and down to Charlotte's Web. He forded Echo River by Chloe's Bridge and cantered through a huge grove of poplars, their quaking leaves afire in gold. Out at Tepee Hill, he scoured the perimeter of the outcropping. Nothing. Daddy rode the entire fence line running north and south from the outer reaches of the Snowy Range all the way up Echo Mountain. Twice. More than a few times he hesitated to look over the barbed wire into Medicine Bow National Forest; nothing but dense woods with too much undergrowth. Others circled Greta Lake and went around Indian Rock doing a figure-eight of Dry Pond and Bear Paw. Nothing. By two in the afternoon two tracking dog teams, commandeered by Aunt Ann, arrived. Bloodhounds, famed for their ability to discern human scent even over great distances or days later, reported for duty. One deep whiff of Grammy's undergarments purloined from her hamper, and the dogs were off to Poison Arrow, up Jacob's Ladder and down again, around Echo Lake, over to Hiawatha and Hart Lodge Dock. A dead end. When a few of my cousins heard the scent had come to an abrupt stop at the dock, they jumped into canoes and began trolling the lake. Our General Manager, Pete Brewster, hit every roadside tavern within a twenty-mile radius and I can just hear him yelling at the men sitting on barstools, *get off your asses, boys, Mrs. Hart is missing!* Every one of those guys climbed into the back of Pete's pickup and went to the ranch to join the search. Volunteers either went east through the Old School Yard, over to Moon

Creek and out to the state park or schlepped up the mountain and over to Snake Cliff. The rest of my family, essentially women folk, prepared food for the over sixty guys and gals who made up the search party. Peanut butter and jelly sandwiches, tuna fish, ham and cheese, chips, bottled water, lemonade or hot coffee. Some great soul even baked ten dozen chocolate chip cookies. As the sun was setting over Medicine Bow National Forest, many began to pray.

Twilight was settling across the ranch like a shroud. I can only imagine Grammy feeling as though she'd been swallowed up by the gloom. And when night plunged her into darkness and Echo Mountain was no more than an inky blue outline flattening against the horizon, she must have been so scared. She probably staggered in circles around and around in a dew-soaked forest, bumping into trees, stumbling over stumps or rocks hiding under ferns. I can see the vapor of her labored breath lifting into the blackness. I can hear her whimper. There was a thick fog that night. The kind which creeps across the forest floor to encircle legs, making first the feet disappear, then one's body. I imagine Grammy found a hollowed out spot at the base of a hemlock into which she hunkered down for the night. That was about the time a cold drizzle began. Even though her dog, Missy, stayed very close, undoubtedly the chill of the night made its way through the layers of Grammy's cotton shirt, blue jeans and tartan jacket. No doubt, she became numb to the bone.

As a silver moon, hiding behind a scrim of cloud made its slow march across the sky, she sat with the stillness of a mouse blinking in the dark while the shriek of a mountain lion circled around her. At some point in the night, a pack of coyotes yowling and chasing prey came too close. Missy kept a faithful watch, making soft woofs yet trembling like a leaf. ELR's barn chimes balefully rang all night in the hopes of guiding Grammy home, and though she could hear them very faintly, she couldn't trust her judgment as to their point of origin. Besides, she knew that at this point it was best to stay put. She was exhausted and too stiff to move any more.

At ten thirty that night, the Sheriff called off the search and recommended getting some sleep before resuming the search at daybreak. A sheriff's helicopter from Laramie would join the search in the morning.

"Too many folks on foot and horseback have confused the dogs," he explained. Before settling into his patrol Jeep, he told my Aunt in a hushed voice, "I think there may be a kidnapping involved. I'm widening the APB." Wow, an all points bulletin!

In the pale pink of early morning, a chopper landed on the golf course. Daddy told the pilot, "I'm convinced Mrs. Hart has drifted into the Medicine Bow National Forest. Go there first."

Sure enough, twenty minutes after heading east, the crew spotted Grammy under an old hemlock. Her pale blue hair caught the light in an otherwise mottled forest green and brown landscape! They landed in the nearest clearing.

"Good morning, gentlemen," Grammy said, standing up and wobbling terribly. "What took you so long?" And just like that, her legs gave out and she folded like a tent.

Back at the barn, headquarters for the search effort, word arrived over the radio that Grammy was found. Whoops of joy erupted like firecrackers on the fourth of July; people began laughing and crying, hugging and dancing, praising God for His mercy. But when Grammy was lifted off the chopper, everyone was silenced by their shock. Her complexion so sallow, her stare vacant, and her papery skin so scratched and profoundly bruised, she was barely recognizable.

As Grammy was loaded into the ambulance, Aunt Ann couldn't resist a bossy scold. "I told you to stay on the blacktop, Mumsie, not veer off behind Crane's Hideaway. What were you thinking?"

Grammy apparently studied her daughter for a second and replied, "I can only regret what I don't do in life, dear."

On the way to the hospital, Grammy stayed awake or alert long enough to pick off every tick and chigger clinging to her body or embedded in her clothing. She was released after lunch and brought back to Echo Lodge by the Sheriff.

As for me while all this was happening, I had just walked in the door back home in Connecticut when I got the call about Grammy's disappearance. So distraught was I, I didn't even think as I turned around, jumped in my car and drove straight back to Westchester County Airport. I was too late to join the search as it had been suspended for the night, but

I was there when she was found the next morning. And was I ever grateful to see Grammy safe and alive. I shed pails of tears that day.

"You were very brave, Grammy," I say. "Chapeau! That means hat's off, by the way"

"I know what it means, dear." When I start to leave Grammy's room, she asks me to bring her her purse.

"Here!" she says, thrusting a crisp one hundred dollar bill at me.

"What's this for?"

"Bring me a whiskey sour. No fruit."

"Grammy, I ..."

"Just an itty-bitty, teensy-weensy little wee one, pretty please?"

How adorable she looks. Enough to melt anyone's resolve. I remember thinking even Gramps, with all his discipline, would have capitulated. My eyes slide over to the monitor and back and just then, the monitor crackles and a few *ahem*'s and *uh uh*'s can be heard. Grammy's fate is regrettably sealed.

"Sorry, Grammy fifteen witnesses just heard you bribe your own granddaughter for alcohol. They'll tackle me to the floor if I go anywhere near that liquor cabinet. Plus, Doc is still here, so he heard you, too."

Grammy produces the biggest pout I've ever seen on a grown-up and crosses her arms over her flat chest.

"You're out of luck, Grams."

"Would you have brought me that drink if there were no hard-hearted heathens downstairs threatening personal injury to you?" she asks, raising her voice and leaning out of bed toward the monitor.

"Of course," I whisper, caressing the back of her hand. Her age spots and knobby knuckles are so dear and familiar to me, I bend to kiss them. "I'll check in on you in a little while. Maybe I can sneak you a piece of chocolate."

I almost lost Grammy that weekend. I'll never forget how afraid I was at the prospect of losing my favorite grown-up. She was the one who most of all, seemed to accept me as I was, often saying that because we were both Aquarians, she understood what made me tick. Whenever I was in trouble as a little girl or later when I was a teenager and at odds with my mother, she'd just say that in the grand scheme of things Aquarians *know what's what and can always adjust.* Then she suggested we play a few hands of her favorite card game, Spite and Malice, and all would be right with the world again.

I realize now that Grammy was definitely suffering from dementia. Since her mood was always so congenial, we never noticed that her ability to think and remember was decreasing as rapidly as it was. She didn't show the other signs of dementia like irritability, depression, apathy or delusions such as suspecting people of stealing from her. Getting so horribly lost not just once, but twice was the wake-up call, though. After the incident at the ranch, we all went into overdrive to keep her safe and most importantly, loved extra hard.

GOODBYE

It's springtime, Grammy's favorite season, and she lies dying. In a room with walls white as alabaster and in a bed of bleached linens tucked tightly across her fragile frame, she is ready. Ready to join, her husband, Jackson, her son, Oliver, and all five babies she lost to either miscarriage or stillbirth.

The only colors keeping Grammy company are the purple hyacinths, daffodils, and pink tulips, bursting from the window boxes outside her room. For four days and four nights, I sit by her side, holding her hand, stroking her hair, which is no longer pale blue but an angelic halo of snow-white. It's as soft as down feathers. By day, sunbeams fall through the window and warm her face, which is turned to embrace its kindness. By night, a crescent moon hangs aloft in an ebony sky. There are no stars. And like so, we wait. Together. One last time.

As we drift in a cloud of shared silence, random memories begin to swirl in my mind's eye like a kaleidoscope. The box of Whitman's chocolate Grammy always proffered after lunch - *just one* she'd caution; or opening the window so her two Bouviers, Bimbo and Buffie, could hop inside and slobber their canine greetings; her taking a rare dip in Echo Lake, wearing a swimsuit dating back to the thirties, a pair of John Lennon shades I'd given her one Christmas and an old straw hat; and sipping her whiskey sours (*no fruit, please*); or the time she displayed every page of *Playboy* to me, including the magnificent centerfold, then making me accompany her twenty blocks down Madison Avenue to throw it away. *Heaven forbid the maids see it in my waste basket. Whatever would they think?*

These and so many more are memories filled with aromas and sounds so dear I'll take them to my grave: Grammy's favorite, the Bench Trail's loamy forest floor; her Lancôme eau de toilette, dabbed at each wrist and in the hollow of her neck; the maze of orange and yellow tiger lilies she planted down at the water's edge to memorialize the babies she'd lost. I will forever hear the music of her joy: the endearing little high-pitched *oohs* and *aahs* whenever she shared gossip; the evil *tee hee* whenever she one-upped anyone at Spite & Malice. The color turquoise will ever be synonymous with Grammy as will the musicals Camelot and My Fair Lady. Finally, I shall always marvel at her fearlessness astride Black Magic, her poise amongst a crowd of strangers, her kindness to all, and most especially, her unconditional acceptance of me.

As I sit at her bedside, her face still turned toward the window, I resolve to try and love as she has loved; to forgive as she has learned to do. It comes to me that this is the only way to be truly free. I know that in a perfect world forgiveness ought not to be given until it is sought, but not everyone knows how to ask for it. It's just too hard. If one can forgive another's transgressions, one is no longer prisoner of that hurt. I lay my head by Grammy's shoulder, grateful for this epiphany she has sent my way and stretch an arm lightly across her body. I listen for her breath, feel the faint rise and fall of her chest, and long to feel her breath on my skin, but her face is averted. Tears begin to slide down my cheeks. I feel so alone. And yes, I'm afraid. Who will love me and let me love her back like Grammy? There will be no other I decide.

On the fourth afternoon, it occurs to me how much she delights in a good secret. She can never keep them, mind you, and is usually giddy whenever sharing one.

"Grammy," I whisper, "I've got a big secret for you." And with that, Grammy slowly rolls her head across the pillow to face me.

"I'm pretty sure Ty is going to pop the question, you know, ask me to marry him."

She opens her eyes for the first time in four days and we look at each other for a very long time. Then the slightest smile breaks across her pallid complexion. And as I remember it today, it was a look no one has ever given me and one I will forever treasure the rest of my life. With that smile came her very last words:

"He's a lucky man, Lexie, a very lucky man."

She died that night, never uttering another word. When I awoke the next morning, she looked as though she'd been carved in marble. Like a porcelain doll, she was fragile but beautiful; serene and at peace. Her dark lashes actually fluttered against her cheeks and I almost believed she was still alive, but her skin was cold and her lips slack with no more breath. I caressed Grammy's velvety brow one more time before the orderlies carried her body away. I remember how I did not move from where I stood at the window. I had opened it the night before in case her soul was ready to reach for heaven. I guess it was.

The emptiness I felt made my whole body ache, and strangely, my tears were slow in coming, so stunned was I by the loss of her. But indeed the tears came; buckets and buckets of them. They still do at the most unexpected moments.

"What's holding me back from searching for Mama? Is it fear of rejection? What if I don't meet Mama's expectations? Maybe I'm a secret she'd rather keep buried. Honestly? I can't blame her, especially since she was an unwed mother. Besides what right do I have for barging into her life unannounced? She'd probably prefer not to be found. On the other hand what if she's hoping I do find her?"

NOW YOU SEE IT NOW YOU DON'T

What made me decide to go digging for any adoption information one night, I really have no idea. Was it that bizarre dream about Sylvia, my doll with her pendant-watch and satchel, niggling away at me over and over again? Or was it something else? All the people who had been essential to my equilibrium were gone. Gramps with his wisdom. Grammy with her abiding faith in love's beneficence. Even Aunt Ann who had suffered a stroke and refused therapy, was instead actively willing herself to die by barricading herself in her room. Daddy was gone, too. That left Mother, with whom I shared less and less affinity, not knowing if it were my fault or hers. Blame was pointless, though. Did I search because all these people left a vacuum in their wake which rendered me needy? Or was it that the memory of these people and their influence on my life pointed me to a path embracing both trust and courage?

I was finally ready to discover more than what the adoption agency gave me, like Mama's name for starters. There's no question that at the time The Cradle's information had been completely satisfying. It was good to know my English/German heritage. It explained my easy fluency with the German language, which I'd always found so curious. It explained my high spatial IQ thanks to my birth father's architectural bent and his before him. Most of all, it explained my size, which had so aggrieved me what with Mother being such a petite five foot five, one hundred and ten pounds. All this was hugely comforting back in the early eighties. Now in the late nineties, it didn't seem enough. So, I swallowed my fear and set sail for the unknown. Looking back on it now, you'd have thought I was Columbus heading for the edge of a flat earth, I was that afraid of what I might find. Besides, sneaking about and violating Mother's trust was not my wont.

Stale air rushes at me when I unlock the storage room. It's pitch dark and as I take a few tentative steps inside, not only is it as hot as a furnace, but the pungent stench of mold immediately slaps me in the face. I gag. In the pitch-black darkness, it feels as though the past is trying to wrap me too tightly in its humid embrace, making me want to bolt. It takes a Herculean effort to shrug it off, but when I finally find the light switch by patting the wall up and down and I flip it on, there they are. Standing like the time-encrusted monuments at Stonehenge are three metal file cabinets which have been hidden from view practically all my life A single lightbulb hangs overhead, casting tall shadows up the sweaty cinder block walls.

Tentatively, I open the first drawer. What dust isn't clinging to the mildew, billows around me. The contents are flocked with white splotches too, making it difficult to read the labels. I remember how at that moment I thought about how exhilarated Howard Carter must have been when he found King Tut's tomb and that this was absurdly comparable. After combing through four drawers I finally find a file labeled *Alex*. Looking over my shoulder at the door which I've left ajar, I make sure Mother isn't lurking around the door jamb. Then I gingerly lift the folder from its brackets, blow the dust from its cover and hug it to my chest. Wow, there really are documents about me! Why did I never think or dare to look before now? I look down at the somewhat thick file in my arms, incredulous. Then my stomach lurches. With a new-found identity am I about to meet myself as a missing ghost?

Wanting to escape the dank and dark as quickly as possible, I seek comfort out on the terrace, above ground and away from the fungal fumes. I want to be gone from this crypt where Mother and Daddy chose to entomb my records. Thankfully, I see a dome of stars hanging low through a veil of ocean mist. I am calmed by its heavenly expansiveness. The moon, a mere pinprick in the gauziness, shines dimly but reassuringly constant. Even the Atlantic's waves, gently lapping at the shoreline, are soothing. I begin to read.

Among all the correspondence between The Cradle and my father is my birth certificate. Its black background with a blurry white print is difficult to read. But my mama's name, age and place of domicile at the time of my birth are recorded. The box for my father's name is left blank. Oddly, that doesn't bother me. Probably because I don't care much for the man who abandoned my mother. I stroke the letters of her name as if this might bring me closer to her.

All that night I sat out on the balcony, intermittently grieving for myself, having lost a mother I'd never known and more than likely never would, and pitying her just as much. Bending over my lap and hugging my knees, I remember rocking back and forth to the point of almost hypnotizing myself. I'd spent a lifetime shellacking my mind in layers of rationalizations of why not to look for Mama, but now, with a name, Anna Jane MacKenzie, she was instantly very real. She came alive on that birth certificate, and I scolded myself for needing a piece of paper to make her all that much more physical. She lost a child, me, and must wonder where I am; if I'm healthy and happy. I should have looked sooner so as to allay her worry.

I wondered if she were still living. She would be sixty-eight, so probably, yes. And as soon as I did the arithmetic in my addled brain, it occurred to me that the name *Anna Jane Mackenzie* could be my Aunt Ann's alias. Yikes! More math proved there could be a bit of fudging about Aunt Ann's birth year to throw off suspicion, but it was all too plausible. Oh my God! Aunt Ann was there for so many of my milestones as if she were gifted these opportunities by Mother and Daddy in exchange for her having given them her illegitimate child to round out a perfect little family. Her affection and interest in me had always been so large, so genuine. If I were Aunt Ann's biological daughter, might that also explain Grammy's and Gramps's extraordinary, unconditional love for me, their daughter's daughter?

All night I sat motionless as the layers of the past began to dissolve. They exposed more and more mystery, possibly even subterfuge. How could Aunt Ann or Mother have maintained, even survived this lie? No wonder they were so jealous of each other, continually competing with each other, putting me in the middle as if I were obliged to choose between them? I spent years begging them to leave me out of their squabbles, but now there seemed to be a reason for them. I didn't like where this line of thought was going. Too many voices were suddenly clamoring in my head. I could scarcely hear my own, and if my many years of reading self-help books had taught me anything, my voice needed to be the most important.

All of a sudden, my mind felt as if it might explode and I shot out of my seat. Both hope and fear jangled in my chest like the wind rattling the mangroves, the waves now whooshing noisily as the tide began to rise. I tiptoed back to Mother's guest room and climbed into bed beside my husband, Tyler. Sensing my return, he probably mumbled something akin to *you okay?* his voice intimate in the dark. I remember he took my hand in his and held it under the covers. It was all I needed to feel safe.

Nonetheless, I lie awake until the slanting rays of sun stretching across the horizon stream across our bed. By the time I'm dressed, I have already concluded that Aunt Ann being my birth mother is utter nonsense and simply a product of too much imagination. I also decide, though I am completely drained and in no position to be making any declarative choices, that a person, once abandoned probably bears that loss forever. Accept it, I tell myself. After all, look at Mother. She has been deprived of so much as a child and young woman she now has an unquenchable thirst for love and attention that is insatiable. It makes her clingy; suffocatingly so. She seems to always be in pain. I don't want to be like that. Losses are a part of life, but we soldier on. I remember thinking there are people all around me, even if they are only ghosts, and I am so grateful.

And so, before Mother rose for breakfast that next morning, I returned all the documents back to that dark and dank storage room, resolutely walking away from my past. It felt like the right thing to do preserving what equanimity Mother and I still shared. After all, I was an obedient child; loyal, filial, conforming. And in so doing, I was probably doing Anna Jane Mackenzie a favor by keeping her secret. She didn't need me interrupting her life, disturbing her husband's or children's lives if they existed. I had her name now, and that was good enough.

Two days later, when I went back to take, and this time, keep my birth certificate, having had a sudden change of heart, it was gone. Everything else in the folder was still there, but no birth certificate. Mother must have suspected something - her intuition always uncanny - or she'd actually seen me in the storage room that night after all. Over the next eighteen years with every subsequent visit down to Florida, my birth certificate has never been returned to the sleeve entitled *Alex*. Am I angry? Sort of, though disappointed is more the sentiment. Hiding my birthright from me is a reflection on her.

Like the ocean tide rolling in and out, my ambivalence about searching for Mama continued to wax and wane. I tried to be content with the comforts I already had, but after my mission to find Mama was actually stolen from me by the sequestering of my birth certificate it was hard to tamp down a fomenting rebellion. As a result, this action of hers waged war with the best of my intentions.

DOUBLE BAREBACK

The Northern lights are once again on display and I am reminded of you, dear Aunt Ann. How can the years have passed so quickly? You were such an eccentric what with your *I insist on winter air being transfused into my tires each and every November then in the summer putting summer air back in,* or *shipping used paper clips back and forth between my homes makes perfect 'cents'.* So many memories flash in a smudge of color: our picnics, golf tournaments, and moonlight rides; skinny dipping, canoe-tipping, campfires and sing-alongs. Most special is the night we fetched Freedom from the herd in the Old School Yard and rode him double-bareback to your cabin.

Astride Freedom, I in front you behind, we set out on the Camp B Road, the aroma of rich dark earth filling our noses as dew began to descend with nightfall. I remember crickets chirring so loudly we couldn't hear our own conversation. When we approached they went silent only to resume again as soon as we clip-clopped past. At Echo River, Freedom drank before we forded the shallows under Chloe's Bridge. The water curled around slimy caramel-colored boulders. Blue flag irises stood as sentries by the water's edge and wild arrowheads peeked from underneath fronds of lacy maidenhair. It was here you pontificated on *how unfulfilling the appeal of popularity can be* and I wondered if you were alluding to Mother's constant need for attention. You were deliberately obtuse, I think, for fear of angering me. After all, I was prone to defending Mother in those days, no matter what she did. Now, when I reflect upon this conversation some forty years later, I know you wanted me to see the truth, but only when I was ready. It's taken me years, but I do see it now. *The faster you run away, the bigger the problems become* - another reference to Mother I think, as she had run from the tragedies borne in her youth and was paying the price as an adult and my parent. Or maybe a reference to me, as I was clearly not willing at age twenty to look at my life objectively. I was still too needy as an adopted child, so you could say I was running away by remaining entrenched. Back then belonging mattered far more than analyzing the to what or to whom I was trying so hard to attach myself.

I remember inhaling the scent of oyster mushrooms clinging to rotted oak, and all at once wanting to cry but withholding my tears as we scrambled up the hillside. I so sensed your profound love and devotion to me but didn't know what to do with it for fear of being a traitor to Mother.

Blue spokes of moonlight stretch across the lake as I contemplate this chapter of my past. Ribbons of purple, pink and orange streak across a blanket of stars, and I'm reminded of your awe, Aunt Ann, whenever you gazed upon such a sight as this one. *The Northern Lights are God's way of showing us the way, right, kiddo?* are words still echoing in my ears to this day.

She borrowed this phrase from her father, my grandfather. Gramps was her rock, as he was mine. Strange that both of us felt so strengthened by his influence while most others, including Mother, were intimidated by him. Could the common denominator be that we were both adopted and craved firm boundaries so we felt as though we belonged? I think we must have gravitated toward his strength of character, too, for the same reason. The confidence and integrity oozing from his pores signaled he was a safe and predictable place. Even if the rules were tough, we knew where we fit. And fitting in is key to an adopted person.

Aunt Ann and I shared more than I knew while she was alive. She lost her father, figuratively speaking after Oliver, her brother died. Gramps was never present for her after that, his grief so profound. I played second fiddle to Mother's grief, too, she having lost Oliver so shortly after they were married and it scarring her for life. I wonder if Aunt Ann, being of a generation that didn't typically permit too much introspection, was aware of her own hurt? Or did she deliberately drown herself in projects so as not to be in touch with it? Did she know about the primal wound and give herself permission to mourn the loss of her birth mother? I'd give anything to be able to talk to her about that today.

There was a brief time when I actually wondered if Aunt Ann might be my birth mom. She was present for so many milestones that I thought it was Mother's and Daddy's way of sharing me with her; all on the QT, of course. I concocted a scenario whereby she became accidentally pregnant with me, gave me to Mother and Daddy who were childless so that she could stay close all the while keeping her giving birth to me a secret. When Mother and Daddy were gone for an entire summer house-hunting in Los Angeles, I was in Aunt Ann's care at the ranch. She taught me how to swim, barrel race Quarter Horses and showcase a five-gaited horse. She tutored me in seventh grade New Math, took me clothes shopping for college, even drove me to Skidmore my first day freshman year. She proffered advice, initiated games and made me feel special. We bunked together when Grammy and Gramps treated the family to Christmases in Zermatt, Puerto Rico and Bermuda. On trips to France and Ireland, Aunt Ann and I always shared a room. After my aunt married for a second time late in life, she kept calling her new step-granddaughter by my name, a faux pas the girl understandably came to resent.

Aunt Ann kept me close. Perhaps, she did recognize her pain and wanted to be there for me should I verbalize mine. The trouble was, I didn't dare take her into my confidence for fear of Mother's jealousy. That is an opportunity I now regret as she was good to me and didn't deserve to be kept at an emotional arm's length.

I've included a poem I wrote about her love for Gramps:

IN GRAMPS' LIBRARY

You've come to the room
of all your Christmas eves
to recover a treasure from your youth.
A book read to you from
Gramps's ample lap year after year
in a library overflowing with tomes

only ladders can reach
if one is to read them all.

You've come to a room
where a spiral staircase climbs
like a corkscrew to a loft,
where you played jacks,
pick-up sticks and cards.
He played to win
and you to learn the hard way.

You've come to the room
where sweet scents of tobacco
still linger tickling your nose.
Do you remember how you
pretend-puffed on his pipes
so you could be just like him?

You've come to the room
where fires crackled and popped.
Flights of sparks pranced
up the flue to light a sky
of velvet-soft darkness
in welcome of Santa and his crew

In a room transformed
his desk set of silver filigree
is tarnished, but no smudge can erase
the shadow of your scrawl on the blotter.
You remember, don't you, Ann,
the day he taught you how to write in script?

Swallowed by the gloom
in the room of all your Christmas eves
everything is frozen now

just the way he left it.
Dust motes shift like tides
of desert sand. And it's dark,
and dank and dreary.

In the gloom of the room
the phone is off the hook
as if it were only an hour ago
he got the call your brother was gone.
It's flocked with dust and grime
no tears can ever wash away, but

You've come to the room you loved so much
to recover a treasure from your youth.
It's where he left it
open
face down
on page three
just as you were settling into his lap.
Here to blow away the cobwebs,
and keep it safe, you recite for me,
T'was The Night Before Christmas
when all through the house…

UNCONDITIONAL LOVE

There's no question my grandparents made a dramatic impression on me. Though not a very big man, Gramps was absolutely larger than life. And Grammy, for all her petite and feminine ways, was a giant of kindness. Together their sober demeanor, refined morality, sense of fairness and steady disposition made them people one could count on. The expectations of others and the boundaries they set for others were always known and understood. So, instead of feeling restricted by them, I actually felt secure in knowing where I belonged. Being with them at the ranch or on vacation were really the only times I felt as though I were connected.

Though I was never aware of it at the time, Gramps's politics and values influenced my choices. His ardent love of country, passion for our Constitution and deep belief in a man's personal liberty live on in me. Despite his wealth, he was neither boastful nor arrogant; this a truly lovely attribute of character and one I have wanted to emulate. He gave his time and energy to many civic endeavors - the New York City school system, the Brooklyn constituency, U.S. Navy, Maritime Commission and later the IMF (International Monetary Fund). Gramps never sought adulation or recognition. He was an upstanding citizen of the very best sort.

Grammy always pushed the proverbial envelope of do's and don't's with impish delight; for example, telling an off-color joke despite Gramps's warnings to refrain. Those were fun exchanges to watch. At opposite ends of the great mahogany table, my head swung from left to right, back and forth watching their game unfold like a tennis match. At first, when she began, he arched an eyebrow in warning. Then as she persevered, he wagged a finger, then a *tsk-tsk* from behind his teeth. When everyone else held their breaths waiting to see if the wrath of God might bellow from his lungs, but did not, gaiety ensued. Grammy graduated from a Carnegie Mellon public speaking course. She was obliged as a Congressman's wife to have that skill. Anyone who knew my grandmother, though, knew how challenging this was for her as she was painfully shy. She even baptized ships by breaking champagne bottles across their bows. It usually took several embarrassing attempts as she didn't have the physical strength, but that made the ceremonies that much more delightful.

Older cousins agree that when they were kids (before my time) they always loved visiting Grammy and Gramps's cabin above all others' in the 2nd Generation. My grandparents made time for each of them. Gramps took time out for a quick game of jacks or marbles; paused for a discussion about the flora and fauna sighted on the trail that morning; or congratulated a child for his catch in Echo River. He showed them how to gut a fish for the frying pan or freeze it in newspaper for the taxidermist. He led bird walks and pointed to the different species; played a vicious game of chess; or asked the kids to describe their favorite book or movie in ten words or less. Grammy encouraged effort at the puzzle table, offered treats from her extra-large box of Whitman's Chocolate. She played countless games of Go Fish, Spite and Malice, Gin Rummy with all of us. The two of them even sang duets under a canopy of stars around our annual Labor Day campfires. Their interest in the young was a commodity none of us took for granted. I always felt ten feet tall after time spent with them. Yes, Gramps was intimidating in his demand for respect, but he returned the gesture whenever it was deserved. He was not miserly with his praise. Grammy was never intimidating. She was a sweetheart and a cuddler.

Grammy and Gramps's love of family was unwavering. They gave of themselves to Mother and me. After the tragic loss of Oliver in the clouds over Mount McKinley, they took Mother in as their daughter, no longer thinking of her as a daughter-in-law. So, when Daddy came along and married Mother in 1948, my grandparents welcomed him as their son-in-law. Upon my adoption in 1952, there was no denying I was Grammy's and Gramps's granddaughter and every bit a member of their family. They accepted me as though I were not only their son's adopted child had he lived, but also as if I were of his own blood. In spite of such a tragic loss, the Harts' hearts were wide open to their newly configured family; one which was stitched together from the tears and tatters left by war and infertility. Joining their daughter, Ann, the Saunders family became part of the Hart family. Gramps protected us right up to the time of his death.

When I was a child until the year I went away to college, Grammy and Gramps made me feel like I was their kin. I suffered from periodic doubt on that score while growing up, but with them, I felt wanted, safe and secure. They were never judgmental. Like any child, hungry for approval, Gramps made it a fun project to earn it. I respected that then and still do to this day. His inner strength and personal resolve were my buttresses. I will always be grateful for his love and generosity; not just of his personal wealth, but of his person. Without his welcome into his world and all the kindnesses along the way, I would not be where I am today or the fully developed person I've become.

Grammy too was grounded in selflessness. She was not in the least bit self-absorbed. She truly had a kind and loving heart. Her demure nature interrupted by moments of mischief made a day sparkle. Her courage with bats, snakes, and spiders was admirable. Her comfort astride a horse standing fifteen hands with the ability to toss her into the bushes at a whinny was laudable. She was a splendid example to us all.

Echo Lake Ranch is where I spent most of my time with Grammy and Gramps. It was and still is, a remarkably special playground where we hunt and fish, horseback ride, golf or play tennis, picnic, water ski and relax far from the madding crowds of city life. It is financially supported and bound together by a myriad of trusts, stockholder agreements, and bylaws which before 1961 reflected antiquated notions regarding blood issue as it affects inheritance. These documents directly conflicted with my grandfather's personal estate plans, strangling his specific wishes within his own last will and testament. Gramps spent the last ten years of his life negotiating with his brother's heirs to make the necessary changes to these documents in order for his adopted daughter, who is my Aunt Ann, Mother and me to be included as legal heirs. Unfortunately, there were a few who needed coaxing to agree. These were stressful times for our family, sadly resulting in some permanent scars. I was fourteen by the time things were finally resolved legally. At the time I knew nothing of it. It wasn't until I was much older all the rumors whispered behind closed doors actually became facts. There were a few who didn't like having to share their toys, as the expression goes. They used adoption as an excuse to justify their avarice.

My experience at Echo Lake Ranch dramatically changed after Grammy's and Gramps', Aunt Ann's and Daddy's deaths. Whenever I do get back there, which isn't often anymore, a few shadows will inevitably blow across my path to remind me of an ugly prejudice; one I can do nothing about. So, I have withdrawn from this idyll I once cherished because the absence of the people who made this place such a Shangri La are gone. This was indeed a magical and enchanted oasis holding many happy recollections, but it's easier for me to preserve those memories by not being there. So, it's the summer sun's warmth, the summer night's sparkle, and the Northern Lights streaking in fluorescent kaleidoscope-brushstrokes across an August canvas I most happily recall. Therein reside the family members who keep me connected to the happiest yesterdays of my life.

"Is guilt holding me back like an anchor wrapped around my ankles weighing me down? How would Mother feel if she knew I was searching for Mama? Pretty devastated is my guess. Can I make her understand it is my birthright? Somehow, I doubt it. She has too jealous a personality."

AT A CROSSROADS

The last time Mother and I spoke intimately was 2002. We were on the terrace in Key Largo and just beyond us lay Card Sound. It was the perfect south Florida evening. I remember how a ribbon of frothy surf was tumbling lazily onto the beach over and over; a never ending drumbeat. Brushstrokes of palest salmon and mauve hung over the horizon, the sun having bid its farewell. Thankfully, nightfall was on its way when I knew speaking candidly behind a veil of darkness would be easier than under the glare of day. So I risked it, beginning with as much empathy as I could convey.

"Mom, the way I see it, the desire to be loved or love has been the cornerstone of your youth. Largely because for you, love was not to be had, not for any length of time, anyway. It was so cruelly snatched from you over and over again." Mother shifts her weight from one hip to the other, crosses her legs at the knees and folds her arms across her chest. Her foot jiggles up and down. When I look back on it now, I was clumsy in getting my thoughts out but wanted to start with bucket loads of sympathy. Maybe it was too much.

"First losing your mother, then your ability to have children and finally, the love of your life, Oliver, all before the age of twenty-five is a lot to bear. One questions God's intentions. One questions oneself. One wants to lay blame for all that hurt but doesn't know where to direct it. I get it, Mother, I really do."

"I doubt you do," Mother says arching an eyebrow. "And why do I think there's a big fat 'but' coming?" Grateful for the dark, I soldier on.

"You've carried this pain with you all your life. There's been no outrunning it. Wounds like the ones you've suffered don't ever completely heal. I'm truly sorry about that."

"Your point is what, dear?" She shifts her weight back again, this time sitting on her hands as if that might help her to use restraint. In fact, she looks like she wants to jump out of her seat, maybe even off the balcony.

"I would have thought that after fifty years of marriage to Daddy and adventures such as our living in Switzerland and London, your wounds would be reduced to a manageable size by now."

"Shouldn't I be the judge of that?" Mother looks at me over the rim of her spectacles.

"I just want you to be happy, Mom, not wallowing in the past, conjuring memories of loss when there's been so much good in your life. Do you realize that's practically eighty years? Four times as many years than your first unfortunate twenty."

"What you're saying is you're tired of hearing about my mother dying of cancer? How brutal it was to awaken from surgery to find not only one ovary but both of them removed? You don't want to imagine what it was like for me when Oliver's plane went down over that damn Mount McKinley?"

"Not true, Mother. I've grown up with your stories and listened closely every time. I've felt your heartache more than you know. Truly, I have. My life has always been centered around your tragedies. But it's a record of a vanished life, Mom, and you seem to be stuck there. I don't understand why you can't live in the present, maybe even look to the future." She glares at me, her whole body rigid. And then I blow it. "Darn it, Mother, grief has caused you to throw so much of your life away!"

"Well, aren't you the ungrateful one," she snaps, standing. "I've heard enough."

As she disappears into the house, I mutter "Why won't you embrace my love or the girls' or that of your greats?"

After she turned her back to me, I remained on the terrace for a long time. Thank goodness the quiet whoosh of the tide coming in was so soothing. It helped me to gain perspective. The scent of jasmine borne by a gentle breeze coming through the screens was sweet. That night, I actually made peace with Mother's choice to remain shut off from all the good which lay around her. She and I would just continue to live in our parallel worlds. Never would we reach a place where kinship might simply mean sitting on a swing together, rocking in silent companionship.

I wasn't so much tired of hearing about her tragic blows as much as I was tired of always being asked to feel sorry for her. It was as if I should live her life as though it were mine instead of living my own. It felt like masterful manipulation, if you ask me. Or was she unaware of what she was doing? The consequences of repeating her saga over and over and over affected me dramatically. If my focus were always on her pain, how could I zero in on my own? Focused on Mother's suffering meant I could make no demands about my adoption. Furthermore, she made reference to her trauma so often, I came to believe I must never add to it. Early on I was convinced that not just asking about my birth mother but actually searching for her would do Mother in. Hopefully, it was unintentional, but Mother knitting her scarf of pity early on in my life and adding another row every so often until it was so long it wrapped around my neck like a noose is what it felt like by the time I was in my late fifties.

Perhaps, Mother thought she rescued me, so, therefore, how could I ever be suffering? After all, there was no visible injury. What do babies know anyway? Right? The consensus of professionals was babies weren't conscious of what was happening to them. The psychiatric community of today, though, would refute that premise. Mother might not have detected any scars on my skin or in my eyes, but my psyche did tell a different story. Throughout my upbringing, there were questions, doubts, insecurities and fears. They grew in number commensurate with my birthdays. None that I chose to express, though, for fear of hurting Mother, and certainly none she ever chose to explore. It was better for her, I'm sure, not to ask.

My not asserting myself with Mother regarding my adoption has been my greatest weakness, my Achilles' heel. Protecting her from my emotional demands because they might hurt her was the way I showed my filial respect, my loyalty. It was also my way of striving for the kinship I so craved. I used to think she was blind to my outreach, but perhaps it was my fault so enslaved I was to bonding at any cost that she mistook my steadfastness for granted. I rocked the boat that night on the terrace;

took a chance I could appeal to her better judgment if I showed empathy. I sort of lost my temper, though, when I accused her of throwing her life away. That was total permission for her to exit the conversation.

I have only myself to blame for never saying to Mother *I lost a mama, too; at least you met yours, had her until you were twelve. I never even got as much as that.* To me, though, that would have been just about the rudest thing I could say. Not long ago she complained of having no photograph of her mother. I said I understood her dismay as neither did I. I think she was so caught up in her own hyperbole she missed my meaning. Maybe not. What if I'd ever asked the question *do you have any idea how guilty I feel about being chosen when I didn't choose to be?* And finally, *why does your hurt necessarily supersede mine?* How the years have slipped through the cracks of time. How the opportunities to truly connect are becoming fewer and farther between. Oh, how I wish most of this had more to do with the vagaries of a typical mother/daughter relationship!

You get so used to whatever you've been raised with. The dysfunctional is as normal as normal. That night I tried to resolve to no longer change Mother, but change me instead. I decided to throw off the self-imposed shackles of subservience to Mother and live my life, not hers. I also opened my mind to the possibility of finding Mama; face down my fear of probable rejection. Perhaps she wasn't even alive. Might I find her if I looked? I deserved to look my own heritage in the face, didn't I? It was my birthright, no? It was high time I made things happen, not wait for life to happen to me. After all, time was running out.

Then again, it wasn't really Mother's fault she didn't understand me, or more specifically what it felt like to be adopted. How can anyone if they haven't been? She didn't know I felt set apart or different because I never told her. Were my parents afraid to ask how I felt? Probably. Yet again, on the surface, our life was pretty idyllic, so why look for trouble if there didn't appear to be any? I was so busy trying to fit in and belong, my compliant behavior masked the truth of my turmoil. Mother and Daddy thought they were doing everything right. And they did, for the most part. No complaints. What I couldn't do was tell them that no matter what they did it would never compensate for the separation I had from my birth mother. For one, it wasn't their fault. Why make them feel guilty or think me ungrateful? Nevertheless, I did feel isolated what with Mother never really grasping the difference between kin and kindred; one being family, whether by blood or adoption and the other having more to do with being similar in kind or having affinity. Perhaps it was my responsibility to just snap out of it; shrug off notions of isolation and get on with life. It is what it is, as they say. So, I decided to bury my truest feelings for the sake of others. Was this conflict avoidance? With Mother or Mama or both?

"It doesn't take a rocket scientist to know that the only person who can ever really make any difference in one's life is oneself. If I want to discover my heritage, it's up to l'il ol' me and me alone!"

NOW OR NEVER

"So, guess what?"

Uh, oh...

"Adoptees can get ahold of their birth certificates now!" Lise shouts into the receiver.

"You're kidding."

"Illinois just loosened its grip on adoption records. They're yours for the asking."

Oh, boy...

"And, it only costs fifteen bucks! I checked."

Mmm, you would...

I can hear Lise lighting a cigarette through the telephone lines. She's exhaling long and slow. Her office is probably littered with at least two ash trays, both overflowing with crumpled butts and ash. And the air around her? So thick with smoke it makes my stomach turn just imagining it.

"It's now or never, girlfriend."

Easy for you to say...

"If you wait too much longer you might be sorry."

She's sorta/kinda right. Daddy's already gone. Mother's ninety-seven...

Outside a layer of frost covers the grass and there are footprints fading on the lawn. I can't help thinking totally out of the blue, *funny how every step taken always seems to leave a trace...*

"You there?" Lise asks. She's prepping another cigarette, tamping it down against her desk. "Do you remember," she continues, "my sister getting pregnant at seventeen and having to give up her baby? You're not gonna believe this, but he just contacted her."

"What? That's crazy! Was she happy to be found?" As she fills me in, I'm wondering, *would Mama mind if I found her? What if she did, and sent me packing?*

"I know what you're thinking, Alex. Stop worrying about your mama's rejection or your mother's hurt feelings. Those are big, fat what-ifs. Aren't you sick of setting up all these self-defeating roadblocks? You could turn this around, ya know."

There you go again, Bossypants…

"None of us are doomed to remain as we are," she persists. "And I'm not bossy."

"Yeah, you are," I mutter. *God, she's always so dramatic! 'Doomed'. Really?*

I get up to let the dog out. The night air is cold and smells like snow. The bare aspens are looking particularly leggy against their black backdrop. *It would be pretty amazing if there were a family out there,* I think for the thousandth time, *brothers or sisters who look like me, sound like me… a branch on a family tree…*

"You can't use not having a birth certificate to justify doing nothing. Stop being such a decision cripple!"

That's harsh, I think.

"I know you think me harsh, but you know it's time."

At the thought of actually finding Mama, I ask, "If I write her a letter what if she doesn't answer me?"

Find her first, is what she's probably saying to herself before she adds more gently this time, "Handle that when and if it happens."

"Better than not trying, I s'pose."

"Listen, Silly, get that birth certificate first. Then find her."

And then what? My whole life will change. Forever. We're both quiet. I listen to her lighting yet another stinky Marlborough.

"Okay, okay! I'll get it," I practically shout.

"Of course you will. You're no chicken, ya know."

Oh, yeah I am…

"Stop thinking you're afraid," she scolds. "You're ready."

"My life's been good. My complaints are no bigger than those who aren't adopted. Yet, I have a right to know. Don't I?"

PAST BECOMES PRESENT

It was an unexpectedly snowy afternoon well into spring when I sat down to sort through the mail. All sounds from the woods outside were muffled, and the trees were tinged with an unearthly yellow cast. In Colorado, it's not uncommon for the sun to shine while it's snowing and I remember marveling at this strange phenomenon. At the bottom of the pile lay a crisp, white envelope with IDPH printed in large capital letters in the upper lefthand corner. It practically radiated in the lamp's arc of light on my knees. Illinois Department of Public Health. The reply I'd been anticipating for so long, I'd practically forgotten about it. Oh boy, inside was information guaranteed to change my life forever. I sat very still, afraid to open the letter while evening began to fill with snow, veils of it flying every which way.

Would this letter hold promise or defeat? For most of my life I'd ask this sort of question, but never fully attempted to answer it. *Only you have the power to change yourself if you choose. You need not be condemned to remain who you are.* These words, or some such, uttered to me by an old friend are what made me realize if I were to go to my grave fearful as opposed to brave, I'd probably never forgive myself. *Living a life rife with ambivalence is a waste of energy* is what she'd said. Oh, Lise, once the queen of funk in your tie-dye t-shirts, sexy Daisy-Dukes, and purple fluorescent flip flops, what a wise soul you've become.

Missing Mama, wondering where or how she is, while feeling remorse for feeling that way in light of Mother's care of me has been totally enervating, particularly the guilt. *The shadow of a guilty conscience is long and dark* according to Lise, but I'm grateful to have finally come to the realization that guilt is only for those who subscribe to it. That last mantra really resonates with me. When I finally realized that an ongoing sadness was dominating my outlook, I chucked it. After all, I was sixty-three and wasn't getting any younger. So, what did I do? I sent my check for $15 along with identification to the IDPH and requested my original birth certificate. Simple!

Through a haze of tears I read:

> I HEREBY CERTIFY that by the authority of 750 ILCS 50/18.1b(e)(1) and (2), I have caused the sealed adoption file of Alexandra Saunders to be opened and the original birth certificate to be opened and the original birth record copied.
>
> Nirav D. Shah, M.D., J.D.
> State Registrar

Running my index finger along the page and stopping at each block, I pick out Mama's name, Anna Jane Austin MacKenzie; her birthplace, Indiana; father's name, UNKNOWN; my place of birth, St. Luke's Hospital, Cook County, Chicago, Illinois; time at birth, 2:16 PM. I read all of it over and over again, finally clutching it to my bosom as if it were a winning lottery ticket. Tears stream down my cheeks.

"You okay?" my husband asks, coming into the library. He lays a gentle hand on my shoulder and drops a kiss on the crown of my head.

"Look! This is my birth certificate!" I wave it at him. "Mine! It belongs to me! Can you believe it? It's mine, really mine!"

He sits down next to me. I remember how a moan escaped from my chest so wretched you'd have thought the floor was collapsing right out from under me. In fact, I actually did feel as though I were falling.

Tyler wraps his arms around me. We perch on the edge of the sofa in silence, he gently rocking me while the snow accumulating outside on the window sash bends the aspen branches toward the ground.

I remember looking down at the envelope lying in my lap and

wondering how incredulous it was that others were allowed to keep this legal paper about me under wraps and I not have it until now.

"Do you want me to get the laptop?" Tyler interrupts my thoughts. "Your sleuthing can begin, now that you have an address." My eyes must have rounded into saucers. "I'll take that as a yes?"

"Ty, this is gonna sound really strange, but holding this birth certificate in my hand already has me feeling differently about myself."

"Congratulations, Honey. You're on your way."

The first thing I do is punch in 6200 Sheridan Road in Chicago and up pops a grainy aerial shot of an urban neighborhood two blocks east of Lake Michigan. It looks like a hodgepodge of apartment buildings; cold, gray and uninviting. I conclude Mama's dormitory for unwed mothers is down there somewhere in those canyons of cement, and I shudder. I swear I even feel the chill as if I were standing right there with her on one of those snow-covered sidewalks. It had to be late December or early January when she was left on The Cradle's doorstep, a harsh Chicago wind pulling at her hair and clothes. Poor Mama. Mama, the gal who dared to leave her heart undefended in the arms of a cad, winding up pregnant and in no position to care for me, her baby girl. I continue staring at the photo so as to soak up her presence in this most unfortunate of places.

She and I are down there, displaced and abandoned, I think as I enlarge the image on the screen. *You but a girl and I but a babe, both of us innocent and clueless about what is to come.*

"I'm gonna find her, tell her I'm okay," I say aloud into the dark. "She deserves to know."

"She'd like that, I'm sure," my husband concurs, though I know he's holding his more pessimistic thoughts in check.

Next, I google the Indiana Census Bureau closest to Anna Jane's date of birth, which is 1930. Finding nothing for that decennial, I punch in 1940 and boom! There she is, her two sisters, mother and father...and unbelievably an address in South Bend! There's no mistaking this is she as the middle name is the same, *Austin.* Oh my God, oh my God, oh my God, this is crazy! Raking my fingers through my hair and clutching my head, I must have been shaking in disbelief when Tyler calls from the kitchen, "Another find?"

"I got her address!"

"Google it, " he yells over the noise of running water. "You might get a hit like the one in Chicago."

With that, my fingers fly across the keyboard, typing in 655 Sawmill. And what do you know but a real estate listing on zillow.com offers Mama's very same address. Incredulous, I click on it. And pow! I'm gazing at the house my mama probably lived in when she was pregnant with me. Naturally, I burst into tears all over again.

Tyler rushes to my side. "Whoa, whoa. What's wrong?" Concern is etched across his brow.

I point at the computer screen. The digital image of Mama's house is a mid-century modern home, obviously remodeled, but revealing much of its original nostalgic 1930's character. *I was actually there!* I say with wet eyes pointing first at me then the picture too choked up to speak. Tyler loops an arm around my shoulders and I collapse my head into the crook of his shoulder.

Continuing to marvel at what I'm seeing through a flow of tears, I suddenly realize this is the house I used to draw and color when I was seven years old. I distinctly remember my Second Grade teacher, Miss Alice, asking me if I might consider drawing something else besides this house over and over again. Did she think me obsessed? I wonder now, too. Was I channeling Mama? How could I have known what Mama's home looked like? Yet here is the very same little house, same as all my drawings: sweet, almost childlike in its personality, authentic Americana. A symmetrical box of white clapboard, a triangle for a roof on top, brick chimney, front door with a little porch, and the American flag waving to the right.

"Isn't that the most adorable house you've ever seen? I was there, can you believe it? I was there." And I dissolve into another round of tears.

Outside, snow is piling up in soft drifts. Our front yard looks like a giant feather eiderdown, the kind under which I used to love burying myself when we lived in Switzerland and didn't use typically American bedding. I could disappear under that comforter for hours with a book and a flashlight. This leads me to think how from Mama's point of view I might have indeed been a child who vanished. Why would she ever have imagined my living so far away on the other side of the Atlantic? Today, though, I am found. I start to cry again, realizing just how much a lonely child I really was. It's as if I went missing; as if I were lost at the mall and not able to find my Mama because I wandered off into the crowd and didn't stay in place as taught. These photos and birth certificate prove I truly am connected to Mama, not some make-believe character in a fairy tale about being chosen. I came to hate being told I was chosen. It implied that at one time I wasn't. Anyway, Mama's out there, hopefully still alive, waiting for me to find her. The great distance separating us after all these years is now only a few more prompts away on my computer. Our shared past and present are about to be stitched back together.

I skipped dinner that night, Tyler left to his own devices to warm a can of clam chowder and grab a sleeve of Ritz while I continued to surf the net. Visiting such sites as ancestry.com, Notre Dame University's alumni records - presuming the sperm donor graduated from there — and a variety of public records, it was all to no avail. Clearly, I didn't know what queries to make. Then I had a moment of sheer brilliance. I asked Google who is married to Anna Jane Austin MacKenzie?

Near to the top of the first page, Mama's name catches my eye. It is attached to an obituary from the Shenandoah Standard. I click on it:

Thomas John Redford II, 85, of Clearwater, FL, passed away December 16, 2014. T.J. was born February 2, 1929 in Crown Hill, West Virginia. He was married to Anna Jane Austin (MacKenzie) Redford for 41 years, taking residences in Indiana and Florida.

Redford is survived by his wife, *Mac*; three stepchildren Maureen Rouse, Molly Harrill and Scott Christie; nine grandchildren; and thirteen great-grandchildren.

Redford was preceded in death by his son, Thomas John Redford III (Red), deceased December 9, 1970, and daughter, Mary Jennifer (MJ) Redford, deceased December 29, 1986.

Redford was most proud of his service to the United States as a Navy Seabee (Naval Mobile Construction Battalion) during World War II, the Korean War and Vietnam. He served around the globe from the islands of Guam, Sicily, and Bermuda, as well as Jacksonville, FL, Phu Bai and Dong Ha, Vietnam. T.J. retired from the Navy on March 6, 1969. and from General Telephone Company (Verizon) in April 1987, where he supervised cable crews which buried thousands of miles of fiber optic cable throughout the midwest.

Thomas Redford will be interred later this spring next to his children, Red and MJ, and his parents in Harpers Ferry, West Virginia.

Have you ever noticed how sometimes when you're reading something you see the words but their meaning simply doesn't register? Well, it took two run-throughs before the words [his] three stepchildren penetrated my emotion-addled brain. Oh, my God, if these three are T.J.'s stepchildren, then they must be Anna Jane's kids... from a former marriage... which means they are my half siblings!

"Aw, no! Ty, you've got to come here and see this!"

Tyler scans the obituary. "Holy shit! You've got to be kidding me!"

"I've got a brother and two sisters!"

"That's not what I'm lookin' at." He points to T.J.'s birthday. Incredibly it's the same as mine. February 2nd.

"What the hell?"

"You know what that means, don't you?" I shake my head, more tears falling for the strangest of ironies. What's the chance, I mean really, that T.J. and I would share the same birthday?

"It means every year she celebrated his birthday, she was thinking of you, too."

I open the laptop again and go to Facebook.

"Now what are you doing?"

"I'm gonna look up my half-siblings. See what I can find out."

"You mean, 'stalk'?"

"I just wanna see what they look like. That's not stalking."

"If and when they get wind of you, Saunders, just figure they'll do the same."

Sure enough, all three have public Facebook pages filled with photographs of their children and grandchildren, homes, pets and travels. With every scroll down the page my family grows larger and my life richer. Most shocking of all, brother Scott lives in Basalt, a mere two hours away. And he seems so like the brother I always imagined having. Tall and rangy with a broad, willing smile, he looks like he loves to kid around. My sisters and I don't really look much alike, though we do share high cheekbones, similar bone structure around the eyes and curvy figures. As I sift through Scott's anthology of photographs on his Facebook page, I finally find a picture of his mother, *wait a minute* I remember saying to myself, *our mother.*

I stare at her for a long time. She is the prettiest girl I've ever seen. Slim with downy waves of auburn hair framing her face, her gaze into the camera lens is beguiling. I swear it would knock any man right off his feet. And though these looks might be how she got into trouble, I smile anyway. She probably had every boy in the neighborhood totally bewitched, a thought that actually makes me proud of her.

"Are you scared?" Tyler asks.

"Yes. No." I pull my hair back and tie it into a makeshift knot. "Maybe a little." I bow my head, rubbing the back of my neck. "Do you think she could ever love me?"

"Are you kidding me, Saunders?"

I caress Mama's photographed face with my fingertips. It feels like hello.

"So. It takes me sixty-three birthdays of standing at that fork in the path before daring to choose the direction of the unknown; to reach for both my past and my future. My birthright. It is high time to hold my fate in my hands, turn it over and feel its varied textures, inhale its perfume, taste it on my tongue. Will it be sweet or bitter? Most importantly, will it fit?"

HELLO

Hello,   June 11, 2015

My name is Alex Andersen. I was born February 2, 1952 at St. Luke's Hospital in Chicago, Illinois and I believe you may be the mother who relinquished me for adoption, which was handled by The Cradle in nearby Evanston.

I found you by applying for my original birth certificate (recently made legally available to adult adoptees) from the Illinois Department of Public Health. Matching that information with other records online, such as the 1940 Census for South Bend, Indiana, I found the address of where you lived when you were ten years old. Believe it or not, a photograph of 655 Sawmill is currently on zillow.com as it has recently been on the market; and when I "googled" you, an online obituary for your second husband, T. J. Redford, led me to where you are today.

No doubt, these words come as a huge shock. Rest assured, the same holds true for me, yet I am compelled, perhaps by a force of nature, to reach out and find the connection that's always been missing. If this is an unwelcome endeavor I will understand, but please know that I bear you absolutely no malice, for I can well understand not just the circumstances facing you in 1951 and '52 but the social pressures of the day and years following as well. I am neither angry nor hurt nor needy. I'm simply looking for a sense of closure.

My upbringing as an only child was a happy and healthy one. In high school I excelled in English Lit and foreign languages, was the school's Swim Captain and VP. I graduated college in 1974 with a BA, and since then pursuits have included voluntarism, reading, prose and poetry-writing, interior design, needlepoint, skiing, hiking, and politics.

I live in Colorado with my husband where the pioneer spirit has captured our hearts and we enjoy an uncomplicated lifestyle among the elk, fox, snow-capped mountains and wild flowers. My two daughters are both married to awesome guys and between them, there are four grandchildren; two boys and two girls.

When my children were itty-bitty I looked in the rearview mirror at them sitting in their car seats and upon realizing they were the only blood relatives I knew, I was motivated to contact The Cradle for genealogical info. At the time (1980) that information was very comforting, though I did not learn your name. Twenty years later I embarked upon a search for you, but chickened out rationalizing a myriad of scenarios why not to make contact. I wasn't ready, I guess. Perhaps, no one ever is. But during this past year, too many people and/or events have pointed me in the direction of searching for you again. So, here I am.

Yes, this is indeed surreal. Please believe I want no harm or despair to come to you upon receiving this letter. I am well aware that your family might not know a thing about me so your secret is safe. Nevertheless, I would very much like to be in touch with you as it would answer questions I've had all my life. Connecting after all this time might be very cathartic for us both.

Your daughter,
Alex

PATIENCE IS A VIRTUE

In early spring 2015 time seemed to stand still. To be fair, though, I was in an extra big hurry. It had been a week since I mailed my letter to Mama and for some unknown reason, it stalled in Tampa. Per my daughter, Emma's advice, I had added tracking so I could follow its progress. Frantically checking on the mailer's march across the country at least six or seven times a day, I ultimately consulted with my own post office, which warned it was probably being returned to sender. At least I knew Mama hadn't received it yet. Had there been no tracking, I'd have worried that she had received it and thrown it into the trash. Rejection was my absolute very worst fear.

After an entire lifetime I'd finally decided to find my way "home" to that place where I began; back to Mama and the safety of being where surely I belonged. Since receiving my birth certificate and composing my letter I spent half the time walking on cloud nine. The other half crying for the me who'd lost her way. I had so much built-up tension I didn't know where to stuff it. No question, I was overwhelmed with all the emotions from the past; a past with which I was well familiar and another past with which I was yet to be acquainted. Winter seemed to return during those two weeks of waiting. A flat light tinged with yellow hung over our woods day after day. When I look back on that protracted waiting period it's as if I were seeing my past unfold in an album of sepia-toned photographs, some curled at the corners and others too blurry to decipher.

One day, I am such a mess of nervous energy, wondering if Mama might send me a reply, I decide to burn off some anxiety by taking a long hike. So, I shove my feet into cold-hardened boots and head out as if on a mission. As I trudge over the ridge line and down to the south fence a couple of miles away, I keep my chin tucked inside a muffler and my hands thrust deep into the pockets of Tyler's old ski instructor jacket. Snow squeaks and creaks under my feet and along my route a delicious scent of pine fills my nostrils, reminding me of the fresh boughs I always lay across our mantle at Christmas-time. It soothes my nerves, much like the fragrance of lavender always has. Snow crystals sift down through branches of ponderosas creating a magical snow globe aura. Otto bounds ahead then back, his tail swirling with each leap in the deep snow, his mouth open in a perpetual smile. Once on the flats, I am able to take in the view of Mount Evans, its fourteen thousand foot peak poking above the clouds. I let my mind wander.

I have good parents, but it doesn't change the fact my need to know Mama or where I come from is justified. I think it is this day I actually realize I knew this to be true all my life, but never gave the thought its wings. I've always lived with a longing for Mama, but never let this emotion see the light of day. I remember my mind sliding guiltily over to Mother, but quashing it quickly. *Finding Mama is not only my birthright* I profess to myself, *but also I shouldn't feel one ounce of remorse about it.* My instinct to bond with Mama is a human instinct for survival, pure and simple. It's natural for me to want emotional and physical contact with her. It's what children crave from their birth mothers. Our separation at birth is neither natural nor resolved. When you stop to think about birthdays, mine are anniversaries of the afternoon I was yanked from Mama, who probably never even got a chance to lay eyes on me, much less hold me in her arms. Then I was passed from one nurse to another until several months later I was placed with total strangers.

Mother creeps back into my conscience. A mother with whom I can no longer connect now that I'm no longer the clinging, compliant adopted child afraid of rejection. I tried to connect. Truly. I'll never forget the absurdity of that night on the porch when the jasmine-scented sea air filled the night and Mother shut me down. As she aged, she withdrew more and more into her head and back to her past. If only she could have said to herself, *I am so lucky; maybe not at first, but now, oh yes, absolutely.*

I have been loved by two wonderful men, and still am by my daughter and her daughters, and I love them in return... But no, Mother is trapped by the losses suffered seventy plus years ago.

Tyler would caution, *you can't write a script for someone...* As my temper begins to flare, I coax the rising anger into submission. This is not the time, I say to myself. Focus on Mama. You have a right to feel the longing you have experienced; regardless of other disappointments. So, I focus on the day I might look into Mama's eyes.

Is my life about to become like a cobweb's design, it's threading a weave so intricate one can scarcely comprehend its pattern? I think about all of the hours, days, weeks, months and years Mama and I have been apart. How would we ever be able to catch up on all that lost time? Share all our memories? Know what it was like for the other during thousands of moments of joy or sorrow? Not only do these thoughts strike hard, but this one, too: whose life have I been living? I remember wondering on that walk, am I more Mother due to the influences of nurture and my experiences living all over the United States and abroad? Or am I Mama's daughter due to blood, a shared heredity, a similar personality? As I turn toward home, I hope I'll find out.

It was growing dark, so much so Tyler was worried and came out to find me. After all, a pale winter sun was fast sinking below Mount Evans and a nasty wind was churning in the trees. I was not far from the house when I saw him coming up the trail. I ran to his open arms. As if knowing my afternoon had been fraught with second-guessing, Tyler had already laid a fire in our kitchen grate. Orange and yellow flames were scampering up the flue when we entered our toasty kitchen. On the counter was a Scotch on the rocks. Double.

WHATCHA GOT THERE?

Poor Mama. I can only imagine what it was like for her when she received my letter. It must have hit her like a Mack Truck, so I pitied her inevitable shock. There was no avoiding it, though, as it was a risk I had to take. The pain was necessary even if it hurt me like hell to cause her any distress.

Perhaps she was sitting in the car when she ripped open the mailer while her daughter ran into the grocery store. Once the photograph of me dropped into her lap she probably only had enough time to glance at it and read the first paragraph: *Hello, My name is Alex Andersen. I was born February 2, 1952 at St. Luke's Hospital in Chicago, Illinois and I believe you may be my mother...*

There she sits, staring out the car window. Stunned. Suddenly, her world has come to a surreal standstill. The sights and sounds outside the car cannot penetrate her mind. They are visible and audible, but disjointed and discordant. A dog near the entrance to Walgreens is scratching at fleas around his collar. Adjacent to the parking lot, white bed sheets flap in the wind. The endless whine of a log splitter is coming from a yard forty feet away. And a little girl with pigtails pedals her tricycle in tight circles on the driveway, handlebar streamers of fluorescent orange and green trailing merrily. Once Mama's heart rate slows is she able to think clearly, or even at all? Does she wonder if she and I can find our way back to each other? Or does she ask herself how in the world do I tell this girl to go away?

"Whatcha got there, Mom?" asks Molly.

"Nothin'."

"It's got a Colorado address. Is it from Scott?"

"Nope."

"Then who's it from?" Molly glances at Mama before looking over her right shoulder to reverse out the parking space.

"Nobody."

"You don't wanna talk about it, is that it?"

"Yup." Mama stuffs the oversized mailer into her pocket book and wraps her arms around it protectively.

Poor Mama. The cage door to all her secrets has suddenly been flung wide open. Like a pretty song bird held in captivity for too long, she probably has no desire to fly free much less have a hand snake its way in to lift her out. She probably hasn't told anyone of my existence so she's terrified. I bet she feels crippled, both physically and emotionally. That's understandable. After all, I've been thinking about finding Mama for years. She, on the other hand, has probably figured I'm long gone. Why wouldn't she? It's been over six decades for heaven's sake! Poor Mama. If she were in any way responding the way I did when I realized we were within reach of each other she'd be thinking good God, I wonder if we can ever stitch our torn selves back together again. Maybe on that ride back to Molly's, Mama refuses to let her memories out into the daylight. I wouldn't blame her. It might be that much easier to just tear up the photo, never read the letter, and declare it junk mail.

Planters of purple lobelia and giant red geraniums are pretty on the front steps of Molly's house. They seem to smile in the sunlight. Creeping ivy and wild roses are wound around a post and rail fence running alongside the drive. There's a slow felty beat of raindrops beginning to plop on the lawn when Mama steps from the car. Not waiting for her daughter to fetch her walker from the trunk nor even an umbrella from the backseat, Mama clutches her handbag to her chest, turns her back to Molly and marches up the wooden steps into the house, down the hall and into her bedroom, slamming the door behind her.

Whoa! I'm not feelin' good about this at all, Molly probably thinks. *I wonder if she's received one of those scams ya keep hearin' about. The ones that steal money from the elderly.*

Fleeing the scene is pretty close to what I would have done if I were in Mama's shoes. I'd have pulled a disappearing act, too, I'm hopeless at cooking up a believable lie or arranging my features into inscrutability. Besides, I'd want time not just to read the letter in private, but also to digest it. I'd want to lose myself in that photo, stare into those eyes so foreign to me, yet so incredibly familiar. That's what I did when I found Mama's photo on Facebook. I went back to it several times a day. Also, I knew she'd want to decide how best to tell her family. And I'm sure she worried about her children and the impact it would have on them. Maybe, they'd hate me.

Had I been there that day, sitting beside Mama at the foot of her bed, I'd have whispered, "The shadows of our past stretch long and wide. Nothing we can do about them. They exist for all of us. So, please, don't beat yourself up. No matter how well-intentioned one is, there are almost always unintended consequences. In your case, Mama, there is no one to blame. You gave me life and found me a home where I'd be safe and loved."

A faraway train whistle shrieks as it hurtles its way west, so Mama barely hears Molly's tentative knock.

"You okay, in there?" Molly pokes her head around the door.

"Fine."

"Still don't want to talk about it?"

"Nope."

"Can I ask when?"

"When I'm good 'n ready."

"Okay. I'm just worried that's all."

"I can tell."

"I'll check on you later then."

"I'm sure you will."

How long did Mama remain barricaded in her room? I can only imagine her marinating in despair, and it grieved me to guess at her suffering. She was being forced to revisit the past and all its subsequent hurts. It frightened me she might actually not respond to my letter, instead believing it some sort of cruel hoax. I couldn't blame her. What if she decided I was in need of something she could not give, like a loan or a kidney? I wanted her to know my character was centered not disturbed, certainly not a burden. She wouldn't know that though unless she was as brave as I and replied.

Throughout my childhood, my dreams of some day meeting Mama have remained constant. The fantasies seeming to grow more frequent with age, that probably having a lot to do with staring mortality in the face. Time has been definitely running out. With the potential of meeting Mama becoming ever more real, I have gone from being ecstatic one minute to panicked the next. She can very well turn me away. Decline a reunion. Ignore the letter altogether. Yet I cling to the hope Mama is saying to herself, *I've waited to hear from my baby girl all my life.* There are no guarantees she'll be positive. Rejection looms large.

What happened later that night probably went something like this: Mama joins the family for supper at the kitchen table. She picks at her food, pushing peas around her plate and piling mashed potatoes on top of uneaten bites of meat loaf. Mama's handbag is parked under her chair, close to her feet and inside the walker by her side. When she retires to the den for a little TV, Mama brings her handbag with her, gingerly tucking it between her left hip and the arm of the sofa. The afghan over her legs supposedly hides it from view, but of course, Molly and her husband are not fooled. When it's time for bed, instead of taking the walker or Molly's helpful arm, Mama limps down the hallway hugging her secret to her bosom. This time she closes the door to her room softly.

As she brushes her teeth that night she might be wondering, *is it even appropriate for me to uncover my past at this late date? What if revealing the existence of my daughter tears this family apart? Could they ever forgive me?* And as she applies moisturizer in upward strokes to her softly lined cheeks, she gazes at the face in the mirror and sees a stranger. Before returning to her bedroom where she has left her bag open on the foot of the bed, she puts a comb through her hair and asks her reflection, *am I who I think I am or am I what others see?*

Meanwhile, while Mama is in the bathroom brushing, flossing and gargling mouthwash, Molly, who's been worried sick all afternoon about the secret hidden in the bottom of Mama's handbag, tiptoes into her mother's bedroom. Leaving the mailer in the bag, she slides the letter half way out of its envelope and begins reading: *Hello, My name is Alex... I* *was born February 2, 1952 at ...and I believe you may be my mother...*When Molly suddenly realizes the bathroom noises have quit, she frantically shoves everything back into the mailer and skedaddles down the hallway. How Mama doesn't catch her is anyone's guess. Maybe it's because Molly has gone as white as a ghost.

With trembling fingers, Molly dials her brother's number. It takes her two tries.

"Hey, sis! What's cookin'?"

"You better sit down."

"What's wrong? Is it Mom? Is she okay?"

"Yeah, yeah. She's fine." Molly takes a long sip from the can of beer her husband has shoved into her free hand. "Scott, listen."

"I'm listenin'." He lights one of his clove cigarettes and inhales deeply.

"Mom had a kid, a girl. Before she married Dad."

"Whaaaaat?"

"She wrote Mom a letter and there's a photograph..."

"You've got to be kidding! Who is she? Shit, I bet she's a fraud. What did she say?

"I don't know."

"What do you mean you don't know? Dammit, Molly!"

"I only got to read the first paragraph before Mom came out of the bathroom."

"Does she want something?" Another deep inhale of clove. "I bet she wants money! Or a bone marrow transplant!" A slow exhale fills the silence.

"That's not nice, Scott. C'mon."

"Well, shit, Molly! How come we never knew anything about her?"

"I dunno." Molly sounds beaten.

"Where's Mom now?"

"She's gone to bed.

"So sneak into her room and grab the letter."

"I already tried that. Her handbag's under the covers."

"That's so nuts." Giggles tumble out of Molly like an unstoppable waterfall. "You're losin' it, Molls," Scott growls.

"You should see Mom clinging to that bag, Scott. You'd think she was guarding the crown jewels!"

"We've got to expose this fake."

"Tomorrow when Mom's back in the bathroom I'm gonna try and take a photo of the letter with my cell phone."

"Now you're talkin'!"

"I'm sorry I woke you, Scottie. Get some sleep."

"Like that's gonna happen now!"

Her next call is to her sister, Maureen, who answers on the fifth ring. She's groggy.

"It's mom. Oh my God! She's dead, isn't she?"

"No!"

"Then why you wakin' me up?"

"Are you sitting down?"

No, I'm lyin' down. Are you gonna tell me what's goin' on or waste more of my rack time?"

"Mom had a kid outta wedlock and she just reached out to Mom in a letter. There's a photograph and I think she's legit. Well not legit, but.... Oh shit, you know what I mean."

"Hey, Molls, I'm kinda not surprised."

"Huh?" Molly rakes her fingers through her hair. "Wha'd'ya mean?"

"Well, Mom's always been a bit of a closed book. Now I know why. She's been keeping a secret."

"I'll say! A big, fat juicy one called Alex."

"Yeah… 'cept she ain't a secret anymore." Maureen's laugh spills from deep within her.

"You're crazy. Go back to sleep."

"Wait a sec! Do you remember how I always said I didn't feel like the oldest? Do you?"

"Kinda. But that's because I was the mature one and you were the goof ball."

"Very funny."

"Then why?"

"Because I'm not the oldest. This Alex chick is!"

"Sweet Jesus! The pecking order has totally changed, hasn't it?."

"Yeah, " Maureen laughs again. "Now we're gonna have to revisit those psyche books all over again."

"I'll call you in the morning, okay?"

"What's the point? I ain't gettin' back to sleep now."

NO MORE SECRETS

Sometimes, night bleeds into the sky gradually, allowing ribbons of pink and lilac, orange and red to paint the horizon. However, the night after Mama received my letter fell all at once. Darkness as black as pitch with no stars at all. Not even the faint smudge of the Milky Way was visible. I imagine Mama at her wits' end, trying to sort through emotions she buried years and years ago. Now they were tumbling into her lap laying her bare. It didn't help having to keep her pocketbook glued to her hip for the last forty-eight hours. How many times had she readjusted the strap slipping off her shoulder? Too many, I'm guessing.

It's night two and Mama sinks into a bath of hot sudsy water hoping to chase not only the dark night away but also her blues. Resting her head on the tub rim, she pulls the bubbles across the surface, over her chest, and under her chin. The sweet aroma of lavender drifts up from her bath water and she sighs. There is a soft knock at the bathroom door.

"May I come in?" Molly asks timidly.

"If you must."

Amid all the cosmetics littering the tight space around the sink, Mama's handbag sits on top of the pink tile countertop like an elephant atop a beach ball. Both women glance at it as Molly enters the bathroom. It looks to Mama, I'm guessing, that her goose is cooked. Molly closes the lid on the toilet and sits down.

"Mom, let's have no more pretending. I…"

"I don't know what you're talking about."

"Mom, please. We both know you've been acting really weird ever since you received that priority mailer from Colorado."

"Why are you buggin' me?"

"Because I wanna know what's going on, Mom. I'm worried about you. Besides, along with that pocketbook, sadness is trailing after you like smoke!"

"Stop your foolin', Molly. I know you already read my letter!"

A cloud of steam billows between them and in the moment before it clears, I can just imagine Mama rolling her eyes.

"Guilty as charged," Molly admits when the fog lifts. Her brown eyes are as big as saucers, her lashes as soft and thick as a doe's. "Give me that sponge. I'll soap your back."

Silence envelops them and then "It's the strangest thing, but I long to just hug her."

"I'm sure she wants to hug you, too." Somewhere outside the bathroom a floorboard creaks and the house settles. Mama feels a silky chill caressing her skin so she sinks back down beneath her blanket of bubbles.

"Free yourself, Mom. No more secrets." Molly stands. "How 'bout I make us some hot chocolate and we sit by the fire while you tell me your story?"

"She seems nice."

"Who? Oh. Alex?"

"Who else we talkin' about?" Molly ducks as a spray of water hits her face.

"Don't get testy, Mom. Yes, she does seem nice. She also seems to have had a good life."

"I bet she figured at her age, mine too for that matter, that there wasn't much time left for us to meet." Molly nods her agreement, eyes brown pools of kindness.

"Ya know, Mom, judging from that photo she looks more like you than any of us."

"Ya think?"

"Scott's the one who noticed and I agree."

"Egad! You told 'em?" She slaps the water with the flat of her hand.

"Mom, it's okay. There's a sister out there and if and when you're ready, we think you should welcome her into our family."

"You guys aren't mad at me?" Mama probably looks pretty forlorn at that moment, certainly vulnerable sitting there naked in a tub of cooling water and dissolving bubbles. Molly shakes her head *no*.

"Really, Mom, you should contact her. You can take baby steps..." She looks away briefly. "Oops, maybe I should amend that to one day at a time."

As a total non-sequitur, Mama says, "They say one remembers a fragrance. I used to wear lavender all the time. Do you s'pose she has any memory of it from the womb? And I always rubbed my belly, which most of the time was probably her bottom. Do you think she might remember that?"

"Anything's possible, Mom."

"Those are the only things I could give her. You know, of me..."

Seeing the tears well up in her mother's eyes, a very rare thing for Mama, Molly pulls the bath sheet from the rack and holds it wide open like an embrace. "Let's get you dried off and into your favorite nightie. C'mon, Mom, up ya go!"

Once Molly has her mother out of the tub and sitting safely on a three-legged stool, she leaves the bathroom flipping open her cell phone as she heads down the hall. Punching in the numbers with her thumb, she calls Scott first.

BUCKETS OF TEARS

It's where heaven bends down to hold Mount Evans in her embrace I come
closest to God. Our home is nestled among granite boulders, ponderosa
pine, and aspen atop a ridge facing her magnificent fourteen thousand
foot snow-capped peaks. Day in and day out our timber-frame house is
kissed by the sun. Most nights we bask under a dome of stars. Herds of
deer migrate through our land to find water or forage. In winter bears
hibernate in our caves. In spring foxes give birth deep within a den of
boulders beneath our driveway. In autumn the elk bugle and fight over
females while mountain lion, bobcat, and coyote follow the food chain
down glades and over meadows. It's those yellow alpine buttercups mixed
with red Indian paintbrush and blue forget-me-nots dotting the landscape
which bring so much cheer. They poke their pretty little heads above
smokey kinnikinnick like alpine nymphs. It's here in this idyllic haven,
where I really have no right to ask for anything more, I receive the greatest
gift of all. Mama's outstretched hand.

Via email, she writes:

Dear Alex,   June 28th, '15

I received your letter on the 25th of June. Your letter was
somewhat delayed because my mail is being forwarded
to Indiana. I am staying with my daughter Molly after
having a pacemaker put in.

Your letter was surreal indeed, I wondered if this day would ever come. I am not sure what to do next. But I am open and hopeful for a new relationship. It is a relief to know that you have had a good life.

I tried once to make contact through "the Cradle" with no success. The files were closed. I have thought of you always and you were never forgotten.

It's normal to have questions, so perhaps we can find answers together. I've told my three living children of your existence and they are excited.

I am not sure how to sign off, but sincerely your birth mother, Mac

She tried to find me! And as sad as it sounds, she missed me which makes me absurdly happy. Overwhelmed with gratitude for her willingness to reopen our mother/daughter story, it occurs to me there'll be no more record of a vanished life. Rather there'll be a book whose pages can be filled with conversation and shared experiences. As I prepare to write back I realize how really hard it is to know what to say to someone who's as close as one's own mother, but who's also someone one doesn't know at all. I think the most important thing I want to convey when I first meet her and can look into her eyes is that she did a brave and selfless thing when she placed me in a situation better than the one she thought she could provide. I've always been grateful for her sacrifice. I always believed her pain outweighed mine.

Dear Mac, July 1st,'15

Your email was so kind and loving and I've been in virtual shock ever since receiving it last Sunday evening. Needless to say, I cried buckets, but then I've been doing that ever since I received my birth certificate, discovered your name, followed by your whereabouts and then composed my letter to you. All just a short six weeks ago.

Thank you for such a receptive response. To my mind there was every good reason, you'd have wanted to let things lie. I would have understood. I've heard plenty of stories where this has been the case. After all, you have a family and your health or equanimity to protect. What a shock for you. I really worried you'd be so startled or upset by my letter that you might become unwell. I felt selfish putting myself ahead of your welfare.

I have siblings! What a joy to know that and to hear they are excited about me, though I imagine they're reservedly so as they must wonder who this stranger is and want very much to protect you...Nonetheless, how wonderful of you all to share your email and cell info. Two sisters and a brother... And Scott is in Basalt? Wow!

Like you, I have no idea how to proceed. I, too, am hopeful for some form of a relationship which can be mutually rewarding and comfortable. I so love the way you suggested we find answers together.

Perhaps, we should follow up with a phone date. What say you? I'll take your lead. In the meantime, I'm glad you are with Molly right now. She seems absolutely darling; certainly as loving as you.

Love, Alex

I've always been drawn to big families. Everywhere we lived I'd meld myself to a big Catholic family: the Bowers in Washington D.C.; Roberts in Los Angeles. The Capidanos in Zürich, the Jamisons in London. I'd pretend I was the fourth or fifth child in their families and quite often I didn't even want to go home, often inviting myself to their dinner table. I think I gravitated to the noisy chaos of multiple siblings ganging up on the grownups. But overnight, I acquired real siblings; no denying it. I'd seen their faces on Facebook while I waited for my letter to reach Mama. Oh, how I'd always wanted to be a part of a brood. And here I was the eldest. Wow!

Dear Alex,   July 2nd, '15

Thrilled to get your email! I am just as excited to learn about you as you are to hear about me. My other children are ecstatic to learn they have an older sister.

Which brings up the fact that Scott would very much like to make contact with you but wants to make sure you are comfortable with that.

We may be more family than you are used to. And we don't want to scare you. I have 9 other grandchildren and 14 great grandchildren and one on the way any day. So you see you have a lot of blood relatives, dear.

I think I would feel comfortable on the phone. We can set up a time at your convenience.

Mac

I could already tell that Mama and Molly, who was probably helping her with her correspondence, understood what affinity meant. It's what I'd always known was missing without really being able to put my finger on it. For the first time, I was experiencing family, in the sense of what it feels like to be connected by blood. What an odd thing to be aware of, but there it was loud and clear.

Dear Mac,   July 2nd, '15

Just thought I should amend your numbers and add my
brood to the mix. You have eleven grands and ninteen
greats, including the one on the way! That is some big
family you have. Your family won't scare me; I so relish
having siblings. So much so that when I was a grade-
schooler I used to tell friends I was separated from them
in a car crash and it was my life's ambition to find them.
How prophetic is that?

My daughters, Sophie (38) and Emma (37) are over the
moon about my finding you and have cheered me every
step of the way. They've wanted me to embark on this
odyssey for years, but respected my ambivalence and
allowed me to be ready when I was ready. Needless to
say, they've cried tears of joy right alongside me.

You see, I was so afraid of being rebuffed, even though I
would have fully understood your rationale, and didn't
want to go through some of the horror stories I've heard.
. It would have been too painful as you can imagine to
come close but not get all the way there. That you have
welcomed me into your life so readily is truly quite
astounding. I'm stunned and so, so, so grateful.

Yes, I've been most amused by the irony that Scott lives
so close by. I don't think we're more than two hours
apart. I welcome a phone call from him or a rendezvous,
whichever... and any time he's ready. You don't mind that
he and I meet before you and I do? I'm fine with it, but I
want you to give the nod.

As far as you and I are concerned with regard to the
phone date, what part of the day is best for you? I think

there's a two-hour time difference, so I'll throw some suggestions out once you tell me what suits.

Love, Alex

PS So happy to hear I look like you! This is still so surreal!

Over the course of a week, the emails and texts between my newfound family and me went whooshing over the ethernet. I've never cried so much or been so grateful for the welcome I feel. I've heard so many stories, either firsthand or in books where the birth mother has moved on and created a new life, never wanting to look back on her past or the child she's given up. I was truly stunned to not find myself in these adoptees' shoes. When my half-brother contacted me, I was overjoyed. His *hello there, you're quite the surprise but a welcome one* made my heart swell to bursting.

THIRTY-THREE MINUTES

It was late afternoon on July 5th when I made the most important phone call of my life. In the gloaming to the east and over the city of Denver, the moon was already rising behind a thin scrim of cloud, obscuring her perfect shape, creating an almost mystical aura. This view suited not only my mood but also the strangeness of the moment. To the west, Mount Evans seemed to melt upward into heaven. I remember drawing on her majesty for strength as I watched the sky fade from robin's egg blue to soft orange and finally to a red ribbon outlining the peaks and turning them into inky silhouettes. Without question, the most important day of my life had arrived. Reconnecting with Mama meant I was about to be reborn. I could already feel my new identity spilling from my pores. It made me tremble as I was unfamiliar with who this person was. So, I paced back and forth in front of our large picture window gathering my thoughts before dialing her number. The forests and moonlit fields running up to the base of Mount Evans twelve miles away from our home were undisturbed by wind or sound. I remember as though it were just yesterday taking a few deep breaths and punching in those eleven digits. I was seconds away from talking to the woman who gave birth to me sixty-three years ago.

"Hello?"

"Hello, Mac?"

"Ye-es." Sing-songy cadence I like right away. Is it because it sounds somehow familiar? Her voice, while a bit husky, feels like a cashmere blanket, soft to the touch.

"This is Alex." *Duh.*

"Hi, Alex." Her voice sounds maternal.

"How are you?" *Can you say lost for words?*

"I'm fine, dear." There's a pause where I listen for her tears, and then she adds, " I can hardly believe this, you know that?"

"I know," I reply trying to corral my nervous breathing. "It's pretty startling."

"You sound great."

"So, do you. I'm sorry to hear about the pace maker…"

When Mama went back to Indiana with T.J.'s ashes to bury him in West Virginia, she fell and broke a vertebra. While in the hospital the doctors determined she needed a pacemaker. Unfortunately, she never made it to his memorial, though my three half siblings did go with their spouses.

Mama suggests if it weren't for Scott writing T.J.'s obituary and including her maiden name, MacKenzie, I might never have found her. To which I add it was the inclusion of her middle name, Austin, that made it that much easier to find her.

"Did you notice his birthday?" Mama asks, still referring to the obituary.

"I did. That was pretty surprising."

"Your birthday has been celebrated every year, Honey. I lit an extra candle for you when I celebrated his." Tears spring to my eyes. It feels really good to know she was thinking about me.

"Oh, that's so sweet…"

Mama asks about Mother, where she lives, if she's widowed and if so, for how long. I fill her in as blandly as possible, skipping over details, fearing I might head in a traitorous direction. Poor Mother, she'd faint if she knew I was talking about her to my birth mother. I remember thinking *I need to shed all this guilt. I'm acting as if it were dirty laundry needing to get tossed in the hamper, better yet, the incinerator. Be done with guilt for God's sake! It's okay to share a little of Mother with Mama. She probably wants to know I was well cared for, that she made a good decision…*

As if noticing that I'm struggling, Mama takes hold of the dialogue. "Well, I love your email… and I think you did the right thing when you said to your kids the less said to your mother about us the better. No sense offending her feelings. You know, with your mom…after all, uh, she's the one who raised you. That's fair."

"It is fair. And I appreciate your appreciating it." I hesitate to figure out what to say that doesn't sound like tattling. "It's hard for her. She's, um, I don't know… somewhat possessive. In fact, that's why I didn't search for you sooner. I've always protected her. It would have caused somewhat of a brouhaha."

"I can understand that."

Wow, that was easier than I expected. "Thank you for understanding."

"That was one of the problems I got with The Cradle. They told me it wasn't my place to investigate."

"When did you investigate?" I probably harbored a dream she'd find or at least look for me more than I realized.

"Well, I didn't have any facts to go on. I was hopin' they'd give me information, and of course, they didn't."

"Mm hm."

"They pretty much just told me, *Lady, forget it!*"

That would have been entirely normal up until four years ago, what with Illinois adoptions back in the '50's all being sealed. She seems a bit uncomfortable at this juncture and changes the subject.

"You were raised on the east coast?"

I explain in chronological order all the places I have lived since birth: Alexandria, Virginia for two years; Washington D.C. for five; Los Angeles for two; Zürich, Switzerland for three; back to L.A. and in the same house for six months; London, England for six years; and college in the U.S., but commuting back and forth to London for four more years until I married in 1974 at which point I lived in Virginia Beach, D.C. again, Hanover, New Hampshire, Los Angeles again, New Canaan and Greenwich, Connecticut and finally, Colorado where I plan to stay. I blaze through this list in almost a single breath and am panting at the end of my litany.

"Wow!"

Little do I know how much Mama has wanted to live abroad or travel as I have so I instantly feel bad about living the life she always wanted.

I tell her how having the birth certificate has made me ecstatic. How

I feel a little more complete, as though the puzzle that was my past has very few pieces left to fill.

"I didn't even know there was a birth certificate." Suddenly, she sounds weary.

"Actually, there were two. The original one names you, but I never got to see that one until a few weeks ago. For adoptees, a new one is drawn up naming the adopting folks as legal parents. But guess what?" I say cheerfully. "Fifteen dollars later my real birth certificate is in my hot li'l hands!"

"Did it have your father's name on there?" I'm not expecting this question so soon in our first get-acquainted conversation. Various articles on the topic of reuniting with one's birth mother advocate not to push for too many answers all at once. The question *who is my father* is right at the top of the list of no-nos.

"No, it did not," I say softly. Dead silence. "It did not," I repeat thinking she hasn't heard me too well. A long awkward pause follows, filling the air like smog.

"Do you wanna know his name?" She sounds grumpy, but something tells me she wants me to say *yes* so we can quickly get over this hurdle.

"Sure!" I say all too artificially.

"His name was Christoffer Schmidt, with two fs. You can look him up on Ancestry.com… You see, my children didn't know about this either… ya know… And so that opened a door, um, and when Molly and I first chatted about this, I said *I might as well tell you, meaning her, who the father is*. So we looked him up. He graduated from Notre Dame in '51. You were born the next year. He was an architect. He's passed. Both he and his wife are gone."

I rush to find a pen and piece of paper as she tells me his name. I remember deciding right then and there I wouldn't likely ever ask for his name again; probably because I could tell how uncomfortable she was just saying as much as she did. Besides, I never spent much time thinking about the spermatozoid anyway. I certainly never longed for his embrace or any kindness, for that matter.

"It wasn't very hard to find you what with the internet being what it is today."

"It's crazy what opens up." She sounds calmer now that we're past any more discussion of Christoffer with the two fs.

"It is kinda scary," I agree.

"Yup." *Is she running out of steam?* I race to fill the void.

"Today the internet makes it so easy to find folks. I'm actually grateful for it. And I can't thank you enough for being so willing, you know, receptive. My letter must have come as a humongous shock."

"I'd kinda given up hope that it was ever gonna happen."

"Aw…"

"I know some kids do look and some don't. Some kids have curiosity…" She hesitates probably thinking she just insulted me for lacking inquisitiveness, then switches gears. "I had nothing to go on…" she blurts. Her trailing voice is melancholy.

"I think I always knew it was up to me to go on the search… I did find out some heredity stuff back in 1980 and, um, I was content with that. Well, I had to be. It was going to be the only info they gave me. Twenty years later I got very close to hiring a detective but was advised that happy reunions scarcely happen. People proffered various scenarios. This could happen and that could happen, blah, blah blah. And your mother could find out…" Mama is actually chuckling.

"This winter a lot of stuff happened. People and events … no guts no glory I've got to do it! Search that is!

"I'm glad you did, Honey. Glad you did."

"I am, too."

There are tears at both ends of the telephone line.

"Well, you've been very sweet to me. Molly has been a sweetheart, too. And I have a note from Scott last night…" The pace of our conversation has picked up. Clearly, we are getting more comfortable.

"You do?"

"Yes! We're having dinner on Tuesday."

"You're having dinner with him on Tuesday?"

"Yup!"

"Oh, that's wonderful."

"Isn't it?" More of my nervous laughter. "It's gonna be pretty weird."

"I imagine you'll get along. You'll like Scott."

"He's got a great sense of humor, " I say remembering his *I'm a six foot five Q-tip with glasses* reference.

"He's a tall drink of water. Are you tall? How tall are you, Honey?"

"I'm tall."

"How tall"

"Five eleven, but shrinking as I speak."

"Oh, my God! I can't believe it! I think you got that from my side of the family." *Sperm Donor was no midget*, but I keep that under wraps.

"Well, I'm glad you're gonna get together."

"I know... it'll be fun...it'll be great. And um, I hope some day you and I can do the same."

"You sound good...Are your girls good with this?"

"They're excited, very excited. They're anxious to get to know you as well. They're very happy for me and I think they probably know how or why this was a good thing for me to do. So..."

"I'm glad."

"Oh, I am, too!"

Our voices fill the air like bright ribbons. Hers is a sexy bourbon voice in shades of burnt umber, ocher, and olive green. Mine is more breathy, uncharacteristically high-pitched what with nerves. There's far too much awkward laughter on my part, but we're happily sharing now, and it sounds like music. Her voice, so like mine, I've since been told, brings immediate comfort. I don't want to stop listening to it, just like when I was a girl and played a favorite song over and over again on my record player.

"Well, my kids certainly did understand. I mean, you know I didn't know what their reaction was gonna be."

"Tell me! You know, I have to be truthful with you. My letter to you was tracked. I was happy to know where it was going, or not going when it was hung up in Clearwater, but when I realized it was going to Indiana, where Molly lives I thought, oh my gosh what if she reads it first? That's not what I planned. I wanted to preserve your privacy, but what could I do if you were living there when you were supposed to be down in Florida?"

"Well, they all know now."

"That took a lot of courage to tell them," I offer.

"They thought it was cool they had an older sister; thought it was wonderful. There's no reason I couldn't have told them years ago. I just didn't."

"I don't blame you. It's a hard, um story to tell... you know, unsolicited or whatever."

"I always felt I was never gonna get to do anything about it because the door was closed in my face." She's referring to The Cradle again.

"Well, I knocked and you opened it!"

"That's great! I'm so glad you did. Are you home during the day?"

"Yes, and you can call me anytime you want."

"And you can call me, Honey."

"Is there anything else you wanna know other than what you already know?" *A generous gesture* I think given how hard this must be for her.

"Probably lots of stuff, but let's take it slowly."

We continue to chat about Scott and his wife, Scott's daughters, skiing in Breckenridge and Vail; Tyler's retirement and a handful of trivia.

"Tell me the birth order of your children. Is Maureen the oldest?"

"Maureen is the oldest. Molly is next, fifteen months younger. She's 56, and Scott was born in '61."

"You had 'em pretty close. Mine are fourteen months apart, so I know how that goes."

"Tyler's going along with all of this?"

"Totally. He's very happy for me. Even though there's been the tears and the fears and the worries he's been right there beside me, rock solid. Everybody has been so supportive." And without taking a breath I charge on, " And I'm just so amazed your kids are too because here comes little Miss Interloper. They're so positive. It's really very, very kind of all of them."

"Well it was really very odd because they said *Mother, this is just so cool, really cool* and they were surprised, you know, that I never talked about it after all these years. There was no sense to talk about it because I couldn't do anything about it."

"I understand."

"Somebody else closed that door." She seems to disappear into the past and I can tell it hurts, so I jump in, motor-mouth that I am.

"We buried Tyler's Mother last fall and he said to me just the other day, *This is just the oddest thing. I bury my mother in September and you meet yours at age sixty-three.*"

"Isn't that funny?" Mama lets go of a wavelet of laughter. "That's really odd, I agree."

"I never would have imagined it. For so long our finding each other didn't seem possible."

Mama follows up with a story about a young woman with whom she worked years before who declared she had no interest in ever finding her birth mother. "I'll tell you the truth. That made me feel kinda bad. I guess there are a lotta people like that."

Now I feel bad, too. "Maybe it depends on the personality."

"If it had been me, I'd a been so curious I wouldn't have been able to stand it." Right away I go into guilt mode. Heaven forbid she think I didn't want to know her; yearn in fact, for her arms to hold me and her words to soothe my aching heart. *Time to share a little bit more*, I decide.

"I have a mother who is pretty jealous and clingy...er, I think... Oh dear, how do I say this without betraying her? I just never wanted to rattle her cage." And all of a sudden I realize that were I to complain too much about Mother, Mama might feel guilty, too.

"I don't blame ya, Honey. I think you did the right thing. There's no sense beating yourself up. I'm sure at age ninety-seven I wouldn't take this news well."

"Unfortunately, she wouldn't have taken it well at any age. You're right, though. The older one is, the harder it is."

"So how come you finally decided to find me? What took you so long?"

"The tipping point came when I was enrolled in a memoir class plus doing a lot of reading about adoption. I learned there are typically two kinds of reactions or behaviors of adopted children. One is angry and aggressive and the other is compliant. I was definitely the compliant one. For me that meant just wanting to fit in; not make waves, you know, be accepted or whatever. I chose to be that way because it was outwardly non-threatening. It kept the peace. Ultimately, it probably would have been better if I'd been a little more aggressive or combative because then I would have been a fighter, searched for you sooner. It would have cost me too much, though." *There I go again; gushing like a faucet.* "When I realized just recently I'd been compliant as a child I was intensely irritated with myself. After all, my current self is assertive, candid and pretty opinionated. I've worked hard over the years to shed any co-dependent tendencies; how to politely say *no* and be comfortable with my attitudes and outlook, even when it differs from those I want to please. Whatever, I've always been slow at growing up." Again, I laugh nervously.

"That's okay, Honey."

"Better late than never, right?" More nervous laughter.

"That's right, Honey."

"I'm glad you feel that way."

We are spooling down; running out of yarn. "You can call me anytime you want to," Mama says in her throaty voice. "I look forward to more phone visits, okay?"

I had so much more to say; stuff I'd stockpiled for years. How would we ever catch up? But it's time to say goodbye. We're both exhausted. "I'd like that," I say in a whisper, gulping back a sob. When I ring off, I'm glad Mama cannot see the tears running down my cheeks, hanging from my scrunched up nose, all red and runny, my chin dimpled and trembling.

Our phone call lasted thirty-three minutes and instantly I was released from my purgatory of neither being here nor there. Pure nirvana. Being entirely accepted by not just my mama, but my half siblings, too, meant the missing piece to that jigsaw puzzle, otherwise known as my life, was finally found. A picture was forming and I could hardly wait to see what the landscape of our conjoined lives might look like. Did they have any idea how hugely grateful I was? Would I ever be able to convey this gratitude adequately? I remember turning to my goddess, Mount Evans. She held all the answers, I was sure of it. Her silhouette etched against a blue-black night was as soft as velvet. The stars cascading over her snow-capped shoulders looked as though they'd been tossed in clusters of gleaming glitter.

That night, when Tyler and I went to bed, he held me in his arms, allowing me to cry until I had no more tears to soak his collar. He told me *you're crying for your former self, your mama, even your mother, and all the years gone by... there's been a funeral... and yet there's also been a birth; a second chance at being the daughter you are meant to be.*

ONE HEART ONE SOUL

Mama was sitting alone on a sofa at my brother's house with her back to the foyer when I arrived. Her hands were folded in her lap as if in prayer. She seemed relaxed as she waited for me to come around to face her. Strangely, I, too, was pretty composed. At least this was true until that unmistakable fragrance of lavender filled the air and my heart skipped a beat.

Seeing Mama for the first time makes all the years we've been separated simply slip away. I kneel before her and take her hands in mine. Both of us are too stunned to speak, words not being at all necessary in these first few moments. We stare into each other's eyes for a long time. I think each of us must be looking for the me in the other, sprinting down the corridors of the other's bank of memories, trying to soak up all which is missing and all which might be familiar. Suddenly a grin lights up Mama's face. Her brown eyes shine like maple sugar and a low chuckle rumbles in her chest. Everything written across her face points to an acceptance of who I am which I've never felt more acutely. No one has ever smiled at me this way, and it moves me to tears.

She places her hand on my cheek. "Don't cry, Honey. Come. Come here, sit next to me." She pats the sofa cushion and as I sit, she takes my hand in both of hers.

We sit side by side at an angle, our knees touching, our fingers knitted together. We remain silent. Both of us seem to agree without saying so that this moment bears a special kind of reverence. All is quiet, though we can hear a child several doors down the street plinking out her scales in halting staccato runs. I imagine her short legs are dangling from the bench as she is bent over her task. Mama wonders aloud if her mama is standing at the door with arms akimbo frowning.

My mind is racing and my heart is fluttering. It means everything to me not to be confronted with rejection. I think she knows it as I feel her love envelop me like a fur coat; thick and soft and warm. The dream of not just finding, but also bonding with my physical and mental roots is coming true as we stare at each other. I can tell by her probing look this is as important to her as it is me. Sitting here with Mama, her gaze and her grin so familiar to me move me to the point I am shaking. I realize at this moment I have rarely felt another's affection so acutely. Is this what kinship is? Not counting romance or attraction, I've usually only felt another's curiosity. I wear a label, *adopted*, and am treated accordingly, whether I announce it or just live it wordlessly. Not today, though. I know right away how much Mama truly cares.

There's no question I belong to Mama. We look like each other from the cheek bones up to the eyes, brow line, and forehead. We sound like each other, too. So much so I was frequently unable to decipher her voice from mine on the recording of our first phone call. I see myself reflected in some of her facial mannerisms and hand gestures. How is that possible? But how sublime it is to share these small idiosyncrasies.

"It's so surreal," I say.

"Very weird."

"Before our meeting were you afraid?"

"No. I wasn't in the least bit afraid. Were you?"

"In disbelief," I say quietly. "For so long I believed my search for you would end in heartache."

"Never, Honey."

We lean in for another hug. I revel in the softness of her skin. It's as soft as butter and there's a hint of lavender at her collarbones.

"What do you tell people when they ask where you're from?" Mama asks, sitting back against the sofa's brightly colored pillows.

"I tell them I was born in Chicago but never lived there and that I'm adopted."

"Well, from now on, you tell 'em you come from Love."

Outside, a recent rain shower has washed the Maroon Bells, making those great layers of granite reaching for heaven appear polished. The fragrance of the wild flowers is all the sweeter now as it wafts through an open window. And the blues of fireweed, flax, and columbine glisten under the sun's warm rays. The scenery is Colorado magic.

"Do you love your mother?" Mama asks, catching me a bit off guard. "Was she good to you?"

"Of course," I reply realizing she needs more than that. "You did the right thing, Mama, placing me in her care." The tension in Mama's shoulders relaxes as she hears what she needs to hear. "She and my father were very good to me, especially my Grammy and Gramps and Aunt Ann, but..."

"But what, Honey?"

"Even though my life was blessed, I needed to find you, my natural mother. You're the one with whom I have an irrevocable attachment. The one of heart and soul."

THE CRADLE

The Cradle has had a long history in adoption services. It was founded in 1923 by Florence Dahl Walrath, who was born in Chicago in 1877. Shortly after her graduation from High School, Florence married William Bradley Walrath. They lived in Evanston, a Chicago suburb along the North Shore, and had four children. In 1914, when her sister lost a child giving birth, Mrs. Walrath put her know-how to work and found a child whose mother was compelled by circumstances to place her baby up for adoption. Due to the success of placing a homeless baby with her childless sister, other couples she knew who were in similar circumstances asked for her help. A few years later, she founded The Cradle and an adoption agency of great repute was born.

Over the decades The Cradle has become renowned as one of the foremost adoption agencies in the country. Since its opening, The Cradle has helped place more than 15,000 children into permanent homes. They have provided lifelong support for all who are touched by adoption -- birth parents, adoptees, and adoptive parents.

The Cradle is the only adoption agency in the country with an on-site nursery. This has proven to be a safe, neutral place for infants to stay while birth parents take the time they need in deciding if adoption will be the plan for their child. The nursery also enables The Cradle to place infants whose special medical needs may mean it takes a bit longer to find them a home which is prepared to help them thrive. They are doggedly committed to finding a loving home for every child entrusted to their care.

In recent years, The Cradle has expanded its scope to include Adoption Learning Partners (ALP), an online training program for prospective adoptive parents and adoption professionals. Through the power of the internet, ALP has made The Cradle's thorough training convenient and accessible to professionals and families all across the globe. Their mission is to benefit children and all others touched by adoption by compassionately delivering exceptional education, guidance and lifelong support to build, sustain and preserve nurturing families. They also connect Cradle friends and families through Facebook and Twitter.

Not that it makes me feel at all special it is fun, nevertheless, to know that Scott Burns and Gracie Allen, Bob Hope, Al Jolson, Donna Reed, Pearl Hart and Gale Sayers have all adopted children from the Cradle.

CPSIA information can be obtained
at www.ICGtesting.com
Printed in the USA
LVHW011409100319
610116LV00002B/339/P